PRAISE FOR J.R. SEEGER'S MIKE4 SERIES

"Seeger has crafted a fast-paced narrative which carries the reader to multiple hotspots during WWII... This book may be fictional, but the accuracy and attention to detail yields a fine overview of the extraordinary contributions of a heretofore under-appreciated wartime agency."

ANN TODD, author of *OSS Operation Black Mail: One Woman's Covert War Against the Imperial Japanese Army*

"Seeger quickly immerses the reader into the world and missions of the OSS, our nation's first special operations and intelligence organization. The writing, the 'feel,' and behaviors of the characters are authentic, with plenty here to engage both the veteran operator, as well as the casual reader interested in better understanding the actions [and] courage of our OSS heroes."

LTG (RETIRED) JOHN MULHOLLAND, former Deputy Commander, US Special Operations Command and former Commander, US Army Special Operation Command

"[Seeger] introduces us to the complexities of the war behind the lines across the globe. He clearly knows his stuff; the combat scenes are vivid, the tactics nuanced and sophisticated, with a host of political problems lurking in the background."

COL (RETIRED) NICHOLAS REYNOLDS, author of *Ernest Hemingway: Writer, Sailor, Soldier, Spy* and *Basra, Baghdad, and Beyond: The United States Marine Corps in the Second Iraq War*

"If you like good tales of the shadowy, often hard-edged world of counter-terrorism, read Mike4! Written by a veteran of 'the community,' it will teach while it entertains."

GENERAL STANLEY MCCHRYSTAL, author of *My Share of the Task: A Memoir* and *Team of Teams: New Rules of Engagement for a Complex World*

The Swordfish Deception

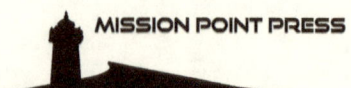

Readers are encouraged to go to www.MissionPointPress.com to contact the author or to find information on how to buy this book in bulk at a discounted rate.

Published by Mission Point Press
2554 Chandler Rd.
Traverse City, MI 49696
(231) 421-9513
www.MissionPointPress.com

ISBN: 978-1-961302-33-4
Library of Congress Control Number: TK

Printed in the United States of America

The Swordfish Deception

J.R. Seeger

book 8 in the   MIKE4 series

Yesterday, upon a stair,
I met a man who wasn't there!
He wasn't there again today,
Oh, how I wish he'd go away!
— Antigonish by William Hughes Mearns

THE COLLECTIVE

The office building in Stockholm was one of many on the outskirts of the old city, the Gamla Stan. It was a square affair in a brutalist style that would be familiar to visitors of modern Europe: Ten stories of grey concrete and glass designed to house a total of twenty different Swedish companies, two per floor. On the top floor, one of those companies was not Swedish. Its heavy wooden door had a simple logo of a 19th century cavalry saber and the name SCHWERT GMBH. The unlikely visitor who managed to gain access through the door's magnetic locks would encounter a simple concierge desk staffed by an efficient male office assistant in a black suit, white shirt and red-and-blue striped tie. The visitor would see that behind the desk was a glass wall, and beyond that a series of desks with men and women working at computers. All in good order, and precisely the appearance for a German company listed as an international business consultancy focusing on accounting and best leadership practices.

It was an appearance purposely deceiving.

This "ordinary office" was actually headquarters for one of the world's most successful mercenary organizations, known as SWORDFISH. In a part of the office no visitor would ever see was a conference room with windows that faced north and east. The windows, designed to prevent any high-tech surveillance, shredded the fading October light sufficiently that it had to be augmented by stark overhead lighting. The long conference table was made in the mid-20th century Swedish-modern style with stainless steel and polished pine. There were eight chairs set on both sides of the table with one at the head. They were also in a blend of light wood and steel with leather seats.

On this autumn day, five seats were filled for a meeting of the board of directors. There were no computers, notebooks, or anything at the table but five glasses and five bottles of mineral water, one in front of each of the men. There would be no record of the discussions at this meeting.

The man at the head of the table looked like most of the current crop of European business executives. Young, tall, and thin with short black hair greying at the temples and a very tightly groomed grey beard. His suit was black wool and his open collared shirt was starched white cotton. His appearance was what could be called "trainer fit" and indeed his day started with a full hour in a gym in his house with his personal trainer. His house was on the shore of a sea corridor between Stockholm and the Baltic Sea and he had a small sailboat that he raced against his Swedish neighbors. As a result, a dark sailor's tan covered his face and his hands.

He had risen to the head of SWORDFISH on the strength of a unique blend of experience and talent. First, his previous employment in the Sixth Directorate of the Russian military intelligence organization best known by its Cold War name: The Main Intelligence Directorate or, its Russian acronym, GRU. Second, he had exquisite skills in reading the sector of the private and public security markets. Recent successes of SWORDFISH were based on the ability to weave in and out of the complex world of Russian oligarchs, Russian intelligence services, and various despots around the world who had enough money to buy "special services." Just as important, he was very good at avoiding competing interests among these clients and other competitors. His final skill was a degree of ruthless focus demanding absolute success in each operation.

The four other men could not have been less like the man at the head of the table if they were from another age. And, in one real sense, they were from another century. While their manager was a child when the Soviet Union collapsed, these others had started their lives as Soviet citizens, fought both internal and external enemies of the Soviet Union and watched what they thought was a completely predictable world crumble in front of their eyes.

As members of the two arms of intelligence, the KGB and the GRU, they were able to create off-ramps for themselves before the end of the Soviet Union and during the lost years while the new Russian Republic descended into the chaos of the oligarchs. They used funds and access available to their services to establish business opportunities outside Russia. As with many startup businesses in the 1990s, their small security and information enterprises could only survive by consolidation. Regardless of their distrust of each other, they knew that success required expanded capability. The senior manager of their firm offered them a chance to accomplish this success.

It wasn't the style of their clothes that separated them from their manager. They had more than enough money to spend on personal items. It was their faces and especially their hands that showed the difference. Their hands were calloused from years of hard physical labor in the Soviet military and intelligence services. Calloused from war zones and domestic raids. Calloused from fights and vicious interrogations. Their faces showed the deep creases of years in desert sun or high-altitude battlefields. Unlike their senior partner, they didn't have a personal trainer. Rather, they were men who visited martial arts dojos or old-school weight rooms where men lifted iron plates and sat together in saunas.

This was the quarterly meeting and these four men at the table served as the representatives for the various teams of SWORDFISH. The senior manager sat quite still, waiting for both the sweep second hand and the minute hand of his large, white-gold German-made watch to cross twelve. One of his quirks was to always start a meeting precisely at the top of the hour. This meeting was no exception. Each of his counterparts wore watches to ensure the same degree of precision. However, their timepieces were stainless steel diver or pilot's watches made in Russia or Switzerland. No matter what brand, they were reliable and had luminous hands that would be visible in the dark of night when precision meant success or failure of a raid or a murder.

These were dangerous men led by a master of the modern, shadow world. A world where they had to balance their capabilities with shifting political power: where an oligarch one day might be a prisoner the next and dead in a month. It wasn't easy, but it was very lucrative. These five men called themselves The Collective and they managed the worldwide operations of their mercenary organization.

The leader spoke just as his watch pointed with precision to ten hours. "We accepted the Iranian project last month. Is there anything to report?"

One of the men on the side facing the windows was a former member of the Eighth Directorate of the GRU, known more commonly as SPETSNAZ. He said, "We are awaiting contact with the Iranian surveillance team."

"When?"

"This afternoon. Misha and his team will act as soon as they have the information. The Iranians insisted on playing a role in this. They paid us extra compensation so they could do so."

"Do we expect any complications?"

"It remains to be seen. The negotiations have been...complex. Misha will take their information, but he only trusts his own men for any active measures. The mission itself will be accomplished with precision."

"Excellent." The leader rarely focused beyond the basics. The other members of The Collective were responsible for the details. He also hated meetings and did his best to limit any meeting to thirty minutes. He looked across the table at another of the hard men. "Have we heard from our new client?"

Across the table with their backs to the windows were two veterans of the KGB, specifically the Second Chief Directorate. When the USSR collapsed, they both stayed long enough to work in the Russian Federal Security Service, the FSB. The man who spoke was recruited out of the FSB to work for SWORDFISH on special projects that linked international criminal enterprises with oligarchs who had fallen out of favor with the Kremlin. His partner was silent. "We met with representatives in St. Petersburg. They want us to recover their lost property and to punish the perpetrators. They promised additional information today. With that in hand, we can set a price and a reasonable timeline for the project. If they have the necessary data, we should be able to satisfy the client."

The senior knew these representatives. For a change, he made clear his own opinion. "They have more than enough money to satisfy our request, but we need to take some care. The Orthodox Church leadership is exceptionally close to the Kremlin. We want no trouble at that end."

"I do not think the requirements will be too much of a challenge. However, my best team is currently involved in an operation in Tblisi. There may be a delay in addressing the new requirement."

The manager looked at his colleagues. "As I said, we must respond immediately to this new client. The Church is a central power in Moscow and throughout Russia. If they wish a problem solved and if they ask us to solve that problem, then we will do it immediately."

Before the FSB veteran could speak, his counterpart across the table said, "Misha's work will be accomplished in short order. He is already in Europe. If the target is in Europe, we can assign the new target to his team. Of course, if the target is in the near abroad or in Asia, then we cannot help. All of my other teams are currently active in Africa."

The FSB veteran looked across the table. He begrudgingly accepted the offer. "I think the target is in Europe. I will know more today. If Misha's team is on site, then it makes sense to use them. I will have a second team available to serve as backup as soon as I can recall them from Georgia."

The man at the head of the table smiled. Running SWORDFISH was like managing a wolfpack. Any weakness among the members resulted in conflict. This was why he insisted on absolute discipline. The Collective was balanced between former competitors — two from the KGB and two from the GRU. Their competitive nature made them successful. It just required a firm whip hand. He was that whip hand. He said, "Enough for new business. We need to review the cost-benefit analysis on our projects in Africa..."

A MEETING IN A CAFE

A fall day in Frankfurt could be a cold, dreary precursor of winter, or it could be sunny and feel like summer was still in full force. Misha realized that he had luck with him. It was sunny but cool, and a light wind passed through the Romerplatz of old Frankfurt. The walking area around the old Roman ruins and in front of the Frankfurt cathedral was filled with a mix of tourists and rich Germans enjoying what might be the last warm day before winter closed in. He had picked a table inside one of the cafés in the old center of town. Now, he wished he had chosen an outdoor table. It would have been most enjoyable.

Misha had waited for this meeting until he was certain that he was clean of surveillance. He arrived two days ago with his five men. They were staying in a pair of pensions in the suburbs of Frankfurt, where the owners were willing to take Euros rather than a credit card. They had to provide passport information, but that hardly mattered because SWORDFISH provided new identities each time they traveled. The team was split, with half in Bad Soden; half in Bad Homburg. Far enough away from the city to avoid any federal police surveillance, but close enough that they could travel in and out of the city on public transportation.

Misha had worked for SWORDFISH in Syria and Central Africa after he finished his service contract with SPETSNAZ. The money was far better, and he no longer chafed at the complex military bureaucracy that was a remnant of the old Soviet Union. SPETSNAZ was an elite organization, but still under the direct control of seniors in the GRU who had little interest and no experience in special operations. His managers at SWORDFISH were far better. His direct supervisor had been a senior in SPETSNAZ, and to use the well-worn phrase from the Soviet Union, he knew where the dogs were buried. Misha liked the fact that SWORDFISH managers simply gave their team leaders a mission statement and then didn't ask any questions about how the team leaders intended to accomplish that mission.

Of course, the one negative aspect of SWORDFISH was that the managers expected absolute loyalty. If you received an order, you obeyed the order. You didn't offer alternatives; you didn't ask questions. You left the meeting and accomplished the mission. Working with the Iranians was not his preference, but like any SWORDFISH instructions, he didn't have a choice.

Misha chose this café in one of the busiest parts of the city in hopes of avoiding notice by the many adversaries of SWORDFISH. It was only a few years ago that a SWORDFISH operation in Frankfurt was disrupted by a blend of US special services and German police. A senior SWORDFISH executive was still awaiting trial and his manager was retired ... permanently. Misha wanted no trouble on this mission. He just hoped his Iranian counterpart was as diligent as he was about security.

Misha's past contact with the Iranian special services had been less cordial. The Islamic Revolutionary Guard Corps worked with the Syrian Military Intelligence Directorate for years and had their own way of doing business. They had no interest in working with "new" allies from Russia, even though Russian military force was critical to the survival of the Syrian regime. The Syrian MID wanted good relations with the Russians, but at a price. The price was that SWORDFISH operations had to be under their control. In Misha's view, that had been a recipe for disaster. While SWORDFISH was an independent organization, it had only one primary client, the President of the Russian Federation. And when the President told SWORDFISH executives, "Make this work," they needed no further instruction. SWORDFISH would make it work.

Misha looked at his recently acquired Swiss-made stainless-steel sports watch. Far better than the Russian made Vostok he had worn in multiple war zones. The Vostok kept reasonably accurate time but had about as much style as a crowbar. This watch fit his new persona as a European businessman sitting in a café enjoying a late fall day. The black dial and large luminous hands would serve for night operations. The shock resistance and water resistance to 100m meant the watch would survive any hard service. But the stainless steel case and thin bezel did not scream "special services" and that also fit his new persona. It had everything he needed in a watch and just the right level of polish that pointed to wealth rather than stealth. He purchased the watch while in the transit lounge in Dubai. After Syria, he felt he deserved a small prize just for surviving.

Gazing at the watch brought back few good memories. He remembered fleeing the Syrian battlefield in two Toyota Hi-Lux trucks, bouncing across the desert, a large field-dressing covering half his face. He remembered hoping the American aircraft would just let them escape. He remembered they couldn't recover the bodies of his teammates. And he remembered the look in the eyes of the Syrian medic who had helped pull him from the wreckage of the SWORD-FISH armored vehicle. The medic wasn't sure he was going to survive but Misha didn't want to die in Syria. Misha knew modern war was dangerous and brutal, but this was his first combat experience facing an enemy that had air superiority. No matter how much money you made, the only value to the money was if you survived. If nothing else, the battle in Syria taught Misha to trust only your teammates and to hate Americans. He had no room for any other emotions.

He looked at the watch again. It was 15 hours. He didn't expect the Iranian to be on time. His experience in the third world taught him that precision was not to be expected. For this reason, he was surprised when the stranger silently came from behind, jostled him slightly and then pulled up a chair at his table. The newcomer waved to the waiter.

"*Café, bitte.*" Misha noted that the order was precise. Another look at the watch. The sweep second hand was just about to hit the luminous triangle at the top of the watch face. It was 1501 hours. They waited in silence until the waiter returned with a small plate with an espresso, a sugar cookie, and a glass of water. The Iranian nodded, handed the waiter a 10-Euro note and said, *"Stimmt so."* The waiter nodded and left.

Misha did a quick scan of his counterpart. He looked to be nearly fifty years old. Clean shaven with short, black hair that covered his head like a helmet. Grey-green eyes. He had what looked to be a long-healed scar running across a broken nose and ending at his left ear. European tailored black wool coat and matching wool slacks. A white shirt. No rings or watch. His nails were manicured, but the knuckles of his hands were scarred. The Iranian looked back. No doubt he was doing the same scan. Misha wondered what the Iranian might gain from his visual interrogation. Misha was wearing black: black jeans and a black leather jacket. Under the jacket was a black roll-neck pullover. Five days growth of beard seemed stylish enough in Europe and it covered the pock marked skin from the shrapnel wounds acquired in Syria.

"Auf Deutsch?" The Iranian raised an eyebrow. Misha didn't respond. *"Francaise?"*

Misha was not certain he could hold a conversation in either of the languages. He said, "English?"

The Iranian smiled and switched to unaccented English. "Of course."

"You have the material?"

"Please, don't insult me. I would not have come if I did not have the material." The Iranian took a sip of coffee, put it down and fingered but did not eat the cookie. "You do know that we could have done this on our own."

Misha nodded. He tried to think of a remark that would have countered the Iranian's arrogance, but his English was limited. Sarcasm in German and French was impossible, so he could only mutter a curse in Russian. Eventually, he said, "It wasn't my idea."

The Iranian smiled. The smile did not reach his eyes. "Then we both are just foot soldiers following orders."

This time Misha decided he did have a response. "Except I'm well paid."

"There is more to life than pay, brother. I have the pleasure of delivering justice."

Misha's English language skills were fine, but he hadn't expected that response. He wasn't sure he understood, so he grunted, "Eh?"

"The target is a traitor. He has been tried in absentia in an Islamic court in Tehran and found guilty of treason. The fact is that I would have preferred to do the execution myself. However, that is not to be." The Iranian turned his hands over revealing his palms. He looked at the ceiling of the café as if appealing to God himself. "As I said, we are both foot soldiers following orders. I just want to be sure you do your job."

Misha wasn't about to debate his skills or how he intended to accomplish his mission. He said, "Show me."

The Iranian smiled and said, "Reach into the right pocket of your jacket."

Misha thought later he should have waited a few seconds before complying just to avoid the self-satisfied smirk he saw on the Iranian's face. Instead, he did as requested and felt a memory stick that had magically appeared. The Iranian was clearly a showman. He said, "How do I know it is all there?"

"Along with our entire surveillance report — written in Russian in case you were worried — the stick also has my contact information. If you need more, all you need do is contact me. But, please contact me soon because we leave tomorrow. We need to be back home in 48 hours." With that, the Iranian took a final sip of his coffee, stood up and left.

Later in his hotel room, Misha inserted the stick into his laptop and read the report. The Iranians might be annoying, but they were thorough. They had identified the target's house and photographed his pattern of life for two weeks. The memory stick included a set of maps identifying the target's routes, his daily routine and even pictures from inside the university where he worked. As promised, there was a file listing the contact information for a man simply identified as Cyrus. A German telephone number and even an email account.

Included in the files were pictures of the target when he resided in Iran along with photos of his family — a wife wearing a headscarf and two children. Those photos were more than ten years old, some dated from before the new century. In the background of some of the family photos, Misha saw mountains and an industrial plant of some type. There were also holiday photos of the target with his family at the beach — most probably the Caspian Sea. Misha assumed the target had been a spy for the Americans, or the Israelis or some other European power. In fact, he had no interest in why the target was on a list for execution.

Misha's time in Syria taught him that Middle East societies were complicated and the line between loyalty and treason was a thin one. He smiled for a moment when he considered whether it was all that different among the oligarchs in Moscow. Misha had grown up in St. Petersburg and had a natural prejudice against anyone who would choose to live in Moscow. Too many years of intrigue, too many chances to make a false step and end up on the wrong side of the leadership or the mafia or an oligarch with his own private army. Better to stay a soldier, take your pay and retire to a bungalow on a beach in Cyprus or a small flat in the Russian community in London or New York City.

When he finished reading the report, he pulled the stick from his laptop. The report was complete. There was no reason to recontact the Iranian. The next step was to gather the team and show them the information. They would not trust any of the reporting until it was checked, but if it proved reliable, their mission would be easily accomplished in the next week. Misha reached into the small refrigerator in his room and pulled a bottle of vodka from the freezer and poured himself a toast to a good day's work.

The Iranian signals officer in the embassy in Berlin reached for the direct line phone that ran to the commander of the office of the Defense Attaché. When the man in the office picked up the line, the signals officer said one word, "*Tamom.*"

The Assistant Defense Attaché hung up. It was late but he always worked late. He lit himself another Turkish cigarette. The room was filled with the acrid smoke from dozens of its predecessors. He smiled and thought to himself, "Finished, eh? Well, now the game has truly begun since we can track the Russian anywhere."

WET WORK

It took two days to confirm everything that the Iranians had provided. Misha and his team were not about to take the Iranian's word without checking. Luckily, the target was very predictable. During the week, he walked to his job as a mathematics tutor. On weekends, he and his wife would take breakfast in a local café and then stroll in the Gruneberg Park or visit the Palmengarten nearby. Misha and his team watched him leave, and they watched him return. He didn't seem at all security conscious. It would be an easy job.

Misha split the team in two. He knew from experience that the only way to guarantee success was to have redundancy built into the plan. Team one rented a white cargo van from a local rental agency in Bad Homburg. Team two rented a large German sedan in Bad Soden. He and the remaining team member had rented a passenger car at the Frankfurt airport. They set up early in the morning and waited.

The target lived in a neighborhood made up of apartments built just after World War II. Most of the buildings served as housing for military and American government personnel until German unification. Once the Americans left, the German government took over the housing and provided it to the various immigrant communities that came to Germany for work or to escape conflicts in the Balkans and, more recently, in Syria. From the German government perspective, the housing was more than satisfactory for these families, and Frankfurt needed workers willing to accept wages far under the requirements of the European Union. The challenge for the SWORDFISH team was to conduct their fixed-point surveillance in a part of the city where there were almost no Europeans. These were the sorts of challenges that Misha enjoyed and his team was equally adept at blending into whatever environment they were given.

Misha was watching the target house from a commercial video camera that his teammate Sasha placed on a lamppost overlooking the sidewalk that the target used every day. It was disguised as a polite, but pitiful request for help finding a lost dog. Even the street cleaners were unlikely to remove such a request. They knew he walked down the street called Hansaallee in the morning between 0730 and 0800hrs heading toward his job at the Goethe Institute. Misha watched as the target walked slowly down the street. He had a distinctive walk. The file said that years ago, when he was a government official in Tehran, he was arrested and accused of corruption. Interrogation at Evin Prison began and ended each day with various means of physical torture. In his case, his interrogators decided to use bastinado — beating the soles of his feet — as a means of gaining a confession. Before they moved to more vigorous means of interrogation, his captors realized they had picked up the wrong man. He was released but would never walk properly again. Misha cared little about the story, but he was pleased that the man had such a distinctive walk. Even in a crowd, he was easy to spot.

After the target walked past the camera and moved three blocks down the street, Misha got out of the car, walked into the neighborhood, and recovered the camera. It was now up to the team to keep an eye on their prey.

As soon as he returned to his car, Misha keyed the microphone on his small encrypted radio. *"Eins."*

"Da."

"Bitte?" Misha was confident that the encryption on their radios would protect them, but you never could afford to slip when you were in a hostile country with an excellent security service. Even a small thing like speaking in Russian might at some point reveal their presence. The number one car was in place, but he needed to let them know that they were taking over the mission.

"Ya."

"Verfolgen."

"Jawohl."
"Swie."
"Ya."
"Der reihe nach."
"Ya."

Team One would take the lead in the pursuit and the second team would serve as the follow-up. Both teams watched as the target disappeared behind a corner kiosk as he prepared to cross with the light at Miquelallee. They each had a small video camera placed on the dashboard so that the image was shared among the three vehicles. Misha knew the target would follow the walk-don't walk instructions. He also knew the target always stepped out into the street as soon as the instructions allowed. Due to his former injuries, it took him nearly the entire allotted time to get across the divided highway.

The target stepped out into the crosswalk. The white Volkswagen transporter van of Team One accelerated through the intersection, avoided the cross-street traffic and collided with the target. The van hit the target with sufficient force to toss him nearly across the westbound two lanes of traffic. The cross-street traffic included a grey Mercedes driven by Team Two making a left turn westbound on Miquelallee. It ran over the collapsed man. There would be no doubt that he was dead. Cameras in the vehicles captured the result. The rest of the traffic stopped, creating congestion that would delay any police investigation. Misha nodded. Mission accomplished.

He tapped his driver on the shoulder. "Nicolai, time to move to the linkup."

The young man in the driver seat nodded and put the car in gear. He pulled away from the side street and headed north on Hansaallee toward a streetcar station north of the city, where the team members would rendezvous after abandoning the two vehicles. After the rendezvous, they would drive to Frankfurt Airport, turn in the rental car and catch a train in the underground station heading south to Munich. By late afternoon, they would be boarding a train to Vienna. They would await their next set of orders while enjoying Viennese hospitality on SWORDFISH accounts. Misha knew there would be another set of orders. There were always more orders.

THE CALL

The call came while Sue O'Connell was drinking her second cup of tea, watching the waterfowl walking along the edge of the property that led down to a dock on the Potomac River. It was dawn and the birds were just starting to wake up and think about food. The house, known to the entire O'Connell family simply as the Potomac River House, was a legacy of her grandfather. It was an old farmhouse that sat on ten acres with a small dock and boathouse on the river. Like everything in the O'Connell family, it looked totally normal. Like everything in the O'Connell family, it was anything but normal. It had security cameras and alarms, armored windows and doors, and two different concealed armories. It had been the scene of one gunfight where a man Sue considered her mentor and surrogate father had died protecting her mother. It was a house with history. Violent history.

Sue was enjoying the quiet Sunday morning, thinking about taking a drive on a lovely Virginia day or, perhaps, firing up her grandfather's powerboat for one last ride on the river before winter. Her mobile phone buzzed. She put down her mug of tea and looked at the screen, which said "UNKNOWN" where it should have registered either a number or a name. Sue knew immediately this was not going to be a friendly Sunday morning call from family. She also knew that someone else had decided what she was going to do today. She picked up the phone and answered with the last four digits of her phone number. "2614."

Jamie Schenk's gravelly voice replied, "Good morning, sunshine."

"Work?"

"Yup."

"Long or short?"

"Yup."

Sue smirked. "OK, wiseguy. Do I pack for hot or cold weather?"

"Definitely cold. And don't drive the T-bird. It may be sitting out-side for a while."

"See you."

"Make it sooner rather than later. And pack a uniform."

"Check."

The phone connection ended. She looked at the watch on her wrist. It was a Bulova from World War II, another legacy of her grandfather. She had it on a grey nylon strap. Not the most stylish, but practical. It was 0622hrs. Sue took one last look out to the water-fowl and said, "It looks like we are all going to be migrating."

A DRIVE IN THE COUNTRYSIDE

Sue was the first to admit that while her commute was longer than most of her colleagues would tolerate, it was a great drive in the Virginia countryside. Sue returned to the US in 2012 and after nearly six months of recovery, she returned to work, this time at a CIA facility. She never tired of the drive from her house along Virginia State Highway 3 to the small CIA office just east of Culpepper, Virginia. It was nearly an hour, but it was a scenic hour. She was convinced that if you were still stressed after that drive home, you needed to see a doctor. And, of course, when she returned home each day, she could look out over the lawn and the trees and watch the Potomac River working its way to the Atlantic Ocean.

Those commutes were especially pleasant when she drove the vintage Thunderbird her brother had given her years ago as a gift to mark her release from Walter Reed Army Hospital, where she had recuperated after losing part of her left leg in a gunfight in Afghanistan. The Thunderbird was a two-seat marvel of Detroit engineering, and it hugged the highway through rolling hills covered in trees.

Based on the phone call, she left the T-bird in the garage and switched to a ten-year-old Jeep Wrangler. It was a reliable partner in the winter with four-wheel drive and large winter tires. A bit less fun, but good transport regardless of mid-Atlantic weather that could be rain, sleet or snow during the winter months. And, as Jamie implied, a vehicle that could sit outside in that weather and Sue wouldn't fret in the least.

As she drove, Sue once again considered how sweet a deal she had. After nearly fifteen years of war zone deployments as a military intelligence officer with the US Special Operations Force (SOF), she was now working in a world where it was unlikely that she would be shot, blown up or captured. She was working with a team of CIA officers led by a close friend, Jamie Schenk. Her last operation with SOF had left her with a gunshot wound to the shoulder. While she recovered, SOF headquarters had reassigned Sue from her previous home base, the Human Intelligence Collection Unit (HICU) in Italy, to serve as the military detailee to Schenk's unit. In DoD parlance, a detailee was a military person who was officially assigned to another part of the US government, in her case the CIA.

At first, this meant very little to Sue but it meant an enormous amount to the DoD and to SOF headquarters. From her perspective, Sue was still paid by the Army and periodically traveled in military uniform. She was expected to check in with SOF headquarters at Ft. Bragg at least once a quarter. From the perspective of SOF head-quarters, Sue was now under the operational and administrative con-trol of the CIA and her SOF contacts wanted to see her only when/if there was something very good or very bad to discuss. While puzzling at first, Sue realized it was a good deal for her as she headed into what would likely be the last few years of her military career.

Sue was proud of her military service. As a chief warrant officer 5, she held the most senior rank in the warrant officer cadre. She had received multiple awards and decorations during her service. She had served most of those years in two elite units in the Army. First as a surveillance operator in the SOF Surveillance and Reconnaissance Detachment and then as a human intelligence collector, a case officer in CIA parlance, running agents providing intelligence for SOF counterterrorism missions. During those years, she had built a new family inside the SOF community. Commanders like Bill Jameson and Jed Smith serving as surrogate fathers, a sergeant major named Jim Massoni serving as a surrogate uncle and her best friend, Sarah Billings, as a surrogate sister. Mission success was important, but the camaraderie from within the very small SOF community was what made the difference when times were hard.

And times were often hard. Sue had paid dearly for her years in SOF. She had lost a portion of her left leg during a deployment in

Afghanistan and continued to serve with a below-the-knee prosthesis. She had just recovered from a bullet wound that occurred while hunting a traitor in Germany. She had spent most of her SOF years living out of a rolling duffle bag as she traveled from one war zone to another. For years, she was a Special Operations nomad and she still was living as a single woman in what was very much a man's world.

She had few close friends and no lovers. Her only opportunity to build an emotional relationship with a man ended badly in the Hurtgen forest in western Germany in 2012. The scar on her left shoulder was a reminder that she carried with her every day. It took Sue nearly a year to recover both physically and mentally from that attack in the Hurtgen forest. The bullet wound had healed relatively quickly but the damage to her shoulder muscles required months of physical therapy before she was fully back to normal.

The more difficult recovery was mental. In that forest confrontation, she found out her lover was a traitor. And before she could get closure on that revelation, he was killed by a sniper bullet — most likely from his foreign handler. The wound, the losses, coupled with her own traumatic loss of a part of her left leg in Afghanistan years ago spun inside her head like a sticky web of a black widow spider. Her move back to Virginia had helped, as had weeks with a SOF psychologist working out of Norfolk Navy base.

Work with the CIA over the past year was never boring, but it was a very different sort of work than the SOF counterterrorism world of "find, fix, and finish." Schenk was a retired Special Forces warrant officer who had worked for the CIA for over a decade. He took it on himself to explain the different culture of the CIA — not always in the politest way. Sue was used to a military structure to everything she did. Sue had been through the CIA training for case officers and her parents and her grandfather were CIA case officers, so she thought she knew how things worked inside what members of SOF called OGA — the "other government agency." She was only partly right.

Sue's new unit served as a team working for the chief of the European Division. Within European Division, the unit had the anodyne title of the Operational Support Unit. Even inside Europe Division, the goal of the unit designation was to deliver the message: *Nothing interesting happens here.* That was not the case. When Sue first arrived, half of the team was out of the office traveling to some European city. That had been a year ago, but her memory was still strong that Jamie had sat her down, poured her a cup of very strong, very black tea and started his explanation of what the office did:

"Sue, our team is best described as 'fixers' for any trouble that might come to the attention of the Europe Division chief. That trouble might include counterintelligence matters, security issues at stations or between station personnel and their many partners." He paused and looked over his teacup, his large, black moustache covered what Sue suspected might be a smirk.

"The chief calls us her plumbers," he had said. "That is, we fix leaks. Those leaks might be associated with counterintelligence threats, but they also might involve patching a leak caused when several organizations want to accomplish the same task in the same place and start making a mess. We don't help station if they have some sort of trouble with the embassy. That's the job of the station chiefs and their minions. Rather, we help when there is trouble between the stations, European liaison partners, the US Special Operations Community and NATO Special Operations units. Oh, and let's not forget that various Department of Justice lawmen who are focused on one thing: their criminal target."

Sue said, "It sounds pretty easy."

"It would be if everyone wanted to work together, but they don't. Everyone serving in Europe wants to claim counterterrorism as mission one. But, it looks different to everyone in the game. US and UK special operations want to find, fix and kill terrorists. OGA wants to recruit penetrations of the networks so that they can prevent the next attack. FBI wants to arrest the perpetrators of the most recent attack. Our NATO allies want to make them just go away without any noise. Then there are the other intelligence targets — Russia, China, transnational criminal enterprises, and cyber criminals who get in the way and have their own nasty agenda. For a COS, success against all these targets means more than just a pat on the head. It means promotion, career advancement, and greater control over resources. OK, that's great in the mind of an egomaniac, but that's not how teams work. I think it was President Truman who said: 'It is amazing what you can get done when you do not care who gets the credit.' So, Patty Dentmann sends us out to serve as her…representatives to make sure everyone plays nice in the sandbox."

Sue knew Patty Dentmann when she was the Chief of Station in Nicosia and Sue was on her first intelligence collector tour in Cyprus. Just over five feet tall, Patty did not look imposing, but Sue knew when Patty walked into a room, she could suck the air out of the room simply by a stern look and a quick word. She said, "So, we are Patty's hammer."

Jamie smiled. "Yup. And when we visit a COS, he does his best to be sure he doesn't become the nail."

After a few weeks "working the desk" as Jamie politely called keeping Sue under scrutiny to see if she was ready to get back in the field, Sue and Jamie had traveled to a pair of embassies in Europe, working to improve relationships and to enhance operations. Sue had never been a great diplomat when it came to bureaucratic challenges. She learned patience and tolerance as well as learning how SOF could work better with civilians. She suspected that was one of the reasons why SOF headquarters wanted her in the Operational Support Unit. Either way, it was hardly heavy lifting. If SOF headquarters wanted a detailee to OSU, then Sue was the commander's woman on the job.

As she muscled the Jeep into the parking lot, she couldn't help wondering what today's assignment would be.

A SIMPLE CASE OF MURDER

Jamie was waiting impatiently. As Sue entered the OSU workspace, she saw Jamie in his traveling clothes, with a rolling suitcase staring at the door she just used. In the past, Sue always traveled with one of the other members of OSU. Most of the time, it was with Jamie and he always traveled in the same clothes: black wool sweater over a white button-down collar shirt, black wool trousers, navy blue blazer — wool in the winter, cotton in the summer. Jamie's outfit ended with black, lace-up chukka boots. The only difference she ever saw was when they visited locations on the Mediterranean Sea. Then the colors changed from black to beige. She wondered how many versions of these two outfits were in Jamie's closet.

Sue barely suppressed a smile. "Have you been waiting like this ever since you called?"

One of Sue's co-workers, Richard Smith, shouted from behind one of the cubicles, "Yes he has, and it is driving me nuts."

Jamie growled, "This is a short-fuse job. We need to get going."

Smith mumbled, "Good riddance."

"Laugh while you can, smart guy. You are coming too as soon as you do your paperwork on the last TDY, so get to work submitting it to Headquarters."

"It can wait."

"No, it can't. We are going to be in Germany for a while. Just get it done, pronto. Then pack and get on the next plane."

The noise from behind the cubicle space continued in a low rumble.

Sue could see this might go on for a few minutes. Jamie and Richard had known each other for years, first in the Special Forces and then in the CIA. Their banter was nearly continuous when they were in the office. It was rarely tedious, but it was not a game Sue liked to play. It reminded her too much of the exchanges she used to hear between Massoni and Flash. And, she was forced to admit, she missed them and their friendly arguments. "Just let me get over to my desk, grab my docs and my travel case and we can be out the door," she said. "My suitcase is in the Jeep."

Jamie nodded toward Richard's location. "See, at least someone has a sense of urgency about all of this."

Sue was halfway across the room. She looked over her shoulder and said, "And what is this op, exactly?"

"Murder, Sue. A simple case of murder. Now, grab your stuff and meet me outside. You're driving."

TRAVELING IN STYLE

S ue had to admit that she hadn't expected to fly to Europe in a Gulfstream jet. On previous trips to Europe, she rode in cargo aircraft or commercial planes in coach-class seating. Either way, the travel meant long, tedious waits at either military or commercial airports, stuffing herself between cargo containers and sitting in a nylon sling seat or in a coach seat that made her left leg ache from the prosthetic limb pushed into a grotto under the seat.

The Gulfstream G5 was one of a small fleet of aircraft leased by the CIA. Known as the "Director's Birds," they were used for more than just ferrying the CIA director from place to place. They were the aircraft chosen when it was important to get someplace quickly or to bypass standard airport security at either end of the trip.

Another surprise when they arrived at the small private airfield south of Middlebury, Virginia: Patty Dentmann was waiting on the aircraft. Sue realized at that point this wasn't a normal trip. Dentmann had never been a part of any OSU operation.

"It's about time."

Sue was surprised at Jamie's demeanor with Dentmann. Jamie was not one to normally apologize or even acknowledge criticism. This time, he said, "Sorry, boss. We had to assemble and get the last of the package so we could talk on the bird."

Dentmann smirked. "Assemble the team? Was it that hard to get O'Connell out of bed?"

Sue could see she needed to defend herself. "It is an hour from my house to OSU and another hour here."

"What were you driving? A donkey cart?"

Jamie replied, "She drove her Jeep. We couldn't ask her to leave the T-bird here for however long this is going to take."

Dentmann shrugged. "Did you tell her what this is all about?"

Jamie seemed to have recovered his normal, sarcastic persona. "Boss, you ever try to have a conversation in an old Jeep? It's like talking inside a blender."

The rest of the conversation was delayed as the copilot walked out from the cockpit and said to Dentmann, "Ma'am, we are ready whenever you are."

Dentmann nodded. "Let's go."

The copilot closed and locked the exterior door and walked back into the cabin. He said over his shoulder, "It's about six hours to Ramstein Air Force Base. There are three box lunches for you back in the galley along with coffee and sodas. I will check in with you once we are at cruising altitude." He didn't wait for any response.

Patty said to Sue, "Belt in and once we level off, I'll start explaining."

Shortly after takeoff, Patty walked to the galley and grabbed a coffee from the Keurig. She turned around and said, "Jamie, there are even Keurig tea capsules!"

Jamie shook his head. "You might as well tell me they have packed rat sandwiches in the box lunches."

Sue added, "It's just not done."

By this time, Patty had already reached the round desk just forward of the galley. There were two captain's chairs on opposite ends of the desk and a long seat on the wall of the fuselage. She settled in against the wall and said, "OK, you two. Forage for whatever suits your sophisticated tastes and get back here."

Sue took the hint. She said to Jamie, "Hot tea?"

"Hot tea if you can make it like a normal person. Otherwise, water."

"I didn't realize you were so fussy."

"Years of practice."

Sue found that the galley had a hot water tank, so she pulled two tea bags from her jacket pocket and poured the steaming water into two ceramic mugs. By the time she arrived, Jamie was sitting in the seat at the forward end of the table, leaving Sue the one closest to the galley. She was thankful for small favors. Sue seldom had trouble with her prosthetic on the ground or even in vehicles. But there was something about air travel — perhaps the irregular surface, perhaps the change in air pressure — that made her unsteady on her left leg. She managed to deliver the tea without spilling any on either Jamie or the Division chief.

Dentmann pulled out a pair of files from a battered briefcase. Sue wondered how many years Dentmann had carried the case to however many places she served. She noticed the files were held in old, brown cardboard jackets that were dog-eared and stained. On the top edge were 201 file numbers. That meant these were personnel jackets.

"Jamie told you this is a murder case. In fact, it is two murder cases. Let's just say I don't think the solutions offered by the local police, the *Landeskriminalamt*, will be satisfactory. I can't tell the Germans I think their decisions were incorrect because I can't tell them that the two individuals were on our payroll for over thirty years. Sometime back in the end of the USSR and after German unification we decided to tell our German counterparts some things and not others."

Sue said, "Like the existence of the Panopticon in Wiesbaden?" During Sue's last case while serving with HICU, Jamie introduced her to an intelligence fusion center outside of Wiesbaden run in partnership with UK intelligence, the CIA, and their respective special operations units. The site was totally focused on counterterrorism — at least that was what Jamie said — and at least officially not declared to the German government. It was that last operation that resulted in Sue's shoulder injury and her return to the US as a detailee. After that operation, her former commander at HICU, Jed Smith, his sergeant major, Jim Massoni, and her HICU pal Flash, were assigned to the Panopticon as the US managers of the facility.

Dentmann looked over at Sue. Sue wasn't sure if Dentmann was irritated at the interruption or was simply trying to decide how she was going to kill her and eat her. Dentmann took a sip from her coffee and said, "Something like that."

Jamie said, "Remember, Boss. I wasn't the one who thought bringing this madwoman on board was a swell idea." Sue looked at Jamie and scratched her nose with her middle finger.

Dentmann ignored the back and forth and continued. "Starting in the 1950s, we ran several propaganda operations in Europe. Some were relatively straightforward, like Radio Free Europe, which focused on blasting radio messages into the Warsaw Pact. Until the Agency role in RFE was revealed in the 1960s, it was considered a non-governmental organization that wanted to deliver news to the people behind the Iron Curtain. We integrated our own, denied area collection into the broadcasts telling the folks on the other side pre-cisely what was happening in their governments and on the streets. We also launched balloons from Germany with leaflets, newspapers and heaven-only-knows what else. The balloons had a timed-release so that they would land near Prague, Budapest, and Warsaw. The two operations drove the commies nuts."

Dentmann took a sip from her coffee cup. She made a face. Sue did her best not to smirk. Dentmann continued, "In response they hunted down some of our RFE broadcasters and either kidnapped them or killed them on the streets. At one point, they even used a car bomb in Munich to destroy the RFE building." Dentmann took another sip from her coffee. She looked over the rim of her cup at Sue and said, "Following me, so far?"

Sue decided she was allowed to speak this time. "Part of my grand-parents' legacy is that same stuff in Berlin."

Dentmann paused for a moment and said, "Sorry, I forgot about Peter. Yes, that was all the same fight."

"But what does that have to do with our trip?"

Dentmann tapped the first file. "Our first victim was an agent for us during the Cold War. He was an East German legal traveler in the '70s and '80s who serviced dead drops and even placed special operations caches in the ground near some of the main cities in

East Germany. He worked for us while also serving as a small-time manager of a tool and die maker in Leipzig. The wall came down, East Germany disappeared, the Soviet Union disappeared, and our relationship ended. We gave him a healthy bonus, a generic medal for "assistance" to the US consulate in Frankfurt, and we went our separate ways. He had an emergency contact plan which none of us thought he would ever need."

Dentmann looked at Sue, "Last month, he used that emergency contact plan to reach out to us. By the time we sorted through the old files and identified the meeting site and time, our team in Frankfurt read in the newspaper that he was the victim of a hit and run. The Frankfurt police investigated the case. Stolen car. Fingerprints from what the German police say is a known people smuggler. Location of said smuggler unknown. The case isn't closed but it is in the dead files."

"But you don't believe it."

Dentmann shook her head. "Well, at first, we all assumed that an elderly gentleman might, in fact, end up a victim of a reckless driver. After he retired, he moved west and lived in Darmstadt along the river. The streets are narrow and often used by street racers. Then…"

Jamie entered the conversation. "Then, we had another agent suffer the same fate."

Dentmann tapped the second file. "He was a former Iranian asset. He served in the Islamic Revolutionary Guards Corps in the mid-1980s. Wounded in action in Iraq, he uses his veteran status to get a university degree in electrical engineering. In the 1990s, he works inside the Fordow nuclear facility as a plant manager. Ahmadinejad becomes the president in 2005 and he fires most of the support staff who served under President Rafsanjani and President Khatami's regime. Ahmadinejad replaces them with his loyal crew inside the Revolutionary Guard. There is a tussle over control of the nuclear facilities and if you were loyal to the previous regime, you were done. Our agent gets out of Iran with his wife and sets up a small carpet shop in Frankfurt. He also moonlights at the Goethe Institute near his house as a tutor for newly arrived Persian speaking refugees. He stays on our payroll as a talent spotter for Iranian exiles in Frankfurt and periodically provides reporting on Iranian government officials and businessmen traveling into Germany. His access eventually disappears. So, he is "retired," given a sizeable termination bonus and a US emergency contact telephone number in 2010."

"We hear nothing from him until last month when he calls into the number and asks for a meeting. The headquarters number was managed by the Iran office in headquarters. It takes a little bit of time for them to send a Farsi speaker to Germany. She arrived last week and went to the initial contact point in the commo plan."

Jamie added, "She waits at the ICP inside the German subway station at Frankfurt airport, no contact. She returns the next day, no contact. On the third day, our folks in Frankfurt are reading the Allgemeine Zeitung with their morning coffee and see a small notice that an Iranian was the victim of a hit and run. No further information."

Sue shook her head. "Two entirely separate cases of retired agents. Both hit and run attacks. One Cold War case, one modern case. How exactly are they related?"

Jamie says, "Remember our pal in Vienna?"

Sue made a slight gagging sound. "The rude geezer?"

"Yup, the rude geezer. He generated a non-scheduled meeting last week. I went out with Richard. You'll be happy to know he remains a rude, chain-smoking geezer." Jamie offered an ironic grin. "He did send his regards."

"Really?"

"No. He says he has heard that there is a wet team traveling around Germany. He says they are former Russian special forces working for a contracting firm."

"SWORDFISH?"

Jamie nodded. "One in the same. They apparently are working on cases based on files they have of retired assets that worked for us in Germany."

Sue looked at Dentmann. "How many so far?"

"We don't really know for sure. These two cases came to our attention because the assets generated an emergency contact. Right now,

I have a team working through the files matching old cases run out of our station and bases in Germany against recent unsolved crimes from the national police service, the *Bundeskriminalamt*. Of course, the problem is some of these cases may never come under the federal authorities, so the BKA records or even the state LKA records may never tell us what we want to know. The team back in headquarters has found two other suspicious deaths that match our agent names and last known locations. And, your old pals have found at least one counterintelligence case from the Army. So, at least five."

Sue said, "My old pals?"

Jamie said, "You have forgotten them already? Smith, Massoni and Flash are still running the Panopticon. We asked them to do a deep dive on missing military assets. They didn't find anything from the Cold War, but they did find an Army counterintelligence special agent from 2010 who recently died under suspicious circumstances. After a couple of tours in Iraq, he returned to Army CI in Stuttgart and married a German girlfriend. From Stuttgart, he ran two CI double-agent cases against Syrian operations in Hamburg. He and his wife died six months ago. House fire. Flash also found the two double agents are also dead. Definitely the same pattern."

Sue nodded. This was serious stuff. "So, our job is to find the crew doing the harm."

Dentmann said, "Your first job is to find the leak from our side."

Jamie said, "I told you when you joined the team that we are plumbers."

Dentmann said, "Study the files and come up with something, anything that might link these cases. Once you get it, pull the thread until this whole thing unravels and we can explain what is going on. Reach out to the Panopticon and sort out what they know. And..."

Jamie added, "I know. Don't get killed."

Dentmann said, "Well, I was going to say don't cause an international incident. But, please, don't get killed."

THE USUAL SUSPECTS

The Gulfstream landed at the US Air Force base in southwestern Germany. As they taxied to the hangar where special operations and aircraft carrying senior officials were housed, Jamie turned to Dentmann. "Boss, did you arrange for my usual toys?"

"You know you are a pain in the ass, right?" Sue wasn't surprised at Dentmann's tone, but a little surprised by her response. Dentmann continued, "The toys are still in the car you used last time you were here. Secured in the trunk." She reached into her purse and handed him the key fob to the car. "The case is still in the same concealment and still uses fingerprint ID. I do hope you don't need most of the items."

Jamie smirked. "I have no interest in most of the toys, but sometimes, it just is something you can't avoid."

The aircraft came to a halt and one of the crew came out of the pilot compartment and opened the hatch and lowered the staircase. As Dentmann left the aircraft she looked over her shoulder and said, "Do your best!"

Jamie did a formal bow and said, "Boss, you know that is my objective."

As she walked down the stairs, Sue heard Dentmann say, "That is what worries me."

By the time Sue and Jamie were down the stairs, Dentmann was already in an armored BMW limousine. Sue saw Dentmann wave to them as the car headed out of the hangar. Sue said, "What was that all about?"

Jamie laughed. "Well, the Boss hired me to fix stuff however I saw fit. Sometimes, my work in Europe has been a little ... unconventional.

You haven't seen much of that so far, simply because our previous jobs were pretty straightforward. This job isn't at all straightforward and I wanted to have all my options covered."

"Hence the toys?"

"Precisely."

"So, what are they?"

"Toys."

"You are annoying."

"So I've been told. It's just my nature. Now, let's pick up our bags and get over to the car."

Sue walked to the rear of the aircraft where the copilot pulled their bags from the cargo door. She hadn't paid much attention to anything during the flight other than the discussions. It was already dark in Germany and the fall air was cold and damp. Sue zippered up her fleece jacket, pulled a knit cap from a pocket and put it on. She took the rolling duffle from the copilot, extended the handle and followed Jamie as he walked to the far end of the hangar. After hours of sitting still in the airplane, Sue was stiff and it took her a bit to focus her gait so that her prosthetic foot didn't trip her up. Jamie already knew she was a wounded warrior but Sue had no intention of letting anyone else know her secret.

When she arrived at their vehicle, she was surprised. On their previous trips, they had no need for a vehicle. They used taxis or trains. European cities were not the best place for a rental car. Parking was always a challenge and most of the cities had extensive mass-transit options. Jamie was already loading his suitcase into the trunk of the car when Sue arrived.

"How do you like it?"

"Are you serious?"

"Of course."

"You do realize this is the twenty-first century, right?"

"And your point?"

Sue looked at the aged Mercedes C-class. Most probably manufactured in the 1990s. The body was relatively dent free, but the paint was a faded green that had probably been lime green when the car rolled off the factory line in Stuttgart. "It is a little … old."

"Trust me, it is just the thing for our current job. In Germany, there are thousands of cars that look precisely like this one. The last time I used it, I had a mechanic tune the turbo-diesel so that it has all the torque needed to get up and go, but also the sort of range we might need if we conduct an all-day surveillance operation. It's perfect." Jamie smiled. "Oh, and it has a few little extras."

"Extras?"

"I have two digital cameras installed — front and back. We can park the car near a target house, turn on the cameras and the car becomes fixed point surveillance while we do other work. I had a large antenna embedded in the roof under the headliner. It can give us mobile telephone range for our phones as well as mobile intercept capability. It is dandy."

"So, this is part of the toys you were talking about with Dentmann?"

"Nope. Those are in the trunk. I'll show those to you later once we get inside the Panopticon compound. Now, hop in and we'll be on our way. Next stop, Wiesbaden!"

Sue got into the Mercedes. She noticed the interior belied the exterior age. The leather seats and the electronic displays inside the car definitely belonged in a car newer than the age of the frame and body.

As they headed out, Jamie took what was clearly the least direct route to the autobahn that would take them to Wiesbaden.

"Tourist route?"

Jamie looked over at Sue, "What? You don't like the German countryside?"

"Anything interesting to see in Nobfelden or Idar-Oberstein?"

"Plenty to see in Rhineland-Palatinate, but mostly what I want to determine is our surveillance status."

"Already?"

"Sue, you must realize at this point, we are involved in an operation where there won't be a ton of folks we can trust. Certainly, your old crew now resident in the Panopticon, but otherwise, trust no one." Jamie smiled. "Except me."

"Did you ever think I trusted you?"

Under Jamie's enormous mustache, Sue saw a glimmer of white teeth. "I certainly hope not."

They drove through the German countryside in silence as Jamie ran the Mercedes at a modest 100km per hour. Sue looked to the surrounding hillsides where the neatly manicured forests were a mix of deep green pines and a mix of reds and oranges from the hardwood trees. Finally, she broke the silence.

"Who are we hunting exactly?"

"Good question, but not precisely the correct one. First, I think we need to sort out if there is a leak inside the US offices in Germany. Given the location of the latest murder, I'm thinking we start with the office in Frankfurt."

"Because…?"

"Because, the last of the agents to be murdered was resettled in Frankfurt and because Frankfurt is close to the Panopticon. While the cyber and signals capability there expands to Europe, our ability to grab trusted manpower for physical surveillance in this case is limited because I honestly don't know who we can trust in Agency offices in Europe. I'm hoping we can convince Smith to release Massoni and Flash for some fun on the streets."

"Like old times."

Jamie looked over at Sue. "Well, in the past, we all worked together on joint operations. I'm not sure Smith would consider this a joint operation and I'm not sure I want to bring in Dentmann as a hammer to make this a joint operation. They do have a full-time job of their own serving Special Operations Command and European Command as well as DoD counterintelligence."

"I reckon we have some leverage."

Jamie said, "And that is why you are in the car instead of Richard."

"And not because of my sparkling personality?"

"Oh, sure. That too."

The blend of the quiet rumble of the diesel engine, the smooth German highway and the comfortable leather seat had a hypnotic effect on Sue's jet-lagged brain. At first, she fought her body clock saying it was the middle of the night. Jamie didn't seem to want to talk and so Sue finally surrendered to sleep.

The racket of 1970s rock woke her up with a start.

"Have a nice nap?"

"What are you playing?"

"Classics!"

"When I think of classics, I think of Mozart."

"I think I have some Bach in here someplace."

"Bach will do."

Jamie smiled and scrolled through his play list. Instead of a mix of electric guitars and drums, a synthesized keyboard playing Bach's Brandenburg Concerto came out of the car speakers. "Better?"

"I guess."

"OK, I just wanted you to be awake when we get to the Panopticon. You were snoring and I really didn't want you drooling when we first see your old crew."

"It would be better if I had some tea."

Jamie pointed to the cup holder off her left hip. "I made up a cup for you when I stopped for fuel."

"I didn't wake?"

"You didn't even move. Now drink your tea and start to formulate how you are going to approach Smith with your plan."

"Not going to help?"

"Well, it's not like they don't know we are coming."

"Dentmann?"

"Of course, Dentmann."

OLD HOME WEEK

Jamie made a call on his mobile phone as they approached the Wiesbaden exits on A66. He offered a code number and received a reply and hung up. He said, "I love it when a plan comes together."

They approached the metal fence that surrounded the Panopticon, and just as they were about to turn in, the gate opened and the Mercedes disappeared inside the walls. Sue had no fond memories from her last time in the Panopticon. She had been involved in what she thought at the time was a hunt for Serbian war criminals. Instead, the operation revealed that her lover was a traitor, and she ended up with a bullet in her shoulder. All of this memory was wrapped inside the four walls of the Panopticon, a US-UK intelligence fusion center. For Sue, it wasn't good to be back.

On the other hand, Jamie was like a kid coming back home from college. He jumped out of the car and ran to the gate. He greeted the gate guards and shouted to some of the Panopticon staff as they walked across the compound. Sue realized there was no good way to face these memories, but she decided to do her best. After all, the closest people she had to a real family were living and working here in Wiesbaden. They would definitely be enthusiastic about Sue's return. She decided to act like an adult and do her best to be equally happy.

Jamie came back to the Mercedes, opened the trunk and pulled their two roller bags out. He locked the trunk and said to Sue, "Shall we make our grand entrance?"

Sue knew Jamie well enough to see through his bonhomie. He understood her challenge and wanted to make it as easy as possible. She recognized being "Ms. Grumpy" wouldn't work with him and definitely wouldn't work with her colleagues inside. She did a formal bow and said, "Absolutely, Prince of Darkness. Lead on."

Negative experiences aside, Sue could not help but be impressed with the Panopticon. The outside of the building looked to be just another warehouse in a string of warehouses along the Main River. The first metal door led to a closet-sized room with a string of cabinets against the wall. Once Jamie and Sue emptied their pockets of all electronics, he tried the cipher lock on the interior door. His combinations of numbers didn't work. "Can you believe it, they don't trust me?"

The door opened a crack and a head popped out. Flash, true name Sarah Billings, looked out and said, "Didn't you see the sign? No solicitors!"

Sue smiled. The same sarcastic Flash. Short black hair, blood red reading glasses pushed on the top of her head. Black sweat suit, black trainers, and a wicked sense of humor. Sue felt better already seeing one of her closest friends in the military. For the first time on this TDY, she actually felt like smiling. She said, "Hey, you never write, you never call. Have you found someone else to love?"

Flash pushed the cipher-locked door open and rushed across the entrance room. She grabbed Sue by the arms, pulled her close and gave her a kiss on each cheek. "You could have visited you know. Once you disappeared into the maw of OGA, it was like you left our universe."

Jamie interrupted, "How come I don't get a smacker?"

Flash turned to Jamie and said in her best coy voice, "That's for later, Klingon."

From inside the Panopticon, Jim Massoni growled. "Close the door, you are letting electrons in."

Flash shook her head. "I tried to explain to the sergeant major the importance of the Faraday cage that surrounds the Panopticon. It's like explaining a wristwatch to a fish." She paused and said, "OK, I have to ask. No electronics, correct?"

Jamie raised his arms and said, "Want to search me?"

Flash smiled, "Later."

Sue said, "Enough already. Let's go inside before the sergeant major has a cow."

They stepped up into the Panopticon. The space was a box inside a box, and as Flash said, the interior was surrounded by a Faraday cage preventing any electronic emanations in or out of the space other than by way of the massive cables that linked the servers inside the building to dozens of different collection sensors, European-based surveillance teams, and satellite imagery downloaded from antenna feeds outside the building.

Sue looked around. The interior hadn't changed much. There were dozens of workstations, some occupied, some empty. The ambient light had a tinge of blue from LED lamps in the ceiling. Sue looked at her watch. It was just after 1500hrs. As she recalled, the entire Panopticon lighting system would change from white light to red light at 1700hrs so that individuals who had street work in the evening would not lose their night vision when they visited the Panopticon.

It was a strange mix of new and old. On her last trip, Jamie explained that the building design and even the concept for the Panopticon was from the late Cold War. As the world shifted from the threat of a nuclear exchange between superpowers to the hunt for terrorist networks, the Panopticon morphed into a 24/7 joint intelligence center manned by US and UK intelligence personnel. Sue wondered what it would morph into as the threat from highly structured terrorist networks receded into history.

Jamie seemed to read her mind. "I wonder what this place will look like in five or even ten years."

Flash was standing next to them watching their gaze as it shifted from ceiling to walls to workstations to a closed center space in the hub of the building. "Well, if you are through gazing at your navels, I think we have work to do."

Jim Massoni's voice echoed across the Panopticon. "Hey, we're working here. Quit sightseeing and go visit the boss."

TREASURE HUNT

It was a crisp October morning and Barbara O'Connell was watching the arrival of geese on Chautauqua Lake. After living several years at the lake, she had grown fond of matching the seasons to the arrival of the geese. In the fall, they stopped at the lake on their way south for the winter; in spring, they retraced their flight heading to Canada. Very few of the geese or the ducks stayed for long in this narrow, glacial carved lake, but those that did gave Barbara great pleasure. The ground floor of the bungalow had a large French door that opened onto a small deck with an unobstructed view of the lake. She had a pair of early Cold War military binoculars as well as a modern spotting scope on a tripod near the window. While she was hardly a committed bird watcher, Barbara was certain that she had spotted several banded geese over the years who stopped by the lake every year on their sojourns.

She was drinking a mug of Earl Grey tea, musing about the interesting turn her life had taken in the past two years, as she remained on call to help an old friend, Beth Parson, who was a troubleshooter at the international law firm of Stearns and Mandeville. In 2012, she and Beth had successfully recovered paintings looted by Nazis in World War II, and helped to return the stolen art to the Mayerhaus family. After that, Beth convinced her firm that there were more such cases in the world, with wealthy patrons willing to support the recovery efforts. Beth and Barbara traveled in search of long-lost family art looted by the Nazis, religious icons stolen by every side in the Balkans wars of the 1990s, and even a few pieces of Scythian gold stolen from the Kabul Museum. Good work, mostly in Europe and, thankfully, work without any risk of violence.

Her son and new daughter-in-law were progressing through the ranks of the FBI, working in the large FBI field office in Washington, DC. Barbara was familiar with the challenges of life as a tandem couple — as married co-workers were called at the Agency. She and her long-dead husband had been CIA case officers at the end of the Cold War, often based far apart, and balancing two jobs as they moved up the career ladder. It wasn't easy in the Agency and she expected it wouldn't be easy in the FBI. However, William and Molly might both be able to serve in the Washington, DC area at any of the multiple FBI offices around the nation's capital. Barbara hoped their careers did not prevent them from having children. While not necessarily ready to be a grandmother, she had to admit the thought was intriguing.

For now, she was pretty sure children were not part of her daughter's life plan. Sue had been a special operations warrior in the counterterrorism wars before the 9/11 attacks. She had sacrificed her leg, and lost more than one colleague in the long wars in Afghanistan and Iraq. Barbara knew Sue lost a boyfriend in 2012 because of those wars. The mental demons from the man's own war wounds had resulted in decisions that led to his death in a German forest. His actions broke Sue's heart, and their final confrontation left her with another bullet wound.

After that confrontation, Sue returned to the US to recover both physically and mentally with help from a physical therapist and a psychologist. And she started a new assignment with a CIA unit in Northern Virginia. The work probably bored Sue to tears, but Barbara was happy knowing her daughter was safe in the USA.

After her morning tea, Barbara started a slow process of fall housekeeping. A cottage on the lake was a wonderful thing, but Chautauqua Lake would turn to ice soon enough. When that happened, the house would need to be clean and sealed tight to keep out the winter cold.

As she moved from room to room, every nook and cranny of the house reminded her of Peter O'Connell Sr., her father-in-law who had lived and died in this cottage.

Peter Sr. was a high-level intelligence officer in CIA headquarters until his retirement, and Barbara's relationship with him had been cordial, but not necessarily revealing. She met Peter O'Connell Jr. while both were attending the CIA case-officers school known as the Farm. After their marriage, Peter Jr. served in Eastern Europe targeting Russians, and Barbara served in the newly established Counterterrorism Center, working against Arab and Iranian terrorists.

The elder Peter was devastated when his son, her husband, was killed in the line of duty by a Russian poisoner. Only later — after Peter Sr. was himself killed by a Russian sniper round — did Barbara learn that he had managed the program that put his son directly in the line of fire of Russian intelligence services and the Russian mafia. She understood then why her father-in-law had disappeared from public life and spent his last days alone in the cottage where she now lived.

During those retirement years, he took interest in mentoring his grandchildren. William joined the Marine Corps after college and served in Iraq before joining the FBI. Sue was strongly influenced by her grandfather, spending weekends at his house on the Potomac River while attending William & Mary. Barbara was convinced Peter was the one who encouraged Sue to join the Army and, once in, encouraged her to join the special operations forces. Peter's legacy to Sue was his house on the Potomac and everything that went with it including a remarkable collection of firearms. Bill received Peter's townhouse in Georgetown which made his life as an FBI Special Agent much easier in an area where housing was nearly impossible on a federal salary. Much to Barbara's surprise, Peter's legacy to her was the cottage at Chautauqua Lake. It took some time, but she had finally started to think of the house as her own, rather than Peter's last retreat from the world.

As her autumn cleaning duties took her around the house, she carefully avoided the hiding places where her father-in-law had cached weapons and diaries inside the house. Over the years, she had discovered several concealments, of varying size. The hidden weapons had done him no good. He was killed by Russian assassins before he had a chance to use them. The diaries were something that

Barbara had pulled out and read, one after the other, as she tried to piece together the life of Peter O'Connell, OSS commando and CIA intelligence officer.

She thought she had found them all, so it was a surprise when the vacuum cleaner bumped against an irregular floorboard in the master bedroom.

There were no clues that would have pointed to a hideaway there. Instead, Barbara found it by accident when she moved the bed to vacuum the ancient Turkish carpet that stretched from corner to corner in the room. The twelve-by-twelve-foot Hereke carpet looked to her untrained eye to be easily over 100 years old. The pile was almost completely worn down, leaving the fabric as thin and as supple as a dish towel. As she carefully worked the vacuum cleaner along the carpet, she noticed a small deformity. Nothing that would have been visible when the bed was in place, but just enough to make her stop her cleaning chore.

Barbara got down on her hands and knees and moved from the edge of the carpet to the center, where she could feel a loose floorboard. She knew that if she didn't make a repair, the edge of the board would eventually tear through the thin carpet. She fetched a small tool bag that included screwdrivers, a hammer, some sandpaper and, for use in a worst-case scenario, a small chisel. She pulled back the carpet and, once again on hands and knees, moved to the offending floorboard. On closer inspection, she saw that the small lump under the carpet was a hinge. She had just discovered the most obscure of Peter's concealments.

It was a single plank, four inches wide and three feet long. She carefully used the chisel to pry up the end away from the hinge. The plank lifted easily, and Barbara could see into the skeleton of the house. Hand-hewn joists, easily sixteen inches tall by four inches wide stretched and divided the first and second floors. In that space, she found an oilskin envelope along with a blue silk bag the size of a woman's handbag. After recovering the envelope and the bag, she smoothed the plank back in place, and returned the carpet and bed to their original positions. Barbara put away the tools and the vacuum cleaner, poured herself a glass of red wine, and began to inspect her discovery.

First, she upended the silk sack on the small writing desk in the upstairs room where she did all her reading. A treasure trove of items fell out, some predictable and some more like wonders from Aladdin's cave.

The first thing Barbara noticed was a carved gold bangle. It was designed to look like a dragon with cabochon-cut emeralds for eyes. The details of the scales, the hands and the wings of the dragon were etched into the gold. The bangle opening was big enough for her to fit her hand through it, so Barbara gave in to temptation and put the bracelet on. Once it was on her arm, she realized that the bangle was heavy. It was solid gold.

The next thing on the desk was a gold men's bracelet known as a baht bracelet. When Barbara first joined the CIA, many of her instructors and early mentors had served in Southeast Asia in the 1960s and 1970s. They all wore these bracelets which they claimed were part of their escape and evasion kit. With very little work, you could pull a link off the bracelet and use the gold to trade for food or transportation. Since no one ever told her about how they used the baht bracelet, she just assumed it was maintained by the Asia hands to distinguish themselves from their Cold-War colleagues in Europe. More symbol than tool.

The third item was much easier to source. It was yet another of Peter's weapons. Specifically, a Smith and Wesson Model 10 revolver with a 3-inch barrel which was a standard weapon in the CIA inventory for over forty years. Instead of the standard hard-rubber handgrips on the revolver, there were a set of engraved grips which looked to be from elephant ivory. The engraving on one grip had the OSS spearhead insignia. On the reverse was an engraved map of Southeast Asia. Barbara thought that this seemed more a memento than the battle-ready weapons she had found in other concealments in the Chautauqua house.

The final items on the desk were more ordinary, and yet even more intriguing: a key and a dozen gold coins with the image of a long-dead

German Kaiser on the front and a gold eagle on the reverse. Clearly, the coins were minted before the Nazis took over and put the swastika on every government item. The key had a small cord and label attached. In careful handwriting that she recognized as belonging to her father-in-law, it read, Banque Marchande, Lugano, account 675221/Dilettante. Barbara decided she needed another glass of wine before dealing with the contents of the envelope.

The flap cracked as oilskin opened, leaving small chips of dried paper on the small table next to the Adirondack chair. The writing was Peter's. While some of his journals were written in blue fountain-pen ink, this letter was in ballpoint pen. It was in a cramped writing style, less controlled than the journals written during his years as a case officer and senior manager at the Agency, but still clearly Peter's hand.

> *Barbara, I'm glad you found this note. I knew you would eventually. I am leaving this treasure hunt for you to follow. I wasn't sure whether Peter would approve, but he passed before I could explain. The story is not one I'm proud of but it is certainly a story that someone needs to read. I'm assuming it is you, Barbara, but it might be one of your children. So, with that in mind, I ask your patience and your forgiveness.*
>
> *Peter*

Barbara flipped the page. Nothing more. Barbara shook her head. It was typical of the old codger to leave a trail of questions without clear answers. It seems that she is going to have to go to Switzerland to find out.

FIND THE FINK

Sue and Jamie followed Jim Massoni toward the hub of the Panopticon. Sue knew the room in the center was the most secure in the building and when she was last there, served as the command post for the multiple shifts of technical surveillance. Massoni knocked on the door, fingered the cipher lock and gestured for Sue and Jamie to enter. He and Flash followed.

Brigadier General Jedidiah Smith sat behind a metal-framed desk filled with stacks of reports. When Sue worked for Smith back in Italy, she always assumed that he was just as hostile to technology as Jim Massoni. His new office proved her assumption. She expected at least one if not two workstations at the desk. None were there. Instead, an old-fashioned, stacked pair of boxes sat on the right of the desk, marked IN and OUT. An equally old-fashioned desk lamp and desk blotter completed the work space. Smith looked up from the stack of papers, wire-rimmed reading glasses perched on his nose.

"It's about time."

Jamie said, "Jed, the G-5 was as quick as we could get here."

Smith nodded and said, "Well, I'm glad to see you brought O'Connell. She is certain to get things done."

Massoni added, "More likely than not with some degree of violence."

Smith looked over at Massoni and Flash as if he had just noticed them in the room. He pointed his pencil toward the small table in the corner of the room. "Why don't you sit down and I'll tell you what we know."

Sue and Jamie sat at one side of the table, Massoni and Flash on the other, and Smith walked around his desk to sit at the head of the table. "The problem isn't all that complicated. Here's what we know: the targets are all long-retired assets or, in our case, a long-retired agent handler and his assets. The perpetrators work hard to make the hit look like an accident or a health problem. We know from the list of victims that their work was either against Russia or the Iranians. So, in a sense that narrowed our search down to three of the usual suspects."

Sue looked up and said, "Three?"

Flash interceded. "Sue, the first two are pretty clear. Russians and Iranians traveling in country. The third is Lebanese Hizballah that are already in Europe serving as Iran's surrogates. It isn't as if the Iranians haven't used Hizballahis in the past. After all, they used the Hizballah goons to murder the Kurds in Berlin in…"

Smith nodded. "No need for a history lesson, Flash. We used the Panopticon capability to search travelers in/out of Germany up to six weeks before and six weeks after the assassinations. In the case of the attack on the Iranian, there were four Iranians who traveled into country a month prior to the assassinations and then left a few days before the hit. There was a slight overlap with a team of five Russians who arrived five days before the assassination and departed the same day."

Flash had been fidgeting in her chair as Smith talked through the results. He looked at her and said, "OK, so tell them."

Flash smiled and said, "SWORDFISH."

Smith decided to reestablish control of the meeting. "SWORD-FISH. It isn't clear if they were simply working as contractors for the Iranians or there is some sort of Iranian-Russian network that is at play, but it really doesn't matter. The profile works: the Iranians surveil the target. The SWORDFISH team conducts the assassination. It is designed to befuddle the German investigators. Now, in the case of the death of our retired CI agent and the Agency's German asset, the trail has gone cold, so we can only speculate. But, in each case, there were similar arrival of five Russian citizens into Hamburg from St. Petersburg. Always different names, but always a group of five. An unlikely coincidence."

Smith paused and looked around the room. He continued, "If we didn't have the resources here that were designed to identify non-standard terrorist patterns…"

"And we didn't have a super genius…"

Smith gave Flash a hard look and continued as if he had not been interrupted, "We would not have sorted this out."

Jamie said, "So, now that we know who is doing this, we have to sort out how they are getting their targeting data."

Massoni nodded and said, "That's your job, Schenk. Find the fink."

Jamie smiled and said, "That is precisely our job."

"Meanwhile," Smith said, "I have to be certain that there isn't an electronic fink inside our system, because there just might be."

DO THE EASY STUFF FIRST

Sue and Jamie were sitting in an outdoor café, drinking herb tea and enjoying the warm morning sun. They left their quarters at the Panopticon early that morning and drove into the Frankfurt traffic. Sue wasn't surprised that Jamie knew the various ways into the city. After all, he had been the boss in the Panopticon and no doubt had made the trip at every possible hour of the day or night. They parked in a ramp near the Congress Center Messe, walked to the closest U-bahn station, and then rode the network across the city until they came out near the Romerplatz.

"So, explain to me again why we are talking to the local OGA chief?"

Jamie looked up from his tea. Sue couldn't determine if he was amused or bemused at the question. He was wearing yet another version of his standard travel clothes. Black wool from top to bottom with a navy wool blazer. Sue always felt a little underdressed. Her wool slacks and rollneck sweater were certainly appropriate for the climate and the venue, but not quite as formal as Jamie's travel "uniform."

Jamie said, "So, where would you start if not with the local OGA?"

"I figured we would start with the old files and look for some sort of connections."

"Someone gave up the current contact information and that someone may work with the local OGA. I figured it made no sense not to go right to the top and rattle the chief's cage. And, I always do the easy stuff first. After all, it might make the hard stuff less hard."

"So, we are the hammer and the chief doesn't want to be a nail."

"Exactly, Grasshopper. Plus, I want to see how nervous the chief is when we start asking questions that must be a little disturbing."

"We are treating him like a reluctant informant?"

"I think I told you before: Trust no one."

"Sheesh."

Neal Bascomb hadn't changed since the last time Sue saw him, nearly two years ago in the commander's briefing room for US Army Europe. He was a fit man, balding with a beard. He was dressed in a pin-striped suit and red tie under a black wool overcoat. His shoes were highly shined black loafers. He wore tortoiseshell sunglasses and was carrying a leather portfolio. Sue wasn't entirely certain what to make of this senior intelligence officer. Her experience had been limited to Dentmann and her instructors at the Farm. It didn't take long for her to decide.

Bascomb shook hands with Jamie and Sue and sat down. After the waiter delivered a coffee, his opening gambit was not friendly. "Look, I've got about fifty people who work for me in three German States. I have the ConGen breathing down my neck about this recent murder and I have two different appointments with German liaison today. I have plenty of resources to work on this murder. I really don't need your help and it is not a good day to have a coffee at an outdoor café."

Sue watched as Bascomb spoke. The veins at his temples were pumping plenty of blood, but his face and bald head were perfectly white. She wondered if she should tell him that he needed to practice some yoga to prevent an early heart attack. Jamie on the other hand appeared to be more than willing to create the conditions for a heart attack.

Jamie stood up and said, "No dramas, Neal. We'll stop bothering you. You don't need our help, then we leave. Just send a note to HQs and to Berlin saying you wanted us out of your turf." Jamie paused and watched as Sue started to get up from her seat. "In fact, you don't need to send the note to HQs. Dentmann is in Berlin seeing your boss, so one addressee should be enough. I'm sure Dentmann will give us our new marching orders after that. Ciao." With that, Jamie stood up and turned to walk away. Sue followed.

As soon as they were a dozen yards away, Sue whispered, "A new negotiating technique?"

Jamie smiled, "Hey, if the guy wants to draw a line in the sand, I'm all for that. He should know better. We are here to help him. I don't have time to waste playing nice with a fathead. He has my mobile number. He can call us when he decides — or when his COS decides for him — that it is better to play nice." Jamie walked over to the cab stand, climbed into the first cab handy and asked in a regional German dialect to be taken to the Palmengarten. As Sue got into the cab, she looked over at Bascomb. He was still sitting at the table, making a phone call. He looked a little worried.

They were quiet as their cab wandered through the side streets of Frankfurt avoiding traffic on the main streets. They pulled up on the side street next to the Palmengarten. Jamie paid in Euros and they got out. He watched as the cab pulled away. As soon as the cab turned a corner and was out of sight, Jamie said, "Up for a stroll?"

"So, we aren't going to enjoy the botanical wonderland of the Palmengarten?"

"Sorry, not on the taxpayers' dime. We have another place to go, but I didn't want the cab driver to know our destination."

"And that is?"

"The scene of the crime." Jamie turned down Siesmayer Strasse and walked toward the entrance to Grüneburgpark. "It's a lovely day for a stroll."

SCENE OF THE CRIME

Sue walked with Jamie through the Grüneburgpark. The groomed mix of stone and dirt on the trail made for easy walking, and for a change, Jamie matched her pace rather than forcing her to try to match his strides. Sue could feel Jamie was using the walk to think about the case so far. The trees around the park were in their last few days of color. At 50 degrees north latitude, fall would soon be over. Freezing rain and sleet would soon be the weather. For now, she was enjoying the sun on her face and the slight crunch of the trail. She had learned over the last decade to appreciate the good times because you never knew how long they would last.

After a few minutes in silence, Jamie finally said, "I think we need to engage the full power of the Panopticon. If Bascomb is determined to be a knucklehead, then we must work another track."

"Do you think Bascomb is trying to hide something?"

"Meaning do I think he is the fink?"

Sue nodded. She had no idea how close Jamie was to this OGA officer and she had done her best to avoid saying it directly.

Jamie shrugged. "Sue, you and I learned the hard way that you never know who a traitor might be or why they might make very bad decisions."

He looked over to see how Sue would take that comment. After all, it was her lover who had proven to be a traitor the last time they were in Germany. Sue was walking with her head down so he couldn't see her expression. Jamie decided to press on. "So, anyone in the mix except for our pals in Wiesbaden, Dentmann, and us kids are possibly in the frame. For now, I'm assuming Bascomb is just being an officious dick rather than trying to hide something. However, he might be trying to hide something in his shop that he thinks might be embarrassing to him. Before I try to squeeze him to see what comes out, I want more data. And data are what we can get from the Panopticon."

They continued for a few minutes in silence. Jamie said, "We are coming up to the murder scene. It is a major road junction between Miquelallee and Hansaallee. Hansaallee is a two-lane north-south street that becomes four lanes headed into the city at this point. Miquelallee is a four-lane city street that quickly becomes A66 heading west toward Wiesbaden. It is a wicked busy intersection. You would have to be confident in your surveillance ability to make sure you get the chance to run over a guy. I just need to see this for myself. A map recon wasn't going to be enough. It has been years since I have been on foot in this side of Frankfurt."

They walked out of the park and then north along Hansaallee. The transition from the quiet of the park to the noise of city streets was dramatic. Inside the park, German landscapers had created an environment that felt deceptively natural. A half block later, that deception disappeared as they entered a major industrial and banking center for all of Europe.

At the intersection, the traffic noise was deafening. Jamie turned to Sue and shouted, "OK. We are going to cross here and walk north on Hansaallee. It is the reverse route of the target. I just want to see something on the other side of Miquelallee." Sue nodded and looked at the four lanes of traffic. It was clear that all the cars passing through the intersection and heading west accelerated immediately to 100km well before the highway became A66. Sue wasn't shy about pushing her prosthetic when needed, but the thought of being caught in the middle of this traffic while trying to cross made her stomach tighten. It was very much like the first time she was a jumpmaster at Ft. Bragg and leaned out the aircraft hanging on the edge of the paratroop door. A little disconcerting.

Jamie looked at Sue and said, "The Germans are very good with their crosswalks. We are going to have a minute to get across." He smiled and said, "If you want, you can jump on my back and I'll run across."

"How about we work our way across with me kicking you in the ass every couple of meters."

Jamie shrugged. "Just trying to help."

Before Sue could think of an appropriate remark, the lights all turned red, and the crosswalk sign turned white. They crossed well before the countdown timer started. Jamie nodded and said, "So, to hit the target, both vehicles had to be prepared to run stop lights and be captured by the cameras. I suspected as much, but it's always good to double-check. So, Flash should be able to get us mug shots of the drivers. Now, let's continue our walk."

Sue and Jamie walked along Hansaallee leaving the roar of traffic behind. The area was residential, with classic 1950s block apartment buildings on both sides of the street. Jamie seemed lost in thought. "Back in the day, this whole area was called HICOG. It stood for High Commissioner Germany and was one of the first apartment complexes that the Army built during the early '50s. This was before the Western allies released authorities to the new West German government."

He pointed toward the east. "Over there was a huge commissary, PX and all the normal Military Welfare and Recreation buildings. When V Corps left Frankfurt, we turned it all over to the Germans and this little suburb, known as Dornbusch, became the place the German government housed refugees and guest workers. I suspect they are still placing some of the Syrian refugees here." He pointed to the west. "Just out of sight is the headquarters of the Bundesbank."

"Did you serve here?"

"Nope. I was with 10th Group in Bad Tolz at an old Wehrmacht compound. But, in those days if you were traveling on an international flight, you flew out of Frankfurt. Munich was too small an airport if you wanted to be low profile. Our PX complex was OK, but the V Corps complex was grand. So, I would bunk with a pal or get TDY quarters near here and then walk the streets. You never know when a little area familiarization might come in handy."

"And is this walk coming in handy?"

Jamie looked over at Sue and said, "Did you notice the various cross streets here? If you had to lay up for a bit and watch the target walk down the street, it would be no sweat to wait in a car until he had passed and time the attack based on his walking speed. It was a pretty good choice. Especially since he lived in Dornbusch and worked at the University. He was going to walk down this road every day."

Jamie stopped and looked at the screen on his phone. Sue assumed he was checking the time or had been timing their walk from the intersection. Jamie said, "Hungry?"

Sue wondered at the change of subject. Was this another Jamie trick to get her to a meeting spot with one of his old cronies? "Sure. Where are we going to go?"

"There is a café back in the park. We can always eat a full meal later, but I would like a little *kaffee und kuchen*."

"Are we meeting someone?"

"How did you guess?"

"Is it the creep in Vienna?"

"What would you think of me if I only introduced you to creeps?"

"Is this all part of the master plan?"

"Of course! Now pick up the pace. We don't want to keep our guests waiting."

A TWIST IN THE PLOT

Sue trudged along next to Jamie. After all this time, she thought she would be used to Jamie's style of keeping quiet about his plans until the last minute. Still, after years working together, she expected to be treated as a full partner. As she walked along, she considered how she would respond. Sue learned over the years that she needed to be better at keeping her temper. It wasn't easy, and as they entered the park she was at a full boil.

Jamie looked at his watch and slowed down. "We are right on time. We'll be at the café in a couple of minutes."

Sue couldn't help herself. Her voice had a serious edge to it when she said, "And exactly when were you going to tell me we were having an agent meeting today?"

Jamie smiled and said, "I never said we were having an agent meeting."

Sue stopped in the middle of the path and exploded. "Enough with the games! What is going on?"

Jamie continued to walk as if Sue had neither stopped nor spoken. He looked over his shoulder and said, "If you would like to walk with me, now that we are in the park, I will tell you the deal."

Sue begrudgingly caught up with Jamie. She said, "Well?"

"I just got a text from Flash. She said that she and Massoni were at the Grüneburgpark Café and needed to see us. That's it. Nothing more than that. I didn't want to say anything while we were on Hansaallee because I didn't really want the folks we passed focusing on our conversation. You never know."

Sue nodded, "Trust no one."

"To do this job, you need a circle of trust. But, in this town, that circle is mighty small."

"As in, the folks at the Panopticon?"

"Well, honestly, inside the Panopticon, I trust only Smith, Massoni and Flash. The other OGA, military and UK folks come and go, and I lost track of my previous team a year ago. Now, I do trust the Panopticon surveillance team I recruited, but I keep them in the dark on the details of their taskings. I think they prefer it that way. They are eastern European gents who grew up in a world where need-to-know kept them alive."

Sue remembered her previous visit to the Panopticon and Jamie's independent surveillance team that he called the Black Sheep. A mix from the eastern states of the European Union, they looked and sounded like all the other guest workers in Germany. They were well trained in surveillance operations. Sue wondered if Jamie used them for other missions. Perhaps she would find out as she continued to work with Jamie and for Dentmann.

They arrived at the café. Massoni and Flash were already sitting at an outdoor table, drinking coffee and eating pastries. Flash took a long drink of her coffee and said, "It's about time." Massoni grumbled, but his mouth was full so no words came out.

Jamie said to Sue, "Sit down and I'll get us something. Any preferences?"

"Tea?"

"Any food?"

"Is it too late to get a sandwich?"

Flash said, "The sergeant major has already had a doner."

Jamie said, "Sue, does that sound OK?"

Sue didn't want to admit she wasn't sure what a doner was, so she said, "Sure."

Jamie disappeared into the café.

Sue said, "I wasn't expecting to see you to until tonight."

Massoni had finished his small piece of cake. "Why don't we wait until Jamie comes back," he said. "I don't want to tell twice. Meanwhile, are the Klingons treating you OK?" For a change, Massoni sounded honestly concerned.

Sue paused for a moment before she spoke. She wondered whether the Agency folks — Klingons in SOF parlance — were treating her well. "It's different. I only worked with two other operators plus a couple of admin folks. We travel to stations to help coordinate Agency relations with SOF and with local liaison. Most of the time, we are neutrals trying to make everyone play nice in the sandbox."

With a great degree of sarcasm, Flash said, "How ironic."

Sue smiled, "OK, so I haven't had a long history of playing all that well with the other sandbox kids."

Massoni said, "Is this the first CI case you've handled?"

"I haven't decided yet if it is a CI case or more like a hunt for terrorists. The murders are way too well designed to be some sort of counterintelligence vendetta."

Jamie returned. He was balancing a tray that had two teacups, a teapot, a plate with a piece of cheesecake and a plate that was filled with sliced lamb and multiple vegetables wrapped in flatbread and held together with white wax paper. On the edge of the tray were two carefully balanced coffee cups. Massoni stood up and captured the two coffees before they crashed on the ground or, worse still in his lap. He handed one to Flash.

Jamie dropped the sandwich plate in front of Sue and said, "Madame, your doner."

Flash said, "I am always cautious about doner because I have real trouble eating anything that is bigger than my head."

Sue looked at it and said, "Utensils?"

Jamie and Massoni looked at Sue and said in unison, "You just eat it."

Flash said, "Sue, I've never seen you eat a hamburger with a knife and fork."

Sue looked doubtfully at the over-filled plate.

Flash shook her head. "Nibble around the edges, you sissy."

Jamie poured tea: "OK, what's the deal?"

Sue knew from experience that Flash was aching to tell the story, but Massoni jumped in. She assumed that if he wanted to get in any words at all, he had to do so first. She smiled as she noticed Flash was fidgeting in her seat like a kid in a classroom who knows the answer to the question and wants to tell everyone.

"The boss decided we needed to move this outside the compound. As we started working on the leads to the Iranians and the Russians, it became clear that we either had to do this ourselves," he looked over at Flash, "or read the entire team into the project. As powerful as the resources are in the Panopticon, the reality is we can't justify need-to-know for the entire staff — Klingons, DoD civilians, and the Brits." Massoni stopped to take a sip of his coffee. If he had intended to continue, it was a strategic mistake. Flash immediately filled the gap.

"If you are wondering why, I'm here to tell you why."

Massoni finished his coffee. "Yup. Ms. Smarty Pants computer geek is going to tell you why."

Sue laughed. "Whenever Flash starts talking geek speak, I am lost."

Massoni nodded. "That's my world, O'Connell. So, don't make fun."

Jamie looked at Flash and said, "Go ahead, Flash. Leave these Luddites behind and amaze me."

"OK, Klingon, but just because you asked so nicely." Flash smiled a completely insincere smile. "As I started using the Panopticon network looking for links between the two sets of travelers — the Iranians and the Russians — I started seeing anomalies inside our databases. It looked as if there were bits and pieces of the story missing. Some of the passport data from the travelers was missing. A couple of the cellphone numbers. Even a couple of the CCTV photographs. Just enough to make the hunt much harder. If it had been just one timestamp of data feed or even one feed related to a venue, then it wouldn't have piqued my interest. I would have just written it off as failures of software or hardware. But it was too curious not to investigate. Today I start digging into our data storage unit. I can see where the complete feed was, and I can see where someone inside the compound decided to delete little pieces. Whoever that someone was, they were good. They disguised their efforts."

Jamie put his fork down. The cheesecake had magically disappeared while Flash was talking. Sue remained challenged by the doner sandwich. Jamie asked, "How exactly did they disguise their tracks?"

"They logged on as me."

Jamie laughed, "Well, then. Case solved. You are the fink."

Massoni nodded, "That's what I said, but Smith was not amused."

Flash looked down at her coffee cup. "Not funny."

Sue said, "OK, so it's someone inside the Panopticon. Could the fink inside the compound also provide the original targeting data?"

Massoni decided he could return to the conversation. "That wouldn't have been easy, but I think they could have if they used both a Klingon and one of our DoD terminals. There are some cross network links between the OGA and DoD servers and even among our terminals, the Brits, and let's not forget the Canadians, but there are also firewalls inside each of the networks. A DoD terminal can't reach back into OGA headquarters."

Jamie said, "So we reach back to headquarters and get a computer forensics on site to sort this out."

Flash said, "Smith said the same thing. However, I can't imagine how we can do that and not have the perpetrator know what is going on. After all, there is really no cover story that works when the forensics guys arrive."

"And they can't do it remotely?"

"They could try. Smith said he wanted us to do our own investigation."

Sue had finally finished half of the doner. She pushed the plate over to Flash and Massoni's side of the table. Flash immediately grabbed the sandwich and started eating. Massoni nodded and said, "Nice play."

Jamie nodded. "So, we are on our own for a bit."

Flash mumbled something through the doner.

Massoni shook his head. "Didn't your mom every tell you not to talk with your mouth full?"

Sue added, "I've always assumed Flash was raised by wolves."

"Or by aliens," Jamie offered.

Flash swallowed hard. "Laugh as much as you want, smart guys."

Jamie said, "OK, so we don't go back to the Panopticon."

Massoni nodded.

"I have a little place we can go," Jamie said. "It's in the Taunus. Lovely."

Flash mumbled over her coffee, "Klingon lovely?"

Jamie smiled. "Definitely Klingon lovely." He turned to Massoni and asked, "Do you guys have wheels?"

"Nope. We didn't take anything from the Panopticon. We used the train."

"So, here's the plan: Take the S-bahn line named S5. It goes all the way out to Bad Homburg. Get off there and wait for us at the station." Jamie looked at his watch. "Given the traffic, you may beat us there. If we aren't there after thirty minutes, call me on this number." He handed Massoni a card with his name and a mobile number with a German area code.

Flash finally had finished eating. She looked at Jamie and said, "Did you expect this problem?"

Massoni grumbled, "When you are dealing with Schenk, there is always a problem."

Jamie managed a hurt look that was insincere and humorous at the same time. Sue laughed. Jamie said, "Hey, let's not forget who destroyed my last two safe houses." He pointed his thumb at Sue.

Massoni nodded. He and Flash said in unison, "And we all know it wasn't Sue's fault."

Flash came back to her question. "Did you know this was going to go down the way it did?"

Jamie finally conceded and decided to answer. "Nope. I just always have a couple of places to hide out wherever I go. Remember the old saying: Two is one and one is none. That works as much for safe houses and it does for kit. Consider this a well-designed contingency plan that we can use."

Sue said, "Since Flash is finished eating, I think it's time to leave."

Jamie stood up and said, "That's what we like about you, Sue. You are an action hero. Always on the move."

Sue gave Jamie a blade hand to the ribs.

"Ow! What was that for."

"Consider it a statement that it is time for action."

Massoni turned to Flash. "And you thought I was a creep?"

Flash stood from the table and watched as Sue and Jamie walked to the taxi stand. "Sergeant Major, that's because you are a creep."

A CABIN IN THE TAUNUS

The safe house was a small cabin nestled close to the Roman walls built to defend Roman legions from the Germanic tribes of the North. The house was a half-timbered white stucco stand-alone building about two miles from Bad Homburg. It reminded Sue of the safe house that she and Flash used when they conducted operations in the Black Sea against a Russian mafia proliferation target. It looked completely normal from the outside and, for that matter, normal on the ground floor. It was in the second story that the CIA team created a small, secure communications information facility or SCIF: Basically, an acrylic box inside one of the bedrooms that served as a Faraday cage allowing no communications out and no electronic penetrations in. As always, Flash was thrilled.

As she walked into the room with multiple computers and a satellite radio rig, Flash said, "Klingon, you made this just for me?"

"Well, there was this other…"

Massoni said, "Never mind, Jamie. Just tell me we can communicate with Smith."

"Jim, when have I let you down?"

"There was this time…"

"Never mind. The answer is yes. However, Smith is going to have to communicate outside the Panopticon. Otherwise, this whole move is pointless."

Flash said, "The Boss said he would set up a separate satellite feed once a day at 1600Z hours for us to chat."

Sue smiled, "Funny, I never thought of a dialogue with Smith as a chat."

"Whatever." Flash looked her watch. "Jamie, we need to get your end of the satellite link up. It's 1550Z."

Jamie bowed. "Your wish is my command, madame." He turned to Sue and Massoni and said, "Our bedrooms are down the hall."

Massoni nodded. "We will eventually need to pull all of our kit out of the Panopticon billets."

Jamie said, "I already took care of that with the Black Sheep. Your kit is already in one of the rooms."

Sue said to no one in particular, "He thinks of everything."

Massoni said, "Except for coffee."

At the appointed time, they were all sitting around one of the workstations in the SCIF. Smith's face appeared on the screen and the conference began. Sue realized that the computer camera made Smith's face look even more cadaverous than usual. Clearly, he had never fully recovered from his wounds in Bahrain.

"I've sent for a cyber forensics team to sort out our problems. We will cover them under the story of a series of tech upgrades to the hardware in the Panopticon. They arrive at the end of the week and we should have something tangible by next week." He continued, "I've talked to Dentmann. She and I have decided you four should shift your targeting to tracking the assassins rather than hunting the leak. Flash, didn't you say you had some leads in that regard?"

"Boss, I have the travel data for both the Iranians and the Russians. I think the Iranians are back home, but I'm not sure about the Russians. It looks like the safe house has the necessary equipment for me to continue the electronic chase. If we get sufficient data to target where they are, we will switch to physical surveillance."

Massoni added, "Jamie has a unilateral surveillance team that we can deploy for this job, so between his team and the four of us, I think we have that end covered if Flash is successful."

Flash snorted. "WHEN Flash is successful."

Jamie decided to add, "We have one more from my office arriving tomorrow. We have the resources to do the job."

Smith nodded. "We'll regroup tomorrow at 1600Z. Out." The screen went blank.

Jamie said, "He's like Dentmann. He doesn't waste any time."

"And that's why we like working for him, Klingon."

"So, get to work, Flash."

"And what are you going to do to earn your keep?"

"I'm making dinner."

Sue raised her eyebrows, but Massoni interceded. "One of Schenk's real skills is cooking. I heard that he took courses in Paris at the Cordon Bleu."

Jamie shrugged and said, "Handsome, a genius, and he can cook too? Sue, didn't you wonder why I was so irresistible?"

Sue did a mock bow and said, "Why did I ever doubt you?"

THE HUNT BEGINS

Sue woke early. It was still dark. She looked at her watch. The luminous hands on the old Bulova barely showed. 0515hrs. It was too late to try to get back to sleep and too early to expect anyone else to be awake. She tossed off the covers and pushed her legs over the side of the bed. Her prosthetic was next to the bed. She slipped it on and stood up.

"Is it really time to get up?" Flash's voice croaked from under the covers of the other single bed in the room.

Sue whispered, "Not unless you want to. I just can't sleep anymore."

"Jet lag. That's your problem."

"My real problem is I need to pee and I need some tea, in that order."

"Bring me back some coffee."

"What makes you think I do room service?"

"Because you love me?"

Sue giggled. It was great to be back working with her best friend. "If I can bring up a cup, I will do so. But, don't expect breakfast in bed."

"Peasant."

Sue slipped a pair of tai chi shoes on and padded toward the door. She knew there was a toilet upstairs, but also one downstairs. Rather than risk waking anyone else, she waited until her eyes fully adjusted to the darkness and then started toward the stairs. By the time she was at the head of the stairs, she realized someone else was in the house. Sue returned to the bedroom to recover a small sheath knife that resided on a chain with her dog tags. A gift from her colleagues in S&R when she left, it had served her well over the years. Flash said, "Back already?"

Sue said, "Someone's downstairs. I'm not going to assume it's a friend."

Flash popped up in bed and said, "Wait for me!" Like Sue, Flash slept in a pair of black nylon shorts known in the community as "Ranger panties" and a black T-shirt. She reached into her rucksack and pulled out a collapsible baton. She looked at Sue and said, "Just in case."

They quietly walked down the stairs. The living room was dark and empty. The noise was coming from the kitchen. Sue pointed to the doorframe. Flash took the right side, Sue the left. She pulled the knife from its sheath, keeping her right hand behind her hip, she walked through the door with Flash right behind her.

Jamie looked up from the stove where he had three different cast iron skillets under heat. He said, "Please don't hurt me. I'm still mixing the eggs and the biscuit batter."

Massoni was sitting on a stool near the stove. "Go ahead, do him harm. He doesn't have any coffee in the place other than some sort of machine that produces one cup of swill at a time."

Flash started to laugh. "Sergeant Major, please make a cup of swill for me."

"It's just after 0500hrs," Sue said. "What are you two doing up?"

Massoni acted as though it was a perfectly normal time to be up and about. "It's just after 0500hrs, why weren't you up yet? It's nearly time for PT."

"A run?" Flash asked.

Jamie said, "Runs are off-limits in the safe house. We don't want the neighbors wondering what sort of madmen are living in their neighborhood. You must go into the basement to use the gym." Jamie pointed with his nose toward another counter. "And, there is a pot of tea ready if you want some. Now, leave me in peace while I finish cooking breakfast."

The early morning breakfast included scrambled eggs, bacon, and fresh skillet biscuits served with butter and assorted marmalades. After the kitchen cleanup, accomplished by Sue and Flash, they settled back to the table with their coffee and tea mugs and started to war-game the next steps in the hunt for the assassins.

Flash started. "Before I left the Panopticon, I set up stand-alone connectivity with the servers. I built the connectivity so that it will take some time for anyone to notice. That means that we have about four days before the cyber forensics folks find my link and shut it down. I will spend the day hunting the Russians. I have software tracking their passport information and their credit cards. We should see where they are staying and where they are headed."

"Meanwhile," Jamie said, "I will use the link upstairs to engage headquarters to see what, if anything, they think are the next targets. Our CI shop is pretty good and I expect they will have some alternatives. If we know where the creeps are and we know the most likely next targets, we might get ahead of them."

Massoni asked, "And, if we get ahead of them? What then?"

Jamie said, "We either work with the local service or…"

Flash said, "We take care of them ourselves."

"We could," Sue smiled. She turned to Jamie. "Using the toys that Dentmann said were in the trunk?"

"With a little help from the Black Sheep. First, we need to pinpoint the targets."

Massoni rubbed his hands. "I love it when a plan comes together."

ENLISTING ASSISTANCE

Barbara folded the letter and put it back in the crumbling envelope. Barbara had more than twenty years in the CIA and had traveled to dozens of countries. She had handled agents in most of those countries. But, unlike spies in the movies, she had no experience with the Swiss banking system. So, she turned to the one person she knew would be able to help: Beth Parsons, former ambassador and current troubleshooter for Stearns and Mandeville.

After a call to Beth arranging the meeting, she packed her single remaining business suit, two sets of what she considered her "street/travel clothes" and one set of workout clothes. She wasn't sure how long she would be gone, but it wasn't as if she was traveling to some remote location. Northern Virginia might be hostile territory to Barbara, but it was hardly the moon.

The trip from Chautauqua to Northern Virginia was pleasant enough, first along the NY Southern Tier expressway through the woods and farms and then along US15 past the Susquehanna, through Gettysburg and Western Maryland, and ending across the Potomac just west of Great Falls National Park. However, once Barbara arrived in Leesburg, Virginia, she hit the DC metropolitan traffic gridlock that stretched to the Atlantic Ocean. Tysons Corners started as nothing more than a road-and-rail junction for agricultural goods traveling from farmlands to Alexandria, Virginia, and Washington, DC. By the 1970s, this bit of high ground became a major business and shopping hub and now served as the eastern end of what was known as the Dulles Technology Corridor. When Barbara and Peter had served in Headquarters, Tysons Corners was simply a pair of shopping malls near headquarters that they visited when they needed something special for a gift. Otherwise, they avoided the area which was infamous for traffic jams where two state highways intersected with two different interstates.

Barbara sighed as she entered the traffic snarl on Virginia Highway 6 heading toward Tysons Corners. She did find it amusing that her old Range Rover seemed to cause the otherwise aggressive Northern Virginia drivers to stay well clear. They knew that any accident between their modern vehicles made mostly of plastic and the ancient Rover made of steel would be unfortunate.

The Stearns and Mandeville offices were in one of the business towers built during the last building boom before the 2008 recession. Close to a new metro station and the major beltway that circled Washington, the law firm purchased the office space before the building was even completed. They owned the top floor of a twenty-story building that overlooked the Potomac River. On a clear day, you could look to the east and see the Washington Monument and look to the west and just see the foothills of the Shenandoah. The offices were designed to impress, and as far as Barbara was concerned, it was mission accomplished.

As she walked into the lobby, Barbara realized this was the first time she had visited the Stearns and Mandeville offices. In their previous work, Beth would call, and they would meet in a hotel room or in a restaurant somewhere in the area. Barbara always assumed this was simply a means of keeping their work relationship confidential. After all, their work in the past had been more than a little unconventional. So, Barbara had been a little surprised that when she called Beth, she invited her to the office.

When Barbara exited the elevator, Beth was waiting. She said, "Dear, come through. I made a pot of Earl Grey for you."

Barbara was wearing the only real business suit she had left: a navy wool pantsuit. Life as a pensioner and an occasional traveler with Beth meant most of the time she was in jeans or khakis and a sweater. She expected to be underdressed in this environment and she was not disappointed. The male secretary in the lobby was wearing a silk tie that was more expensive than her entire outfit and Beth... well, Beth always looked like she had just returned from a photo shoot for *Vogue* magazine.

Beth's office was surprisingly spartan. A chrome-and-glass desk with a phone and a laptop was in one corner of the room facing windows that looked west. Four leather chairs surrounded a small, chrome-and-glass coffee table. A large Caucasian rug on the floor offered the only real color in the room.

Barbara said, "I expected walls covered in books."

Beth laughed. "The law library is in another room. If I need a reference, that's where I go."

"Or you dispatch a minion."

"Very few minions in this office, dear. A few interns, but they work for the senior partners. I do my own work, and as you well know, it is mostly internet research rather than research into the arcane world of international business law."

Barbara smiled and thought about their retired Special Forces colleagues who were regularly called to do work for Steans and Mandeville. "And the crew from *Condottieri Malatesta* would not consider themselves minions."

"Hardly." Beth looked discretely at her Cartier watch. "So, what can I do to help you? You said it was a complicated little puzzle."

"It is and it is a puzzle outside my toolkit. It has to do with a Swiss bank account and what I assume is a Swiss safety deposit box."

Beth had been pouring a cup of Earl Grey tea into a porcelain mug. She looked up and said, "Swiss bank account?"

"It is another curious piece of Peter O'Connell's legacy." Barbara pulled a small box out of her shoulder bag and opened it on the coffee table. It included the letter and the key. Barbara had left the firearm back in the concealment and the jewelry in her bedroom. "I haven't worked all the way through the notebooks that Peter left behind, but it would appear this has some ties to his time in SE Asia. What I need to know for now is how do you access an account and after all these years will the account even be active?" Barbara thought for a moment how she had carefully avoided the complicated parts of the story. Well, everything she said was completely true, if not truly complete. If, at some point, Beth needed to know, then she would tell her.

Beth looked at the paperwork. She walked over to her desk and started typing on her laptop. Whatever query she started took only a few seconds. "This is a small bank and, somehow, it has survived the banking consolidation that has occurred throughout Europe. Assuming the account had money in it when Peter last used it, then it should still be there. There are annual fees that banks charge and Swiss banks are very thorough in capturing their fees from accounts that are inactive." Beth walked back to her chair and her tea. "What do you want to do about it?"

"What can I do about it?"

"Well, you could travel to Lugano and simply ask to see the account. You will need the number, the code word Dilletante, and your passport. They will show you the account information, and it would appear from the key, they will let you access the safety deposit box. If they used up all the available funds on fees, there won't be an account and the box will have been emptied and whatever was in the box became the property of the bank."

"Any way I can sort this out from here?"

"Dear, the short answer is no. The Swiss are very diligent about how they provide banking information. If you had encrypted internet access from the bank, of course you could access it. But if this is all you have, then you will have to go to Lugano." Beth smiled over her teacup, "But who wouldn't want to have a trip to the Italian Alps in the Fall?"

"Well, it's not as if I have anything else on my agenda."

"Hmm, we just might be able to solve that problem. I have been working on another European engagement. This time focusing on a Russian Orthodox religious icon. It would mean working for a few days in Austria, but after that, we could drive to Lugano."

"Another adventure?"

"Well, let's hope it is less of an adventure than our first trip to Germany. Mostly, this is about the art and antiques world."

"I seem to recall that was what you said then."

"Well, this time I really mean it."

"So, when would you like to make your work trip?"

"Now?"

Barbara laughed. "I think I might need my passport and a change of clothes."

"Next week?"

"Earlier if you like. I can be ready to leave over the weekend."

"Excellent. Why don't you come down on Saturday and we'll leave early Sunday morning. I'll have the office arrange our travel."

Barbara smirked. "Was this always the plan?"

Beth looked up from her teacup. She smiled her most dangerous smile and said, "Perhaps."

A FLIGHT TO VIENNA

The flight to Europe was uneventful. Especially since Stearns and Mandeville arranged first-class tickets on Austrian Airlines. The first-class section of the Boeing 777 aircraft was spacious, with each seat its own small cubicle with table and a seat that could fold flat into a bed. The nonstop flight took just over eight hours. After she and Beth were served a very European three-course meal with sparkling wine and then coffee and dessert, Barbara thought she would be able to rest. The seats were comfortable and the gentle sound of the aircraft engines should have been perfect for a few hours of uninterrupted sleep. The story kept calling to her.

What in the world was in the safety deposit box? And, why was Peter O'Connell ashamed of his actions? After dozing for two hours, she woke and decided to open a book she had on the official history of CIA actions in Southeast Asia. It wasn't light reading, but perhaps it would help provide some context. As she read the history, she realized for the first time how complicated the operations were and how intertwined they were with White House hopes and fears. Barbara was a teenager for most of those years, and few of the CIA operations were declassified until she was already in the Agency and busy with her own career. The glow of the reading light above her circled the book in the otherwise darkened cabin. Barbara finally fell asleep dreaming of the highlands of SE Asia.

The lights came on in the cabin and the flight attendants started setting up for the breakfast service. Barbara reluctantly put the book back in her shoulder bag and stretched. Coffee and breakfast sounded like a good choice after a fitful night of dreams. The flight attendant walked up and asked if Barbara needed anything. She asked for a cup of tea. He brought it and a heated washcloth scented with lavender. Barbara nursed the tea and her thoughts as the cabin came alive for breakfast.

When the flight arrived in Vienna, Barbara was far less jet lagged than she expected, given her long night. The day was bright and sunny as they walked down the jetway to the terminal. Beth showed an exceptionally sunny disposition and Barbara struggled to keep up with Beth's long strides through the airport. As they cleared customs and collected their bags, they met a driver holding a Stearns and Mandeville card. A quick drive in a Mercedes S-class limousine ended at the Hotel Imperial.

As a CIA case officer targeting Iranians and terrorists, Barbara had traveled many times to Vienna. Due to her work and the threat from her targets, her travel into the city was always low profile and her hotel accommodations were classic Vienna, but consistent with the effort to remain unnoticed by both her targets and the Austrian police and security services. That meant an inexpensive hotel in the outer ring of the city with easy access to the train station and the airport. When they walked into the Hotel Imperial lobby, Barbara realized, yet again, that traveling with Beth Parsons was never going to go unnoticed. They were greeted at the front desk by a young man in a black suit, white shirt and brilliant maroon tie. "Ambassador Parsons, it has been too long. Welcome back."

Barbara whispered, "Are you greeted like royalty in every hotel in Europe?"

Beth whispered back, "Hush. Enjoy the ride."

"Louis, it is always a pleasure to visit Vienna and stay at the Imperial."

"Madame Ambassador, your suite is ready. Jochim will take you." He nodded to another young man in another beautifully tailored black suit and crisp white shirt, but this time wearing a turquoise tie.

"Ladies, if you will follow me."

The suite was exceptional. The Imperial was an old hotel that prided itself in both its 19th century furnishings and its 21st century infrastructure. The sitting room of the suite had Turkish carpets on the floor, brocade on the overstuffed furniture, and what looked to be a highly polished 18th century table with four matching chairs. The walls were painted a pale yellow in the Maria Theresa style with white baseboards and carved crown molding. At the far end of the room was a set of French doors that opened out on a small balcony overlooking the old city of Vienna. Barbara did her best not to say anything at all until Jochim and the two bellmen delivered their luggage and left.

Barbara pointed to the balcony and said, "Is that where you give your address to the people?"

"Barbara, you have to understand two things: When I was an ambassador, I regularly arranged conferences in Vienna." She waved her arms around the room. "This is why I used the Imperial. And, it turns out one of the Stearns and Mandeville clients is on the board of directors here. So, they always give us this treatment."

"I'm sure you get used to it after a bit."

"Never, dear. You well know, I have traveled to war zones, into the collapsing Soviet Union in the late 1980s when capitals were nothing more than collapsing infrastructure, inconsistent power, bad water, and little food. Not like this environment at all. There is no good way to *get used* to any of it. However, I certainly don't mind. Now, I am going to take a long soak in my bathroom. I recommend you do the same and then we will get out on the street and let the October sun improve our jet-lagged dispositions."

Barbara nodded agreement. Beth turned to the right set of doors and Barbara turned to the left. Her bedroom suite included a queen-sized bed, a walk-in closet, and a bathroom the size of her living room in Chautauqua. She decided once again it wasn't too bad working for Stearns and Mandeville. Suddenly, jet lag called to her. Barbara found it hard to keep her eyes open as she took off her travel clothes and headed to the bathroom.

THE START OF A VIENNESE ADVENTURE

It took all of Barbara's determination to claw back from the late morning doze that could easily have resulted in a deep sleep. She had set two alarms in the room to make sure that she was awake when Beth knocked on her bedroom door. She dressed and was ready in a few minutes. As she did, the last remnants of the dream she had stayed with her. It was a mix of a battlefield on the Plain of Jars in Laos and the images of a ballroom filled with 19th century Viennese dancers. Barbara attributed the mix to jet lag. As she left the room, she made sure the key to the safety deposit box and the instructions were all in her bag.

They left the hotel, walked across the boulevard called the Opernring and headed north toward St. Stephen's Cathedral. The weather was unseasonably warm for October. Soon both Beth and Barbara had taken off their coats and were basking in the sunshine. As they walked along Herrengasse past the Schweizerhof palaces of the old Austro-Hungarian Empire, Beth said, "I think a café mélange and some kuchen at Café Central is in order."

Barbara smiled. Café Central was a Viennese icon, a 19th century style coffeehouse that was attributed to be where great intellectuals, revolutionaries and exiles visited during their stays in the city before and after World War I. It was well and truly "central" to the city, so it was a good rest stop after an hour walk. Barbara always wondered how Beth kept fit given her penchant for rich, high-calorie meals followed by very sugary desserts. She supposed Beth had a personal trainer who otherwise guided her through her daily routine of cardio and weight training. In Chautauqua, Barbara simply focused on yoga, walking and a careful diet. They both were fit women in their 60s, but Beth looked more like the star of an action hero movie while Barbara looked more like what she was — a fit widower.

Café Central was perfect: booths with a mix of polished wood and brass, tables set amid plaster pillars, and floors polished to a mirror finish. It was just as Barbara remembered it from her case-officer days. As they entered, Barbara noticed Beth made some mysterious sign with her right hand and they were guided to an isolated booth next to a window overlooking the street. Barbara said, "So, this isn't just a lovely excursion today?"

"Well, it is lovely and it was an excursion, no? But, it is also the beginning of our work here in Vienna. I'm meeting our contact who is going to guide us through the very complex world of Russian icons and, most especially, stolen Russian icons."

"Antique dealer?"

Beth shook her head. "He is an art restorer who works as an expert for the Belvedere Palace. His personal expertise is in Balkan religious iconography. Catholic and Serbian Orthodox religious art. He started working as a consultant for Stearns and Mandeville when the firm was involved in some of the war crimes investigations in 1998. That was before my time with the firm, but we have him on retainer as our subject-matter expert on European art, especially European forgeries."

"Did you use him with the Mayerhaus family paintings?"

"No, we didn't. Remember, the Mayerhaus paintings were modern works. We have used him in other looted art projects, but only for works that the Nazis stole when they occupied the Balkans. Like many in the arts, his expertise is very narrow but exceptionally deep." Beth looked up and said, "And, here he is."

Barbara looked up at the man approaching the table. In his late 60s, he was dressed in a very conservative black suit with a light grey vest, white shirt, and a burgundy tie. In his left hand was a grey homburg hat. He was a small man, just a bit over five feet, with an immaculate groomed grey beard and equally well-cut grey hair brushed back over the balding dome of his head. His eyes seemed an exact match to his grey vest. Beth and Barbara stood up. He came to the position of attention, did a short bow and said, "Madame Ambassador, it is always a pleasure." His English was perfect with a slight accent that to Barbara's ears didn't sound like a German or French speaker.

Beth stood between Barbara and the man. She said, "Count Andrassy, I would like to introduce you to my friend and colleague, Barbara O'Connell."

Barbara had little experience in looking down on men, especially European men. Barbara was five foot, eight inches tall and Beth was at least two inches taller, so in this exchange, they towered over the man. He seemed unperturbed by the size differences. "Ah, Madame O'Connell, Beth has said you are an adventuress. It is a pleasure." With that he offered another bow and continued, "But please do not pay any attention to Madame Parsons. Hungarian royalty deserves a place in history, but they have no place in modern Europe. Please call me by my Christian name, Karol."

Barbara did her own version of a bow and said, "Karol, it is a pleasure. My name is Barbara."

With introductions complete, they sat down. Almost immediately, two members of the staff arrived with a silver coffee pot, three crystal glasses resting inside silver holders, a pot of heated milk, a silver sugar bowl, and a plate of very delicate looking cakes. Beth said, "I shall play mother." With a flourish that Barbara had not seen from Beth in the past, she poured the coffee and offered milk and sugar. Andrassy took sugar and stirred it into the jet-black brew. Barbara took milk until the coffee was caramel colored. Beth poured her coffee and added milk as well. She offered Andrassy the cake tray and he took the smallest on the tray — a small chocolate tart. Barbara took what appeared to be a lemon tart and Beth took a slice of chocolate cake. They each took a small bite, and the discussion began.

Beth said, "Karol, when we last talked, you said there was a growing trade in Russian icons here in the city. Honestly, I was not surprised. I remember when the Soviet Union collapsed, many communists smuggled icons out and exchanged them for hard currency. How is this icon any different?"

"It is the provenance, Madame Ambassador. I believe there is a piece that comes from St. Catherine's Monastery."

Barbara almost choked. She swallowed, took a sip of coffee and said, "As in St. Catherine's Monastery in the Sinai?"

"As you say. The icons there are some of the most exceptional in the entire world. The Russian Orthodox church has sent icons to the Monastery for as long as there has been a Russian Orthodox church and the Greek Orthodox church sent icons well before that. They are perhaps the rarest icons on the planet."

Beth said, "Why is it in Vienna?"

Andrassy shrugged. "Who can say? All I know is that *if* it is from St. Catherine's there are collectors who will pay a king's ransom for it, there are governments who would demand its recovery, and there are many who would kill for it."

Barbara knew this was not her show, but she had to ask the question that hovered over the table. "Have you seen the icon?"

"Yes, I have. I was obliged to do so by one of the most senior patrons of the Belvedere. I do not think he is involved. I think he was obliged to assist based on some previous commitment that he would not share. He promised me that I would be safe and that all that was asked of me was my usual role as an expert in such things. There were three icons that he wanted me to see. My role was clear. I only had to offer an opinion on subject matter and, ideally, age. Nothing more. I agreed with the clear understanding that I could not verify the provenance. Only if it would be an appropriate subject and the age. It was a most exceptional request, but I agreed. After all, when a senior patron of a museum as grand as the Belvedere asks for a favor, the staff are obliged to do our best."

Andrassy took a sip from his coffee. "That evening, I met two young men dressed in suits at the staff entrance of the Belvedere near the parking lot. I was taken by a limousine from the Belvedere in the early evening to a compound somewhere outside Vienna on the

Danube. The windows were all blacked out so that it was impossible for me to see."

Beth said, "And your opinion?"

"Many years ago, when I was a student, I visited St. Catherine's Monastery. It was a sort of pilgrimage for me. I saw some of the icons there. Of course, I was younger then and did not expect to ever have to use those memories for work." He paused again. "When I saw this icon, I could only say that it appeared to be the right size, generally the right age, and a proper subject. Finally, it appeared to me that it had been in an exceptionally dry environment for years, perhaps centuries. Remember, some of the icons were painted with pigments that were made with blood and crushed jewels and all were painted on wood, not canvas. No matter where they are kept, they are going to be coated with candle smoke and the smell of incense. A good forger can try to match some of these aspects, but I have yet to see a forger able to match all of the aspects.

"The subject was an Orthodox saint, Metropolitan Michael of Kiev known as *The Enlightener*, and the style was of 16th and 17th century artisans in the Russian court. That was the best I could do without my equipment in my own studio at the Belvedere, and the patron made it clear that the owner was not going to release the icons for a more scientific assessment. There was a man who remained in the shadows in the room. He thanked me for my opinion and the other men took me back to the Belvedere. It was an interesting experience."

Beth asked, "Could you make out their nationality?"

"They spoke so little. I can say they were not native German speakers. Other than that, I cannot say."

Beth filled their cups and added milk and there was silence at the table as they finished their coffee. Andrassy pulled an antique, gold hunter style pocket watch from his waistcoat pocket. The watch filled his small hand. He said, "I apologize, Madame Ambassador. I must return to the Belvedere."

Beth and Barbara stood up and shook his hand. He turned and

slowly walked toward the door. He put his homburg hat on his head and disappeared into the street.

Barbara had held her tongue for nearly an hour. As they sat down, she asked, "What is this all about? A Russian icon stolen from St. Catherine's Monastery? Who in the world is your client and what are we expected to accomplish?"

Beth smiled over her coffee cup. Barbara recognized the smile. It had no mirth to it. It was more like the smile captured on the Renaissance painters of the Medicis. It was a smile that accepted the irony of the world and offered no insight into what the owner thought. Beth paused to sip her cup and said, "Well, you wouldn't have expected me to invite my fellow adventuress to something that wasn't extraordinary."

Barbara nearly laughed out loud. "When he used the term, I assumed he was thinking of something in German or Hungarian and adventuress came out instead."

"Oh no, dear. He is a precise man and fluent in at least five languages that I know of, so his description was precise. And, I think perfect."

"OK, I've accepted the effort to avoid answering my questions, but I would very much like to know what we are doing here."

Beth waved to the waiter and he took the silver coffee pot and the silver milk pitcher away. He bowed to Beth and disappeared. Beth said, "I think it is best that we go for another walk."

"And the bill?"

"Oh, I paid the service bill this morning. I didn't want anything like waiters to interrupt our meeting. Now, let's walk."

After the cozy setting of the café, they walked out into a cool late afternoon. The wind was running along the Danube and brought a slight chill to the air. They both put on coats and started walking toward St. Stephen's Cathedral. While not exactly the center of old Vienna, it was certainly the heart of the city. Beth pulled Barbara to her side and they interlocked arms. As they walked, Beth started to explain.

"Two months ago, we were approached by a member of the

Russian Orthodox Archdiocese of New York. We have worked on small affairs for them related to the Russian exile community and they keep Stearns and Mandeville on a retainer for special projects that they prefer to handle sub rosa. There are plenty of law firms in New York, but they are well known and the Archdiocese would prefer a different face handling their affairs."

"Enter Ambassador Parsons."

"Indeed. So, one of the priests visited the offices in Tysons. He had a situation that might become a problem. He wasn't sure and asked for our assistance. Basically, a member of the congregation had been approached by a well-respected art dealer who offered to sell him an icon as well as a dozen antique Turkish carpets. The dealer said the items were from Russia, but the owner had run afoul of the Russian authorities and needed to liquidate his collection to pay the necessary bribes to avoid jail. The dealer promised that the sale would be conducted in his office in Vienna and would be transferred to New York through the standard customs process between Austria and the United States. As far as that goes, it sounded like a perfectly standard story of art transfers among the ultra-wealthy who buy and sell their treasures for millions of dollars."

"The priest said after his parishioner saw a picture of the icon, he was suspicious and before he transferred any money at all to the dealer, he wanted the Church to confirm that the item was not stolen from some Orthodox church or monastery in Russia. While many of the members of the Russian Orthodox community in New York are recent émigrés, some are exiles who left the old Soviet Union one step ahead of the KGB. They are rightfully cautious, and they want their lives in the US to be free from fear of reprisals from the Russian federation and the arms of the state security."

"As in the FSB or the SVR."

"Indeed. In an effort to resolve the request while keeping our commitment of confidentiality to the Archdiocese, the firm decided to use Karol as a cutout. We guided him to the seller and hoped for a result. So, we are here to determine if this is just some sort of cautious business transaction or an effort by some criminal enterprise to acquire clean hard currency in exchange for stolen property."

They had reached the magnificent cathedral. The setting sun was illuminating the multi-colored roof panels. Most of the pedestrians were rushing through the streets on their way home from work. Few took the time to enjoy the scene. They had seen it all their lives and it would be there tomorrow and the next day and the next. For now, it was just a landmark to be passed.

Barbara never tired of the scene. As she looked up at the cathedral lighted by the setting sun, she said, "Send in the adventuresses!"

"That wasn't exactly what I said, but it was my thought exactly. The world of extreme art collectors is filled with intrigue. Honestly, I think the ultra-wealthy are drawn to the intrigue to break free from the humdrum of counting their millions."

Barbara smiled and said, "Not a problem we face."

"Indeed. But I do appreciate the fact that this particular buyer was concerned enough to engage the Church. Most are not in the least bit interested in how the items arrive to the market. Generally, they are only interested in authenticity. They may like intrigue, but they really don't like being conned."

"So, now what do we do?"

"First, we report back to the office. Then the office engages the Archdiocese and then we do what we do best: continue to pull the thread on this story until something unravels."

"Ideally without any damage to us."

Beth nodded. "Especially without any damage to us."

When they got back to the hotel, they ordered room service and relaxed over a meal of grilled fish, baked potatoes, and a spiced salad. They shared a split of champagne over the meal. Over coffee, they talked through their day. Beth was the first to speak.

"Given the strange nature of how the owner handled the meeting with Andrassy, we have to assume that there is some sort of criminal enterprise, no?"

Barbara nodded in agreement. "That would be my first thought. Of course, it is entirely possible that the owner is also worried about theft and wanted to be sure that Karol wasn't working for villains. However, I think this feels like the worst possible sort of criminality. We might have some sort of Russian mafia connection and these guys would be hunted by the FSB or some other mafia family. I think the best answer to the client is to drop it like a hot rock."

Beth smiled, "Dear, we aren't paid to offer our opinions. Remember, our client isn't the guy who wants to buy the icon. Our client is the New York diocese of the Russian Orthodox church. And, those seniors are going to want a better answer than 'we think it's a problem.' They want to know what sort of problem. If it is theft of church property, then they decide how to handle the problem. If it is theft of personal property, then we make our recommendation to the FBI and they get to work."

"Which means we need to dig a little deeper."

"For now, it means we wait for instructions. I will send the email tonight and I suspect we will get an answer by tomorrow night. In the meantime, we can relax or…we can make some calls tomorrow and see who wants to talk to us."

"For a price."

Beth nodded. "There is always a price."

PULLING A DIFFERENT THREAD

Sue never was good at waiting. Long before she went to the Farm, long before she passed selection and served in Surveillance and Reconnaissance Detachment, she was a military intelligence officer working for 18th Airborne Corps Headquarters. She hated the daily grind of waiting for the intelligence feed followed by the manic effort to produce an intelligence picture for the command using threads that came from some unknown collector or some sophisticated electronic sensor. She wanted to be doing something, anything, other than waiting. More than one member of S&R, as well as her mother, had made it clear that patience was an essential skill in the intelligence trade. In her darker moments of reflection, Sue realized she lost a part of her left leg because of impatience. It still didn't make the waiting any easier.

After a few hours of watching Sue pace up and down in the safe house, Jamie said, "Will you please just go into the basement and work out or go up into the attic and howl at the moon? Do something other than pace around my chair?"

"How exactly do you sit there reading when we need to sort this out?"

Jamie pointed to the paperback now on his lap. "I told you on our last trip to Vienna, it's important to have a book that will capture your attention. I'm currently reading Hannah Arendt's essays on totalitarianism. There are books over there in the bookshelf. Pull one down and read. It is good for your brain."

Massoni walked into the room. He was in a black sweat suit and had a towel wrapped around his neck and the top of his head. He said, "O'Connell, have you worked out today?"

Jamie said, "She's knocked out a couple of miles pacing in the room."

"O'Connell, let me offer some advice. Work out. It will put blood and oxygen into your knot, make you smarter and reduce the tension. And, it will make you stop bothering the Klingon."

Jamie smirked. "You know why she is here? It's because Flash exiled her from the computer room. She spent a good portion of the morning just lurking over Flash's shoulder and periodically asking if there was any progress."

Massoni used his sergeant major voice and said, "O'Connell, I know you outrank me, so I can't give you orders. However, I can give you instruction. Go change into your sweats and work out. The Klingons have a pretty good gym in the basement…for civilians."

Sue knew they were both right. She begrudgingly went to the stairs. As she climbed the stairs, she heard Massoni's voice. "And don't bother Flash."

At mid-day, there was a buzz from the door alarm. Jamie got up, checked the screen in the kitchen and then opened the door. He shouted, "It's about time!"

Richard Smith walked in with a black rucksack on his shoulder and pulling a rolling black duffle bag. As with Jamie, Richard's traveling attire was a mix of grey and black wool with black shoes designed to look appropriate with a suit but could easily work for long hours of street surveillance. He looked at his left wrist. The steel GMT watch was still on US East Coast time. He said, "I haven't even had time to change my watch. It was a crazy haul across a couple of stops in Europe to get here today. I didn't get the VIP treatment like you and O'Connell, and the rental car agency only had some sort of Eastern European copy of a FIAT. It made it to the Taunus, barely. I'm tired, I'm stinky and I am very hungry."

Massoni walked into the kitchen. He said, "Hello, pilgrim! It has been a while." As he got closer and prepared a bear hug, he said, "Whew, you are stinky."

"Thanks, Jim. Nice to see you as well."

Jamie said, "OK, so go upstairs, clean up and come back here. I'll make you an omelet and we can catch up."

As Smith hauled his duffle up the stairs, he passed Flash as she ran down the stairs. She was dressed in black sweats and black high-top trainers. She stopped on the stairs and said, "Hello, handsome. Who are you and why haven't you been in my life before? You come to join the fun?"

"That's the plan."

"Well, start by taking a shower."

Smith continued to climb the stairs. "Thanks for the advice."

They gathered an hour later in the small, upstairs SCIF. Flash was the one and only speaker. She started by saying, "It isn't all that complicated. Well, it is complicated, but you don't want to hear about that."

Massoni jumped in, "Flash, we really don't care."

Jamie said, "Flash, that's not entirely true. Massoni doesn't care. The rest of us aren't going to check your homework. We only want to know if we have targets."

Flash looked up at the new arrival who was dressed in black sweats and strange little rubber shoes with toes. She decided he might be a kindred spirit. "Richard, do you want to know?"

"Nope. At this point, I barely know why I'm here."

Massoni smirked. "You are the muscle in this operation."

Sue added, "Except for me."

"OK, Flash. Let's hear the good stuff."

Flash decided to deliver the good stuff. "Here's the deal. Sometimes teams get sloppy after an operation. Everyone is focused on security in advance of an operation. They don't want anything to go wrong. When the operation is completed, and especially when the operation is a success, that's when folks tend to cut corners. I assumed that the SWORDFISH crew would be like that. So, I started looking for leads after the assassination. And, in this case the SWORDFISH team left just a few breadcrumbs. Specifically, they all booked train tickets together on a single credit card. I don't know if the card is an alias or true name, but they also used the same credit card to book a series of rooms in a hotel on the outskirts of Vienna. Beats me why, but they did. The best news is that hotel had crap security so I have their check-in date and their departure date. They are spending the next week in Vienna." Flash stood up and took a bow. Richard offered unenthusiastic applause. Flash responded with a single-fingered salute.

Jamie nodded and took over. "Flash, that was some sweet work. I will be sure to offer my thanks later." Flash blushed while Jamie continued, "Meanwhile, we now have the targets in Vienna. We don't know if they are operational or simply waiting the next set of orders to go someplace else. If the latter, then they may leave before their scheduled departure date. We need to get hot. Meaning, we need to leave this afternoon. I will send a note to the Black Sheep to get ready to travel."

He looked at Massoni. "Jim, can you sort out surveillance kit for us? There is a locker in the basement that should have just about everything we need." Massoni nodded. Finally, Jamie looked at Richard and said, "Last one in, so you get to travel in style with the Black Sheep."

Richard nodded. "I've gotten used to traveling in the convoy with those guys. Not super fun, but at least they don't talk much so I can get some rest."

Flash said, "Can I travel with Richard?"

Massoni looked back from the hallway and said, "No."

"Why not?"

"Really, unleashing the Flash on a group of unsuspecting men? I wouldn't be doing my job as a sergeant major if I let that happen. You travel with Jamie."

Jamie nodded. "Jim, I leave it up to you to decide if you want to travel with Richard or with us."

Massoni laughed. "Really? My choice is to travel with Richard or Flash?" He looked at Richard. "You got room?"

"Jim, the Black Sheep will travel in a van and a sedan. I will be driving the OSU office car we used to get here. Either way, we got room."

Massoni made his choice: "I claim shotgun with Richard."

Jamie said, "OK, you two take the rental and get back to the Panopticon. The guys should be ready for you when you get there. Jim, would you let Jed know the plan? I can't risk sending anything to him without compromising the op."

Massoni nodded. "Done."

"And what do you want me to do?" Sue asked.

Jamie said, "We go in the Mercedes. It has a concealment in the trunk that is big enough for Flash to take her laptop and a SATCOM rig as well as basic surveillance kit. You need to sort that out with Flash."

Sue smiled, "And I get to check out the toys."

Jamie nodded. "Yes, we can't go to a party without some toys."

"I love toys," Flash said. "Especially Klingon toys."

Jamie looked at the tritium hands on his dive watch. "We leave in an hour. Start packing." He added, "And, please try not to leave a mess. The staff hates it if you leave a mess."

Sue said, "The staff?"

"Yes, Sue. That's Richard and you."

Jamie walked out of the SCIF and his laughter followed him down the hall.

NEW ORDERS

Misha was lifting weights in a gym managed by another of the brotherhood. The Soviet KGB and GRU had a strong presence in Vienna during the Cold War, and many Soviet professionals from the 1980s established businesses that offered good cover for long-term residency. When the USSR collapsed, the KGB became SVR or FSB. Most of the GRU personnel stayed in the city and established themselves as sleeper agents available when Moscow called. SWORDFISH was not an official SVR or GRU entity, but it was still part of the brotherhood. So, when SWORDFISH teams needed someplace to serve as an informal headquarters, there were many choices.

In this case, Misha's choice was a martial-arts club and gym in the Viennese suburb of Meidling near the Franz Josef train station. Misha was never going to completely let down his guard, but it was good to be in a place where he knew the owner and the owner knew him. The gym was by no means modern. First, there was the smell, thick with sweat and leather and some type of vinegar based cleaner. Second, the equipment was old and very much in an Eastern European style. There were racks of dumbbells and kettlebells, five weight benches and a dozen weighted bars next to the iron plates. Next to the weight room were five old, leather heavy bags that were currently in use by two of Misha's team. He could hear them as they punched the bags. Pale green paint covered the concrete floor and ran up the walls to the white ceiling. In the next room, there was a martial arts dojo in the same color scheme with thin forest-green mats on the floor.

While he had been involved in his kettlebell workout, he periodically heard a thump as one of his two remaining teammates completed a judo throw on the other teammate. It was a gym for men who wanted nothing more than an opportunity to work up a serious sweat. It could have existed almost anywhere in Russia, and to Misha it felt like home. The gym was not very popular with Austrians who wanted their fitness routines to be managed by trainers and where exercise was something accomplished by stationary bicycles, treadmills, and specialized weight machines. They didn't like the smell or the style of the members, who wore old cotton sweat suits or tank-top shirts and shorts. Everyone wore canvas high-top sneakers. They kept a towel handy to wipe the sweat and, perhaps just to annoy an Austrian visitor, to cover their face when they sneezed or spit.

The fact that well-to-do Austrians did not like the gym was fine by the owner. He wasn't in the business of training Austrians. His gym was simply a platform for the Russian security services to use as they saw fit. If there were some working-class Austrians or Balkan émigrés who wanted to use the gym, all the better. It provided the cover story for the other work and there was always the chance that one of the Austrians might become a target for one of the GRU visitors.

Misha was the oldest man on his team, but he was the most fit. He learned long ago — while serving first in the Soviet 331st Guards Airborne Regiment and then in the Russian Federation military intelligence special purpose forces known as SPETSNAZ — that fitness was what kept you alive in combat. You had to have the strength to accomplish the mission and the endurance to get home alive. Unlike most of his peers, Misha decided long ago that along with fitness, he needed to stay clear of alcohol while on a mission. It wasn't that he didn't like drinking. It was that he liked drink too much. He was convinced such a small sacrifice was worth it to have a clear head and to come home alive.

He watched in dismay as some of the younger members of SWORDFISH seemed convinced that fitness meant you looked like the action heroes in Western and Russian movies. They were certainly strong. The real question was whether they had the mental and physical endurance to survive. And, they had yet to realize that heavy drinking clouded their thinking. A man with a hangover is not a man you want by your side in a firefight.

So far, the younger ones on his team were successful in balancing their mental image of themselves with their ability to perform the mission. They had survived two tours in Syria together and that meant something. SWORDFISH missions were always dangerous and always violent. In Syria, they had accomplished assassinations of Kurdish resistance leaders, kidnappings of foreign fighters, and even two reconnaissance missions against the US Special Operations forces operating on the Iraq-Syria border. These missions were more about brains and less about brawn. He hoped over time they would prove themselves to be subtle as well as violent. The operations in Germany suggested that they were up to the challenge.

Misha was interested in keeping his body strong but flexible and stayed focused on endurance. After all, work at SWORDFISH required long hours either on patrol or, more recently, on the street when endurance might mean the difference between success and failure. A fit man was an alert man. He tried several times to point out to his team that their massive frames made them stand out in any normal crowd. They ignored him and continued to lift massive weights. As he thought about the generational difference between them, he heard two of his men tossing each other onto the judo mats. At least Sasha and Alex were keeping themselves fit in a manner that might be useful someday.

Misha was swinging a pair of 10kg kettlebells when his phone began to ring. He put down the weights, grabbed a towel to dry his hands and picked up the phone. He recognized the number. It was the local cutout that SWORDFISH used to maintain contact. He answered on the third ring. "6 Kostroma." When asked what name he wanted for his team, he decided on his Guards Regiment garrison. SWORDFISH headquarters agreed.

The voice on the other end said in German, "6, check your computer." The caller then hung up.

Misha toweled off his face and hands. The call meant a new job.

His computer was in his locker in the gym. He expected the message to be short. All operational planning was conducted face to face. This one would be no different. A few minutes in the sauna and then a shower and he would be ready.

Thirty minutes later, Misha was dressed and sitting on the locker room bench with an open laptop next to him. Given the quarterly GRU security checks on the gym, he knew Wi-Fi in the gym was far more secure than that in his hotel. He already let Alex know they were operational again. He opened the encrypted message board and read: Franz Josef Bahnhof. Gleis 6. 18hrs.

A new mission. He smiled. Another job. SWORDFISH paid men like Misha a small retainer and then a substantial fee for each task. More money in the bank for him and, honestly, something to keep his mind and body busy. It was a good life. He looked at the black face on his new watch. Now the only thing he had to decide was whether he would take Ivan or Alex as backup. Perhaps both. They would either keep him safe or be able to report back if anything went wrong. He had six hours to make the rendezvous.

The cyber clerk from the Iranian Embassy in Vienna knocked on the heavy metal door. It was the entrance to the Iranian Ministry of Intelligence and Security representative in Vienna. The door opened and flooded the hallway with a cloud of cigarette smoke. The clerk recognized the man at the door not as the MOIS station commander but as the deputy military attaché who everyone in the Embassy knew was a member of the Islamic Revolutionary Guards Corps. The clerk wasn't sure which of the two men he feared the most.

"Sir, an immediate message from the office in Berlin."

The IRGC officer took the folded message and closed the door. The clerk was relieved. It would appear he would have no more contact with the security men, and that was fine by him. His wife and children still lived in Tehran and his parents lived in Esfahan. The MOIS and IRGC security personnel in Iran were more than willing to apply various types of pressure on families if embassy employees were considered inefficient or, worse still, not sufficiently loyal to the Supreme Leader. No further contact with these men meant there wasn't any chance of a false step today.

"So, what was that interruption?" The MOIS station commander looked up from the backgammon board on his desk. The pieces were in play, and he had decided how he would win today's set of three games. He didn't want anything to distract him from his plan. Ali Hussein Rashti was a good ten years older than his IRGC counterpart and had grown tired of hearing "Rashti" jokes about his origins in the hinterland. He understood why his hometown was considered backward and its citizens less civilized than their counterparts in Tehran, Esfahan, or Shiraz. But, he had served the revolution since its inception, first as a young Revolutionary Guard foot soldier during the Iran-Iraq war of the 1980s and then as one of the early IRGC officers dispatched to create the MOIS.

Rashti's war wounds acquired on the Iranian front in the marshes of southern Iraq were just severe enough to force him to leave the IRGC infantry, but not severe enough to gain him any sort of veteran's pension. When the call came out for volunteers to join a new intelligence service that would encompass both domestic and foreign threats as well as collect key technology for the Islamic Republic, Rashti was one of the first to raise his hand. Now, almost thirty years later, he was the MOIS senior in Vienna after serving years in Beirut and Sudan. Vienna was likely to be his last posting and he intended to make the most out of his time here.

Rashti looked at his backgammon opponent, Mohammed Hussein Ibrahimi, holding the single sheet torn from the printer in the communications office. Ibrahimi was of a new generation. His lean body, hawk nose, and finely groomed beard made him look the part of the revolutionary warrior. Ibrahimi joined the IRGC after graduating from Tehran Polytechnic University and early in his career moved from conventional IRGC units to the IRGC special operations unit known as al-Qods. After years training dozens of Islamic resistance fighters in Lebanon, Afghanistan, and a secret desert outpost in Yemen, he transitioned again to IRGC counterintelligence. For a man in his late 30s, Ibrahimi had progressed quickly up the chain of command and was now a lieutenant colonel in the IRGC and the deputy military attaché. Rashti knew Ibrahimi intended to be a general officer and Vienna was just one stop on the way. Rashti also knew that there were always obstacles in the way of the ambitious. He did not intend to be one of those obstacles, but he wondered if Ibrahimi knew that his boss in the military attaché office was one.

Given a choice, Rashti would have preferred not to spend his days with this ambitious young man. But he knew full well that if Ibrahimi denounced him as disloyal, no matter how unjustified, he and his family would be on the next flight to Tehran and shortly after that he would be provided with a cell in Evin Prison. So, every day, they met in the afternoon, talked some about their ongoing intelligence operations and played backgammon. Rashti served tea and ghaz, the sugary sweet Iranian pistachio dessert, endured the inevitable Rashti jokes and the less-than-subtle jibes when Ibrahimi pointed out that he had a university degree and Rashti did not. Rashti allowed Ibrahimi to beat him three out of the five days they played backgammon simply to ensure he remained in control over their relationship. Rashti had decided today would be the day to show Ibrahimi something about backgammon and he had fully intended to beat him all three games. Now, the interruption prevented that small victory and he was irritated.

Ibrahimi opened the note which was marked "eyes only, Rashti." He scanned it and passed it on to Rashti. The note was from the cyber communications cell in Berlin. Rashti knew that the Berlin team had emplaced a worm in the computer of the Russian mercenaries who had been contracted to execute a dissident in Germany. Precisely why they did so was still beyond him, but he expected he would eventually find out if the operation ended up in Vienna. Now, it seemed it was already in Vienna. The message read:

IMMEDIATE IMMEDIATE IMMEDIATE

To: EYES ONLY Vienna commander

From: Berlin Cyber

Subject: Russian mercenary meeting in Vienna

Russian mercenaries will meet in the Franz Josef Train station, track 6 at 18hrs today.

Photo of mercenaries to follow. Also, we will report tracking data real time through your phone.

HQs requests you observe meeting. Report back and await orders.

END END END

Rashti looked up from the paper. Ibrahimi's expression reminded him of the hunting dogs his parents used to own before the revolution. As soon as they saw his father pull out his coat and his shotgun, they would quiver with excitement. Rashti just hoped Ibrahimi didn't pee on himself the way the dogs often did if they got too excited. He said, "It looks like we have some work." He looked at his watch. It was his only real indulgence. An antique Swiss Patek Philippe he found in Beirut years ago. It was 14hrs. "Four hours to design a surveillance at a busy train station at the end of rush hour."

Rashti thought about Ibrahimi. The IRGC officer would want to take charge of the operation. With his connections to the Hizballah cell in the city, he would have the necessary street power. Rashti's men were involved in intelligence collection operations against the offices of the International Atomic Energy Agency in Vienna and surveilling Iranian exiles in the city.

Rashti thought: Well, why not? If the operation was a success, the information would be transmitted through his channels and he would have the benefit of the success with little risk. If the operation was compromised, then Ibrahimi and his Hizballah thugs would be the ones facing the consequences. He nodded and said, "I suspect you have the manpower to do the job?"

Ibrahimi smiled. Finally, the old man acknowledged his capabilities. "Yes, I do. I can mobilize my team and be there well in advance of the meeting. All I will need is the photo and some warning that the target is in the station."

"I will be sure to give that to you. I will provide the top cover in case something goes wrong. Otherwise, I will stay here and await your report."

Ibrahimi knew that Rashti's top cover would be non-existent if the operation failed. If it succeeded, he would find some way to report back through his channels that operational success was entirely the result of his work. "Thank you, Brother Rashti. I will make this happen."

Rashti gave Ibrahimi a wave of dismissal and watched as he left. He looked down at the backgammon board and thought: Well, this might be an even better victory today than I expected. Ibrahimi walked down the hall with a smirk. He knew the old man was trying to box him into a corner. He was just as committed to doing the same to Rashti.

Ibrahimi sat in an old Mercedes box truck parked in the large parking lot of a set of abandoned warehouse buildings. The parking lot was close enough to the Bahnhof that he would have excellent mobile connectivity with his team, but far enough away so that if he needed to break contact and leave the area, he wouldn't be caught in any police cordon. On the metal side of the box was a sign in German identifying the truck as a food-delivery van. Reinforcing the food-delivery van cover, there was a medium sized air conditioning unit on the top. The unit served to disguise the various cameras used in the past when the truck served as fixed point surveillance against other adversaries.

Ibrahimi checked his watch. It was a large analog-digital Seiko that had served him well over the years in the various war zones where al-Qods worked with Islamic resistance movements. He no longer wore the large, black watch at the embassy or on the street. It was too conspicuous. At the embassy, he wore a simple Casio watch. Unlike Rashti, who seemed willing to flaunt his affiliation with European decadence, Ibrahimi was convinced that everything about his demeanor had to reflect his commitment to the Islamic Republic and to the IRGC. Both watches were watches that average people wore. Rashti either didn't realize the message he was sending or he didn't care. Ibrahimi put that idea aside as the second hand on his watch touched the 6 marker. 1730hrs. It was time to focus the team.

Years ago, Ibrahimi received training from what he thought was an ancient member of the IRGC. The man, who only offered the first name Ali, served in the Shah's intelligence and security service known as SAVAK. Most members of the SAVAK either fled for their lives or were executed in the early days of the revolution. Ali tried the former and was caught. Rather than suffering the fate of other members of SAVAK, he was "rehabilitated" by the counterintelligence arm of the IRGC. Those early members of the IRGC CI understood that a man who had spent his career surveilling revolutionaries would be very useful in training a new generation of individuals committed to destroying counter-revolutionaries. By the early 1980s, Iraq had recruited more than a few of the less dedicated revolutionaries to work for them. Through Ali's training, the new members of the IRGC intelligence arm destroyed the counter-revolutionaries inside Iran and forced any survivors to flee to Iraq or Europe. Ali had earned his freedom.

By the time Ibrahimi met Ali, he was a wizened old man who only worked two days a week out of his apartment in Esfahan. Ibrahimi traveled to Esfahan to sit in that apartment and learn the sophisticated trade of surveillance. Ali lived alone in a one-bedroom flat that had a small sitting room and kitchen and an even smaller bedroom. The room was filled with books and rolled up Persian carpets. A large tribal carpet covered the sitting-room floor. They sat on overstuffed chairs, with Ali facing the door, Ibrahimi facing the window that overlooked the old city including the Esfahan covered bazaar and, in the distance, the turquoise-blue towers of the main mosque. Ibrahimi was from Tehran and had heard all his life the saying *Isfahan, nesfe jehan* meaning Esfahan was as beautiful as half the world. Even from the tiny apartment window, Ibrahimi could believe the saying.

Ali started the one-on-one training by saying, "My son, I wonder if you are too young to be a surveillant or manage surveillants. You have seen wars and have succeeded because of your bravery." Ibrahimi started to speak, but was silenced by Ali who simply shook his head and quietly clicked his tongue. He would have no argument. "It takes patience to be successful in this trade. I wonder if you have patience."

Ali poured himself some tea into a crystal glass. He took a cube of sugar with his cadaverous hand and put it in his mouth against his left cheek. Ibrahimi wondered at that point whether Ali would die sometime during this interview.

After a sip from the tea glass and a long drag from his smoldering cigarette, Ali began. "I was always a patriot and more than willing to fight against those who would undermine our country. After the revolution, I was happy to use my skills to continue my work against the Mujahedin-e-Khalq." Ali took a sip from a small, crystal teacup. "I know, you think all of the SAVAK were working against Ayatollah Khomeini's organization." He made a sound that Ibrahimi thought might be a chuckle or perhaps a cough.

"We honestly didn't think much of the Grand Ayatollah or his followers. We were worried about the communists, the Tudeh party, and the violent MEK. I suppose that is why I wasn't hung in 1980. I was useful, I knew how to track and destroy Tudeh and MEK cells. You boys who grew up after the revolution, don't realize how dangerous it was with Iraq attacking our borders and supporting the MEK to attack from within. I definitely earned my freedom." Ali took another sip of tea and lit a new cigarette from the stub of one burning in the copper ash tray.

Sitting in the box truck, Ibrahimi understood Ali's commitment to patience and to the first lesson: "Ibrahimi, the mistake men make as they rush to accomplish a surveillance mission is they follow the target. A good surveillant doesn't follow a target. A good surveillant controls the target. What I mean by that is the surveillance operation must be designed to create a bubble large enough and flexible enough that it can adapt to any moves a target might make. You control the environment and that means you control the target."

Over the years, Ibrahimi followed Ali's guidance. He created surveillance teams in southern Lebanon, in Iraq, and in Yemen large enough and sophisticated enough that he always controlled the target. In Vienna, his team included a mix of Lebanese Hizballah and Iraq refugees. They were street cleaners, garbage men, and shopkeepers. They ran small, pushcart food stalls and they were paid well to avoid the biggest counterintelligence threat — a willingness to commit petty crime to add to their salary. Ibrahimi knew that many exiles worked day jobs and then joined small gangs to enhance their income. He made it clear that if he heard any of them following that path, the path would lead to an early grave. After two years working against over a dozen targets, including European targets who worked at the various UN facilities, he was confident in his team's work.

They were in place in the train station. Invisible men and women who the Austrians walked by without a second glance. Each had a small, portable video camera either on their person or placed somewhere on their stall. The IRGC technical branch in Tehran was more than willing to work with him to design and deliver the equipment. Ibrahimi's degree was in electrical engineering. He always checked the equipment before each operation. Now, he sat in the truck in front of six different monitors. The entire train station was covered. He was ready to control his target.

Two minutes before the meeting, he watched as three men arrived at the hall where all the train tracks converged. There were six tracks. He already knew the meeting was scheduled and Rashti was good to his word, so he had a photo of one of the Russian mercenaries. Now, all he needed was to capture images of the person or persons who arranged the meeting. He whispered in the microphone. "Two, push your rolling bin toward track 6. Don't worry about keeping track of the targets, the camera in your bin will do the job. Just sweep up garbage." Ibrahimi smiled as the camera marked No. 2 moved slowly along the platform. Periodically, the camera was obscured as this

Hizballahi walked to a garbage bin or when he grabbed his broom, but the camera was centered perfectly on the three men.

Ibrahimi looked at his watch. It was 18 hours. He checked the other monitors. Number 4 had a small kebab stand in the center of the hall. The camera on the stall captured the entrance to all the tracks as well as the large clock on the wall. The second hand of that clock made an electronic shift from 1759 to 1800. It was showtime. Ibrahimi remembered Ali's instructions: keep your team calm. They will give themselves away if they know the precise time or the precise nature of their mission. Ibrahimi informed the team that the meeting would take place at 1815 hours. That way, they were still calm and thought they had a quarter of an hour to go. Ibrahimi, on the other hand, sat on the edge of his seat.

Misha wasn't nervous, well not exactly. This sort of brief encounter was stock-in-trade for his operations over the past two years. Still, he had to work hard not to be excited about a new mission. Excitement would give him away both to any train station police who could observe in his eyes or in the sweat from his handshake that he was excited. He walked up track 6 with Ivan and Alex at his side. They had taken nearly an hour to get to the train station even though their hotel was only a ten-minute drive. Misha knew that any operational act required certainty that they were not observed. They saw no surveillance during their foot and vehicle route. The SWORDFISH contact would have done the same, no matter where he started his day.

He expected a senior from SWORDFISH to walk out of the recently arrived train. The plan would be to greet the senior, take his suitcase and walk back to the waiting car. Somewhere along the way, the senior would visit one of the various toilets and Misha and his men would continue to the car. The plans and funding for the new mission would be in the suitcase. And, that was precisely what happened. A tall man in a black wool coat and homburg hat walked off the train carrying what looked like an overnight bag. The man was dressed in standard European business attire: black suit, white shirt, burgundy tie, with a small gold watch peeking out from his shirt sleeve. He looked like every other businessman who departed from the first-class cabin of the train. Misha knew him only as Jan or sometimes through his callsign, Control5. When Misha started working for SWORD-FISH, it was a small enough organization that he knew his entire chain of command. After the expansion of the company, he lost that feeling of a family business, but Jan was still part of the brotherhood. In a previous meeting, he noticed Jan had a small tattoo on his right forearm — a representation of a Russian parachute badge. Jan was one of the brotherhood to be sure.

He greeted Jan in what Misha knew was a European style. Normally, he would have given Jan a bear hug. Instead, he offered his hand. Jan took it and greeted Misha in German. "Brother, it has been some time." They turned and walked up the platform toward the exit. As they walked, Jan said, "I wanted to thank you personally for the job in Frankfurt. It was precise. The client was pleased."

Misha nodded and said, "Thank you, sir. We did our best and it seemed to me we accomplished the task with little risk to us or to the company. Is there a new mission?"

"It is in the case. Now, if you will excuse me, I must use the toilet."

"Best wishes, sir. I hope to see you again soon."

"Misha, after you finish this job, I want you to take your men to Cyprus for a holiday. We have included funds for both this mission and the holiday. I will contact you there. Good luck, my friend." With that, Jan walked toward the toilets and Misha and his men walked toward the exit.

Ibrahimi could not believe his luck. His team had captured a Russian meeting and now they would follow the Russians to their lodgings in Vienna. He clicked on his microphone. "Two and Four, well done. Stay for a bit and then go home and await further orders. One and three, there are three men leaving the station, most likely heading for a car in the carpark. Follow them discretely. I want to know where they live. That is your only mission. Five, there is a tall businessman who just went to the toilets. Watch where he goes when he leaves. He may board a train or he may take a taxi. Six, if you can serve as his taxi, do so. If not, identify the cab and ask the driver later where he went. Well done all. Out."

Ibrahimi looked over at the driver who had waited patiently inside the box truck with little to do but drink tea. He said to the driver, "Please take us back to the safe house." The driver nodded, opened the door at the back of the box and walked to the front. Ibrahimi thought to himself, a good success. Rashti will have to admit it was perfect and will be forced to explain to MOIS headquarters the importance of the IRGC contingent in Vienna. Now, he had to complete the report and decide what he should do next.

CURIOUS ANSWERS TO EASY QUESTIONS

Beth made a series of calls the morning after the meeting with Andrassy. Once completed, she said to Barbara, "We have an appointment with a retired Austrian diplomat. He said he was delighted to meet us for coffee. Ready for a Sacher torte?"

Barbara knew that the last thing her body needed was another Viennese pastry, but clearly the purpose of the meeting wasn't to enjoy coffee and kuchen, so she said, "Absolutely."

It was another glorious autumn day in Vienna and they took their time walking the few blocks to the Sacher. Barbara was certain that it was no coincidence that Beth's route to the Sacher was circuitous to the point of absurd.

"Are you checking for surveillance?"

"You can't be too careful."

"Did you ever receive any training on surveillance detection?"

"I've watched movies."

"OK, well movies aren't the best teaching tools for surveillance detection."

"So, are we being followed?"

Barbara's inside voice said *you know better than to work with amateurs.* What she said to Beth was, "If you had asked me to design a route, I could have done so and answered your question one way or the other. Your route wasn't very helpful. All I can say is, I think we are clean."

Beth smiled. "Good enough because here we are!"

The Sacher restaurant was another place that had everything you might expect from old Vienna. Dark woodwork; highly shined brass railings. dark wood furniture sitting on a deep, blood-red carpet that matched the wallpaper; white tablecloths and bone china. For once, Beth was playing the guest rather than the host. An elderly gentleman stood as they entered. He offered a slight wave and Beth walked quickly to the table he had near one of the windows.

"Barbara, I want to introduce you to my old friend, Doctor Hans Friedberg."

Friedberg did a slight bow and in perfect English said, "Enchanted, Barbara."

Beth continued, "We worked together when we were both young diplomats during the last days of the Cold War and then again when Hans served as one of the seniors at the International Atomic Energy Agency here in Vienna. He and I have had a few adventures together as we worked to secure nuclear weapons as the Soviet Union collapsed."

Hans smiled. "Adventures indeed! We both survived our exposure to heaven-only-knows-what in various former Soviet republics. Now, I know this is a work call, but we must have some kaffee and kuchen before we get serious." He waved to one of the waiters and in minutes there was a tower of sweet and savory treats on a tiered silver tray and a pot of coffee and, for Hans, a separate pot of hot chocolate.

After nearly an hour enjoying both the meal and discussions of family and friends, Hans finally said, "So, what is this challenge you raised on the phone."

Beth smiled. "As you know, one of my passions has been art theft and tracking international art criminals."

Hans looked at Barbara and said, "Even when we were tracking radioactive material, she always talked about art theft. She isn't lying about passion."

"Oh, well do I know. We had a bit of an adventure in Germany linked precisely to that passion."

Friedberg smiled and said, "Ah, another story for another day. What is it this time?"

"A Russian icon."

"On the market here?"

"Yes. A US client wants to know if it is genuine as well as if it is legal."

"I suspect you have already talked to Andrassy."

"Yes. He said it was both genuine and likely stolen."

"Well, he would know. You realize he has not always been so honorable."

"Hans, what do you mean?"

"According to my files, long ago Andrassy was a member of the AVH."

Beth looked at Barbara. Barbara nodded and said, "Hungarian secret police. State Protection Authority. The Hungarian initials were AVH."

"Exactly. Beth, I suspect your friend Barbara might have had a small role in that world of spy versus spy."

Barbara said, "Perhaps."

"Well, Andrassy appears to have wiped this history off his records and now he is simply a well-respected antiquities expert at the Belvedere Palace." He took the last sip from his hot chocolate and then a sip from his water glass. "As you know, I am retired diplomat now and have little to do with any of this."

Beth smiled. Her bright red lipstick revealed startling white teeth. It was not necessarily a friendly smile. "But, Hans we both know that you were more than a diplomat in the past and certainly more than a pensioner now."

Hans nodded. "As Barbara said. Perhaps. Well, I know nothing about any Russian icon on the market, but I do know that the Austrian authorities keep a careful eye on Andrassy. He is far more than he seems and has deep connections to his old Russian colleagues."

"Retired Russian colleagues?"

Hans smiled again. "Perhaps."

They returned to the hotel in the late afternoon. As they entered the lobby, the night manager walked up to Beth and said, "You had a visitor. I told him you were otherwise engaged and that he should call back tomorrow."

"Did he leave a name?"

"No, Madame Ambassador. And, if I might be direct, I don't think he is precisely the sort of man that I see here in the hotel. Could he have been some sort of security guard from the Embassy? He looked more like a soldier than a diplomat."

Beth nodded and said, "Thank you, Gerhard. Your response was most correct. I did not expect any visitors, and honestly, I don't expect any visitors in the future. All of my work is currently related to working with the Belvedere Palace Museum on an art collection and none of the men I have met so far look anything like the man you described. Was he Viennese or…"

"Madame, I cannot say. His German was precise but his accent argued that it was not his native language."

"Again, you have been most correct in this. I will engage my museum counterparts tomorrow to determine who he might be. If he should return, please do not give him our room number. If he insists on a meeting, we can do so in the lobby." The night manager did a small bow and returned to the front desk.

The discussion had been entirely in German and Barbara had been unable to follow the details. As they got into the elevator, she asked, "What was that all about?"

Beth shook her head. "I don't know."

"That bad, eh?"

"Perhaps. All I can say for certain is we need to contact my office in the morning and sort out what they found out and how they want us to proceed. I will also call Karol to see if he has heard anything else." The elevator door opened and they walked to the suite.

When they arrived, Barbara did a very quick check of the suite both for intruders and any sign of tampering. She unplugged the telephone, television and radio. She looked for any telltale signs of what she called a "quick-plant" receiver and then said to Beth, "Please give me your phone."

Beth complied, though with an astonished look on her face. Barbara went back into the bedroom, took out a small bag, placed their phones in the bag, rolled and sealed the top. She said, "It's a Faraday bag. It blocks transmissions out from the phones. That means if someone is tracking your phone or working the software to enable the microphone to listen in on our conversations, our phones just went silent. I suspect we need to keep the phones in the bag until you contact the firm. I recommend you contact Karol using the hotel phone. Once those calls are complete and we know where we stand on this job, we put the phones back in the bag. It isn't exactly a cloak of invisibility, but it does make surveillance harder."

Beth nodded. "Is this really necessary?"

Barbara shrugged. "Beats me. Better safe than sorry, no?"

Beth smiled, "Can we at least plug the house phone back in to call for room service?"

"Sure. Go ahead and do that. I will be right back." Barbara went back into the bedroom and opened her suitcase on the bed. On one side of the case, she used her fingers to open a small hook- and-pile slit in the fabric of the hardside case. From between the hardside and the fabric, she pulled out a pair of hard ceramic stiffeners that were integrated into the suitcase. Both of the stiffeners had been sharpened to a knife edge on one end and had finger grooves on the other end. Not a perfect fighting knife, but one that traveled with Barbara on more than one occasion. Next, she spun the suitcase around. This time, she reached between the fabric and the hinge side of the case. From that space, she pulled a thin, flexible, eight-inch, rubber handled rod. It looked, more or less, like a very thin nightstick. It was called a cosh and was liberated years ago from Peter O'Connell's OSS weapons cache in the Potomac River House. The collection she had in her hands weren't ideal weapons, but they were better than nothing.

Barbara changed into a track suit and T-shirt and tai chi shoes and walked back into the living room carrying the three weapons. She found Beth dressed in a black Aikido Gi. Barbara said, "Well, all right then! It would appear you are ready for a fight."

"After our previous encounter in Germany, I decided if I was going to hang out with you, I needed to study martial arts. I found an Aikido master willing to work with me one-on-one. I'm still studying the basics, but I reckon I know enough to break contact with an assailant and run away!" Beth laughed.

Barbara was convinced that breaking contact and running away would not be in Beth's DNA, but she responded, "That's always been my plan."

"Hmmm, that didn't seem to be the plan in Germany."

Barbara decided to change the subject. "I have a couple of toys here. I offer them just in case." She laid out the ceramic knives and the cosh on the coffee table in front of Beth.

Beth showed no surprise at the arrival of a series of weapons. She looked at them with the same intensity as if Barbara had laid out fine jewelry or antique coins on the table. "These arrived in the suitcase?"

"Yes, indeed. They have their own little home in my hardside check luggage. The blades are sharp so you want to be careful that your hand doesn't slide down the shaft toward the blade."

Beth looked at the cosh and said, "I think this is better suited to my personality."

Barbara nodded. She picked up the two ceramic knives and placed them in sheathes sewn into the calf sections of her track suit. She said, "Dinner?"

"On the way. I think I will put the club away for now."

"It's called a cosh."

"Of course, it is."

Barbara thought to herself that this was probably not what Stearns and Mandeville considered to be an appropriate business discussion. She smiled and realized she could be wrong. This might be precisely what Stearns and Mandeville thought was appropriate for Beth Parsons and her colleague, Barbara O'Connell.

WHAT IS THE PLAN?

The drive from central Germany to Eastern Austria was scenic if not necessarily relaxing. It was only an eight-hour drive and the German and Austrian roads were built for speed and for large European cruisers like their Mercedes. What should have been a fun road trip through the German and Austrian Alps was filled with distractions inside the Mercedes: Jamie and Flash.

Jamie seemed to believe that any long drive required music and that music had to be the rock music of the 1970s and 1980s. This was an attribute that Sue first realized in Iraq and it was reinforced during their work together in Afghanistan. Jamie implied that any good case officer needed a soundtrack for his adventures and this music was his. The good news in that regard was the Mercedes's excellent speaker system and sound insulation. That meant that even at high speed, the only thing that you should have been able to hear was Jamie's music.

Unfortunately for Sue, the music was not the only distraction in the car. At the best of times, Flash was a distraction: generally amusing, usually informative, and always over caffeinated. While the Mercedes cabin was large for a road car, it was not large enough to avoid the constant commentary from the back seat. First it was about the operation, then it was about life in the Panopticon, and finally, it was a question-and-answer period where Flash asked Jamie pointed questions about his work, the office in Virginia, and even his love life.

Sue was sure that Jamie would eventually surrender and stop answering in short, monosyllabic sentences and periodic grunts. For six hours, he held to the plan. Finally, he gave in. "Flash, I'm willing to trade love stories. You game?"

There was a pause in the back seat. Sue wondered if Flash was just taking the moment to drink from one of the eight bottles of iced coffee that she had in a soft-side cooler next to the computers. Finally, Flash said in her most cautious voice, "OK."

"Excellent. So, where do I begin? As you already know, I am a handsome and exceptionally smart guy. And, I am a great cook. I'm surprised that I haven't been married yet."

Sue smiled and said, "Perhaps, your quiet demeanor and introversion has prevented the women of the world from finding you."

"Sue, you might be right. Massoni said something like that to me over fifteen years ago."

"Something like that."

"Well, his comment was slightly less polite."

Flash's voice from the back said, "I can imagine."

"I was engaged once, years ago. It was an excellent match. She was a sergeant major in one of the SOF units and I was a senior warrant officer in Special Forces. We were in love and the fact that we didn't see each other much because of our work made it a match made in heaven. Then, events got in the way."

Flash offered, "You mean she finally realized your true personality?"

Jamie was quiet for a second. "No. I meant 9/11."

The car went quiet for a moment. Sue wasn't sure if Jamie knew about Flash's background and the loss of her parents on September 11, 2001. She only found out about Flash's family during a Thanksgiving weekend while deployed in Afghanistan. Massoni was the first one to let her know that 9/11 was a touchy subject for Flash. Could he have let Jamie know as well? Jamie had shut off the music and the silence owned the car for miles as they drove on the Austrian superhighway.

Flash broke the silence. "What happened?"

"Sergeant Major Bea Knox was in the Pentagon on 9/11. She was giving a briefing on women in the SOF community. She had subtitled the presentation: "The good, the bad, and the ugly." We had worked on the Power Point presentation together. It was excellent. I was serving as a jumpmaster on a freefall training jump over Ft. Bragg that day. It was a dawn jump. Beautiful. I saw dawn on the horizon. We opened at 6,000 feet and steered our chutes over Ft. Bragg and landed in Camp Mackall. We were packing our chutes and getting ready for a road march home when the unit sergeant major picked us up in one of the battalion Suburbans. He told us about New York and the Pentagon and Pennsylvania." Jamie paused. "I heard from Bea's unit that she was missing and presumed dead. I wasn't officially next of kin and I had a team that needed to get ready to take the fight to al Qaida. In October, I learned they never found any of her remains. Vaporized by jet fuel."

Flash reached over the seat and grabbed Jamie's head. She kissed him and said, "That's my story as well. Except it was at the Towers." Sue realized Flash was crying.

After another five minutes of silence, Jamie said, "Before we all start crying, I think it is time to pull over at this rest stop and use the facilities. I'll wait while you guys go and then you can wait for me."

Sue smiled, "Dad, don't you trust us?"

Jamie said, "Remember, we have toys on board. I really don't want to come out and find the car and the toys on their way to some chop shop in Albania."

Flash laughed. "Fair. Sometimes I forget that we live in a dangerous world."

Jamie pulled into the rest stop and said, "It's easy to do when you are traveling with The Jamie. I exude safety the way most men exude sweat."

Sue said, "Well, if you don't mind, I think I'll go exude in the restroom."

After they resumed the drive, Jamie started the conversation. "OK, so have we had enough revelations for the day."

Sue jumped in. "Yes."

Flash replied. "No!"

"Well, we either focus the conversation on work or we return to the greatest hits of 1972."

Sue and Flash spoke in unison, "WORK!"

"Excellent. So, here's my plan. We have a safe house in Schwechat just north of the Vienna airport. Station set us up with a space big enough to house all of us including the Black Sheep and all of our vehicles."

Sue did her best diva imitation. "I suspect it will be marvelous."

"No doubt. The last time I was in Vienna, I had a few words with the station chief of ops and this will likely be his revenge. So long as we have power and privacy, I don't care." Jamie took a sip of the rest stop restaurant tea. He said, "Blech" and put the cup back in the cup holder.

Flash offered one of her cold-brew iced coffees. Jamie shook his head and then continued. "Once we are on the ground, we need Flash to come up with some details fast so we can start the surveillance operation."

Flash nodded. "I can make that happen, but once we know where they are, what can we do? In the SOF world, it is called find, fix and finish. I'm just not sure what a finish piece looks like in Vienna."

Jamie nodded. "It all depends on what we find when we start the surveillance. If they are comfortable enough in Vienna and leave their bed-down location unattended, we will do a covert entry. If not, we just surveil their activities. *IF* we are lucky, we find they are doing something illegal here in the land of *gemutlich und schlage sahne* and we let station call their liaison counterparts."

"And they get the credit?"

Jamie nodded. "And, we disappear like the shadow warriors that we are. That's what we do in extraterritorial operations in Europe."

Sue looked over at Jamie. She hadn't noticed in the past that he had a very large scar running from his hairline and disappearing under his shirt collar. "And if they don't do something illegal?"

Jamie smiled. "Then we do something illegal and let them get the blame. We aren't leaving here without disrupting whatever operation they are doing. We want these guys in detention. It would be great if it was our detention, but I'll live with Austrian detention and months of legal wrangling while they wait in some Austrian jail. No doubt without *schlagsahne.*"

Flash said, "What?"

Sue said, "Whipped cream, sweety. It's on everything in Vienna."

"Yum! OK, so you are relying on the brilliance of the Flash."

Jamie nodded, "Indeed, Flash. As we often do."

"Don't forget that."

"Don't worry, I'm sure to offer my thanks later."

"I'm holding you to that, Klingon."

Sue rolled her eyes and decided that trying to keep up with the Jamie and Flash show was a fool's errand. She asked, "Are we certain the SWORDFISH crew are operational and not on some break after Germany?"

"Dentmann thinks they are operational. She said guys like this don't spend their holidays in Vienna. They go to Cyprus or some island on the Greek or Turkish coast, swim on the beach and sharpen their knives. If that's what Dentmann thinks, I'm all in."

They left the A1 and joined the A21 Vienna ring road heading south toward the Vienna International Airport. One of the last exits before the airport took them into the town of Schwechat. Like many suburbs of large European cities, it was little more than a bedroom community for middle-class Austrians who left home every day and took the train into Vienna, to work at the International Airport or the nearby oil refineries.

As soon as they arrived in what was a classic, quaint European town, Sue said, "What is that smell?"

"That's the byproduct of heavy industry, Sue. In this case, oil refinement. You will get used to it. Don't worry tomorrow morning when you wake up and your mouth tastes like you had a lead lozenge in your mouth all night. It's not unhealthy so long as we don't stay too long."

From the back seat, Flash said, "You must have pissed the station COPS off. This is not exactly a garden spot." As she spoke, a giant Emirate Air Airbus 380 flew overhead. The noise was deafening.

"Flash, you have to remember, we can't always live in high-quality places like my old safe house in Northern Afghanistan. This blue-collar town will work great for us. Most especially for the Black Sheep who are all Eastern Europeans. They will fit in nicely." Jamie's white teeth appeared under his moustache. "And, yes. I did piss off the station COPS."

GETTING TO WORK

Richard, Massoni and the Black Sheep arrived in a three-vehicle convoy much later that evening. They pulled into the fenced-and-gated compound of what looked and smelled like a heavy vehicle repair shop. Inside one of the corrugated walled buildings was a series of rooms created by wooden frames and plywood walls.

Jim Massoni looked around and said, "Now we're talking. This feels like home."

Sue was working on her second cup of evening tea and said, "I knew you would like it. We even saved the best room in the house for you, sergeant major." She pointed to a cot next to a very rustic set of gym weights and benches.

Massoni smiled and said, "Never miss an opportunity to train, O'Connell."

The next morning before dawn, they gathered in what could have been called the mess hall if one had a sense of humor. That said, Jamie had gotten up early and made a very good meal of bacon, eggs, and hash browns. He apologized that he didn't have any fresh bread. He tasked the Black Sheep to find the best bakery in town and deliver bread to the team before the evening meal. One of the surveillance team nodded and promised to do so in a Slavic language that Sue assumed was Polish.

After breakfast, Flash started the briefing. Overnight, she identified the targets' bed-down location in the Vienna suburb of Meidling or, as she pointed out with greater precision, the BDL for the targets' mobile phones. She noted that the phones' tracks for the previous thirty-six hours looked to be the perfect display of a working surveillance team. The phone tracks started in the BDL, traveled together to the city of Donaustadt on the east side of the Donau River and then moved in regular patterns that Flash assumed reflected the moves of their target. The pattern included a trip into Vienna proper and then a return to Donaustadt circa 2100hrs. After that, the phones moved back across Vienna to the BDL.

Jamie said, "Where are they now?"

"As of breakfast, they were still in their BDL."

Before Jamie could say anything, three of the Black Sheep got up and left. Jamie scribbled on a sheet of paper and handed Flash a pair of mobile phone numbers. "Send them the coordinates and any movement over the next hour. It is going to take them at least that long to get set up at Meidling." Flash nodded. Jamie continued, "OK. We work in shifts and track these guys. I'm not sure we are going to be able to identify their target at first, but that is the goal. We need to know the target if we are going to disrupt this operation." He looked at Flash. "Flash, can you work your magic off of a mobile platform?"

Flash looked at Jamie as if he had asked if she knew how to add and subtract. Her response was sarcastic. "Of course."

"Great! So, you work with Richard in the car on the second shift. Jim, Sue, and I will serve as reserves and once we identify the target, we might do some of our own digging to sort out why the SWORD-FISH creeps are in Vienna. Check?"

With a nod, the meeting broke up. Flash and Richard went over to his rental car to check out how they would work her electronics in the car. The Black Sheep started a double check on their van and Jamie walked over to one of the work benches. He pulled out four sets of Austrian plates and said to Sue and Massoni, "We put this set on the Mercedes, this other set on the rental and the third set with commercial plates goes on the second van. When the other van gets back, we switch out the plates that are on the bench."

"Gift from the station?"

"Yup. Even if the station doesn't like us, our guardian angel makes sure they help us."

Sue said, "Dentmann?"

"Who else? Remember the hammer and nail analogy?"

Massoni said, "Eh?"

"If Dentmann is the hammer, no station chief wants to be the nail."

Massoni smiled. "Check. Sort of like no one wants to be on the bad side of a sergeant major."

Sue nodded. "Exactly."

Four hours later, Jamie walked over to a bench where Flash and Richard were planning their routes to and from the BDL. They had been tracking the surveillance operation through the Black Sheep mobile phones. It would be relatively easy to switch coverage at this point because the SWORDFISH phones were in a single part of the first district of Vienna. The team identified the make, model and license plates of three of the SWORDFISH vehicles and forwarded ground photography of three of the surveillants.

Flash looked up at Jamie. "They are really good."

"And you doubted me?"

"Well, I mean they are *really* good. How in the world did they get ground photography of these villains?"

Jamie smiled. "I could take credit for this, but the truth is pretty mundane. They look like immigrant laborers and no one in Europe pays any attention to immigrant laborers dressed in coveralls and moving in and out of what looks like a cargo van." He paused and said, "Here's proof that they are good. Not only have they found the targets, but they have identified two individuals who are conducting surveillance of the surveillants."

Flash's head snapped back like she had received an electric shock. "Excuse me? Surveillance of the surveillants? Isn't that our job?"

"Seems someone else is in the game."

"Any thoughts on who?"

"Well, one of my guys identified three guys loitering in the area. Deployed in a classic fixed-point surveillance technique. He identified all of them as Middle Eastern descent. And, before you ask, he got ground photography of them." Jamie passed Flash an electronic tablet. On the screen were three photos.

Richard said, "It's like a parade. Have we sorted out the SWORD-FISH target?"

Jamie said, "It looks like a Russian target this time. An émigré who runs a high-end antiques shop."

Flash shook her head. "Sounds familiar, no? Wasn't that our target set last time? And, by the way, where's Sue and Jim?"

Jamie said, "I had them put their heads down for a bit. Once I realized we had multiple target sets, it was clear we were going to be running shifts overnight." Jamie looked at the large steel dive watch on his wrist. "Aren't you supposed to be taking over shortly?"

Richard said, "We were about to leave when we were interrupted… by you."

"Well, excuse me! Go ahead and get out there. Jim will handle the call from Smith and I will share the details of the SWORDFISH target and the Iranian complication. I already sent Dentmann the same data. I hope someone can help us figure out what is going on. In the meantime, do me a favor and make sure you stay outside the Iranian bubble, OK? I really like this safe house and don't want to make a run for it."

Flash smiled, "Remember, it wasn't the Flash that destroyed your safe houses."

Richard interrupted. "Now that we may have Iranians in the game, don't you think it's time to break out the toys?"

Jamie said, "I already put yours in your car."

Flash looked hurt. "Don't I get any toys?"

"Flash, these are Klingon toys. I think Massoni brought yours."

Flash stood up, gathered the map, her laptop, her cellphone, and a camera with a catadioptric lens attachment and headed to the car she was sharing with Richard. She said, "I love surprises."

WHAT DO WE DO NOW?

Barbara and Beth sat in their room looking out over Vienna. They had a tea tray that could only be delivered in Vienna. A mix of tea and coffee, a three-stand tray of Viennese pastries, a separate tray with cheeses and sliced meats, a bowl of olives and pickles and two different types of sliced breads. Barbara balanced a small plate on her lap. She decided to start with the savory offerings first, though she had her eye on a dark chocolate torte. Beth was far more catholic in her tastes and had a mix of sweet and savory on her plate. She had a long-stemmed glass of sparkling wine. As she explained when she ordered the delivery, it was late afternoon and about time for a cocktail.

Between bites, Barbara started the conversation. "So, what do we know from New York?"

Beth raised the forefinger on her right hand to ask for a bit of time while she worked through a piece of cheesecake. Barbara always assumed that Beth had the metabolism of a hummingbird because she ate anything she pleased any time she pleased and yet remained remarkably fit. Beth took a sip of wine and said, "The office said that the Russian Orthodox church had no doubt that the icon was stolen. It is complicated because there isn't any direct proof that it is stolen and that means they can't, and we shouldn't, inform the Viennese police. Stearns and Mandeville talked to the Washington Field office of the FBI who forwarded their call to the Art and Antiquities section of FBI Headquarters. Every DC official they talked to said the same thing: It isn't their business unless the US buyer closes the deal. Then, it might — but only might — become a subject of an FBI investigation."

130

Barbara took a sip of coffee. The chocolate torte still commanded some of her attention. "So, that's it?" she said. "I suppose we accomplished our mission. The church wanted to know if the icon was stolen, we have given them a best guess. No doubt they will tell the parishioner to stay clear of the deal and the US end of the story ends."

Barbara was about to grab the torte when Beth said, "Unless…"

"Unless?"

"It turns out the Archdiocese would like us to find out as much as possible about the seller. They have their own interests in both the icon and any threat to St. Catherine's Monastery. They would like to know as much as possible about this entire scheme and have asked the firm to do what it could to make that happen. And the firm has two people in Vienna who can do the job."

"And since we are adventuresses, we are going to take the job."

"It does mean a few more days in Vienna and a substantial bonus payment for you if we have any success."

"What about you?"

Beth laughed so hard she nearly spilled her drink. "Barbara, I am already very well compensated, and this is so much better than paperwork and some of the small-scale stuff they ask me to do in northern Virginia." Beth waved her hand around the room and over the tray of food. Like an amateur magician, her hand passed over the chocolate torte and it disappeared and reappeared on her plate. "Besides, it isn't like we are suffering." This time it was Barbara's turn to laugh. Beth continued, "OK, if this was one of your old operations, what would you do next?"

"I would follow up on the lead we already have. I'm sure the Count has more to tell us. I would also very much like to have some reinforcements."

Beth had already placed a small piece of the torte in her mouth. After a moment she said, "That's a good idea. I have already made a call to Longstreet. He has something pending in Germany, but promised to get here as soon as he could. In the meantime, I will make another with the Count. I agree he deserves another interview."

Barbara decided that the chocolate torte was not too great a loss as she found a small lemon torte on the tray. She poured herself some excellent Viennese coffee and said, "Let's hope we can meet him tomorrow. I think that is a good place to start."

WHO ARE THESE GUYS?

Richard and Flash sat in the sedan monitoring the activities of the second shift of Black Sheep. The sun was setting and they had the car placed in a carpark of the Schweizergarten. They were about a mile away from the surveillance team. Just close enough to maintain electronic coverage and just far enough away to avoid the surveillance bubble around the SWORDFISH team and the yet to be identified second team.

Surveillance operations are always complicated, but this one had three levels of uncertainty. First, who was the target of the SWORDFISH surveillance? Second, how many SWORDFISH surveillants were operating in their area? Finally, who was following the SWORDFISH team? Both Richard and Flash knew that Vienna was and had always been a town favored by spies. It was a crossroads of Europe and the Middle East reaching back to the days of the Austro-Hungarian Empire. During the Cold War, the Austrians had preserved their sovereignty by remaining neutral. And like any state that declines to take sides in a conflict, it became the venue for clandestine competition between adversaries. They both realized it could be any number of different teams focused on the SWORDFISH team.

Austria was still a neutral country, and both the government and Austrian industries profited by that neutrality. In this post-Cold War world, Austrian hospitality and goods attracted the elite from Russia and China, wealthy Middle Eastern exiles, and a host of equally wealthy European businessmen and women. The Austrian security service and police force were determined to maintain that status quo. However, status quo did not mean disinterest. It was entirely possible that the second surveillance group was an Austrian team.

Flash said, "This would be much easier if we just tagged their vehicles."

Richard looked over at Flash. Her face was bathed in blue light from the laptop she was using to follow both the SWORDFISH phones and the GPS trackers the Black Sheep were wearing. "If we tagged their vehicles and then the Austrians found the tag, it would be real trouble at the Embassy as well as the end of the mission to track the SWORDFISH team. I don't even want to talk about how pissed Dentmann would be if we lost government equipment. This is an entirely extraterritorial operation. We don't have any authorities and no backup. So, the Black Sheep are running loose surveillance and they rely on your technical coverage. No pressure, Flash, but it's all up to you."

Flash smiled and said, "Remember, you have a super-genius on board so we can easily compensate. At least between the two shifts, we now have descriptions of the SWORDFISH creeps. Five ultra-fit guys who barely fit into their leather jackets and one guy who looks more like a long-distance runner than a bodybuilder. At least I give them credit for style — they are all wearing spy black." Flash looked down at her own trousseau. Black fleece jacket over a black T-shirt. Black jeans and black hi-top sneakers. She had even added a black watch cap for the evening. "Now, while we are killing time, why don't you tell me your life story?"

Richard smirked. "Where do I begin?"

"How about whether or not you are married."

Richard laughed. "Not likely. Life in the special operations community both before and after 9/11 was pretty darn hectic. And after I retired, Jamie made me an offer that simply was too good to turn down. No, Flash. Not married."

"Excellent."

"Anything else?"

"I understand you were in one of the Tier units?"

"Yup. I passed selection in 1999 after ten years in Special Forces. In the units, it takes about a year before you know what the heck you are doing. Just about the time I was ready to go to work, 9/11 happened and it was one rotation after another. Afghanistan and then in 2003, Iraq. It was a merry-go-round, Ft. Bragg to Balad in Iraq back to Bragg, so on and so forth until I retired."

"Assault team?"

"Nope. Sniper."

"Me too!"

Richard looked over at Flash. "Eh?"

"So, my first SOF unit was the Human Intelligence Collection Unit based at Bragg. Periodically, they got a slot for various post schools like jumpmaster, loadmaster, and even sniper school at Bragg. I raised my hand when they said sniper and they sent me. You should have seen the looks on the faces of the instructor cadre when I showed up!"

"I can imagine. I'm assuming you did show up in uniform. The guys from the 82nd Airborne Division can be strict about that."

"Oh, I learned that in jump school. Luckily, by the time I attended, I was already a warrant officer coming from an unnamed SOF unit, so they couldn't be too goofy. It did piss them off when I was one of the top three in the class." Flash looked down at her computer and said, "Well, it looks like we must stop our chat and get to work. The SWORDFISH team is on the move."

"Where are they headed?"

"They set up a bubble around the Belvedere Palace Museum. It looks like their target just left the museum. They are headed south. Given the speed of the phones, it looks like a mix of foot and vehicle surveillance."

"The target might be on a tram."

"Fair point. The Black Sheep are in trail six plus blocks behind them. I really wish we could get some coverage on the other team."

Richard smiled and said, "One of the toys we brought with us is designed to vacuum up cellphone numbers. It uses a technology that I don't understand, but the software will eventually give us a map of all other phones that are following the SWORDFISH phones. The Black Sheep have deployed the collector in one of their vehicles, but we needed to have the SWORDFISH team on the move to make it work. When we get back to base, we will build a new network you can track. Well, that's the idea at least."

"Are you a techno-phobe like Massoni?"

"Nope. I'm just a realist. I know that tech works sometimes and doesn't work other times. Basically, if it has a battery, it can fail and usually fails when you need it most."

"Well, I just keep my stuff charged and hope for the best. As much as being parked with you has been a treat, we need to jump to the next park." She looked down on the map display and said, "Forget that, it looks like everyone is moving south by vehicle. The general track is toward the Vienna main train station. We can cover the team from here until they move past the train station." Flash looked at the very large, very black Casio G-shock on her wrist. She hit the lume button and the yellow glow from the LED inside the watch showed the time. "It's 19hrs. It just might be the target is headed home. If the target catches a train, we are sunk."

"The Black Sheep will handle the train and any other option. Trust me, these guys are the best surveillance team I've ever used."

"Better than the MIKEs?" Flash was referring to Sue O'Connell's first SOF unit, the MIKE team from the SOF Surveillance and Reconnaissance Squadron.

"At least as good and since they are a mix of Eastern European nationalities, they are better than S&R because they are invisible."

Flash nodded. "Fair. Looks like the SWORDFISH team is moving toward a suburb south-southwest of the city. Alt Erlaa."

Richard nodded. "OK, then we need to move. I will head west first and then south. You tell me when we start to lose signal with the team."

"Check."

For two hours, they played cat and mouse with the SWORDFISH team as the SWORDFISH team tracked the yet-to-be-identified target. Finally, at 2130hrs, Flash announced that SWORDFISH had returned to their bed-down location. For the first time that night, Richard made a call on his phone to the Black Sheep team leader and said, "*Schlaf.*"

Flash looked up from the laptop and said, "RTB?"

"Yup, return to base. And, with luck, the Black Sheep will have plenty to talk about before we call it a day. Let Jamie know we are headed back."

Flash nodded and typed RTB into an encrypted SMS connection. Jamie responded RR meaning roger, roger. Flash watched as the lighted streets of Vienna passed in front of her and they headed to what was certainly a relatively dismal part of the great city.

NIGHT VISITORS

Barbara and Beth debated whether they wanted to go out to dinner after their extensive afternoon room-service tray. Instead, at 8pm they decided to order another, less sumptuous meal from room service, plan for the next day and then have an early evening. Barbara was not upset with the decision. During her days working counterterrorism cases throughout Europe and the Middle East, after an agent meeting, she regularly stayed in her hotel and lived off room service until it was time to leave. She assumed the more time she was out on the street, the more chances she had to run afoul of the local security service, street criminals or, worse still, adversaries looking for an American spy. Plus, the living room in the Hotel Imperial was comfortable and the balcony offered a spectacular view of the city.

In less than thirty minutes, there was a knock on the door and a voice from the hallway said, "Room service for Madame Ambassador."

Barbara looked at Beth who was lounging on a chair near the balcony. "Your food is delivered, Madame Ambassador."

Beth did her best diva imitation and said, "Let them in, dear. The minions will be upset waiting in the hallway."

Barbara chuckled as she opened the door. A waiter in the hotel uniform pushed the cart into the room. He was followed by three other men. Before Barbara could react, two of the men had secured her hands with nylon flexicuffs and put a black nylon bag over her head. The waiter and the last man ran past and did the same with Beth. Barbara fumed at the fact that she had been so careless. She heard a quiet voice in her ear. He spoke English with a Russian accent. She could smell a hint of garlic and possibly lemon on his breath. "Mrs. O'Connell, we do not wish you any harm, but if you resist, I will have to do something you will find unpleasant. Please don't force me. It will be best for everyone."

Barbara knew there was precious little she could do, given how quickly and professionally she had been captured. This was not the time to resist. There would be time later. She said, "I understand."

"Excellent."

Two very strong hands guided her back into the room and sat her gently down on one of the chairs. As soon as she sat down, she heard and eventually felt two long zip ties securing her legs to the chair. Barbara had heard nothing from Beth so far. She hoped that Beth was being equally compliant. This was going to be an interrogation — at least at first. It seemed unlikely that a team this efficient would intend to kill them in the hotel where it might only be hours before their bodies were uncovered. It was important to play for time. And, Barbara reminded herself, it was important to do her best to stay calm. She took several deep breaths to flush some of the adrenaline that was coursing through her veins. Adrenaline for a fight or flight event would be useful later, but for now, it would simply add to her mental confusion. She didn't need that.

The voice said, "We have taken your companion into another room. We are quite alone now. As I said before, I'm not interested in hurting you. I am only interested in knowing why you are here and why you are in contact with Karol Andrassy."

Barbara thought about her resistance to interrogation training. In the opening gambit of an interrogation, the interrogator asks questions where the answers are already available. He asks those questions to determine if the captive is going to be compliant. Even if the captive isn't compliant, the questions are useful because they will reveal how the captive intends to deceive the interrogator. In sum, it never makes sense to lie in the early part of an interrogation. Instead, resistance to interrogation starts with the truth. Small bits of truth to begin so that when or if you need to lie, that lie will have logical consistency with the truth. Short, polite answers. Barbara remembered her instructor saying, "It is a chess game. The opening moves are critical, but they are not the most important. Save the important action for later."

The thoughts flashed through Barbara's head in seconds. She replied, "We had coffee with Andrassy at the Café Central. He works at the Belvedere Palace Museum. It was the first time I met him."

"Once again, excellent. Now, tell me why you wanted to see him."

Barbara wondered how sensitive the relationship might be with Beth's client. She had to say something and she still didn't know what her interrogator knew. For all she knew, Andrassy might have had an earlier visit from these same men. "There is a piece of Russian art on the market. We wanted to determine if it was stolen."

"And the answer?"

"He thought it was stolen."

"Did that make a difference to you?"

Barbara decided it was time to insert just a small lie to build some sort of rapport with her captor. "It does to both of us. We have no interest in stolen art. Of course, if the art was stolen, it will be important to bring the thieves to justice, but that is not our job."

"And what is your job?"

"To determine whether the unknown seller is legitimate. We have determined that he is not. We are done."

"Returning to the USA?"

"As soon as we can."

"Mission accomplished?"

"Yes."

"Mrs. O'Connell, please don't think I am a fool. I know your background. You were in the US special services. Your husband was as well. You work for Ambassador Parsons as her...what shall we call you? Perhaps, her security advisor? You are not interested in determining the rest of the tale? You don't care about the theft of the icon?"

Barbara smiled under the hood. Her captor had just revealed three things. First, he knew precisely who she was. That meant this was not an impetuous interrogation. Her captor had focused on her background. Second, she had used the term art rather than icon on purpose. Now she knew her captor knew the icon was on the market. Finally, his tone of voice suggested that he might be sympathetic to the victim rather than the thief. It was too early to tell and it would have been far easier to determine if she could look at his face and his body language. She decided to pay greater attention to the tone of voice and the use of language. Her captor was fluent in English but not overly so. That meant he might not even realize when he gave away more details. She needed to leverage this point.

Barbara opened emphatically. "Of course, I care. But I am no longer in service and I realize that I have to observe and report and then let others who have authority deal with this crime. Theft of religious art is the worst possible crime in the art world."

"Then perhaps we are allies in this little drama." Suddenly, Barbara could feel her captor's breath as he whispered in her ear. "But, you need to know something. Andrassy is one of the thieves. That makes it complicated, no?"

Barbara was surprised and didn't know how to respond to this point. "If that's so, then there is little I can do. I will recommend to the Ambassador that we leave it to the authorities. We can point them in the right direction, but if Andrassy is part of the conspiracy, then there will be many who will not want him to face a criminal charge."

"Indeed. As I said, complicated."

Barbara heard, more than felt, the zip ties freed from her legs. She waited for a few seconds. She could hear no sign of her interrogator. She reached up and pulled the nylon bag from her head. The night visitors were gone. She reached down and pulled one of the nylon knives from its sheath and carefully cut the nylon cuffs.

Barbara quietly walked over to Beth. She was trussed up in a separate chair in the same manner. She quietly and calmly spoke to Beth. "They are gone. I'm going to take the hood off your head."

When Barbara took the hood off Beth's head, she was surprised that her friend was not distressed. Beth shook her head as if to clear her vision and said, "Well, wasn't that interesting?"

"I wouldn't describe it quite that way." She carefully cut the zip ties off Beth's ankles and did the same with the nylon cuffs on her wrists.

In the past, Barbara had used medical shears to cut cuffs off captured individuals. The carbon-fiber knife was certainly sharp enough, but a false move and it would also deliver a deep cut into Beth. It took Barbara longer than she expected. When she was done, they were both free and neither was bleeding.

"Beth, don't tell me you have been through something like this before."

"I was captured in the late '90s while visiting the battle lines in Nagorno-Karabakh. Same deal. Flex cuffs, hood, and an overnight interrogation. I always assumed they were either Azeri security or, perhaps, Russian GRU. Of course, once they realized I was a senior at State, they were apologetic and drove me all the way back to Baku and dropped me off at my hotel. I won't lie. I was pretty shaken when I finally got to my room. I made a cup of tea and watched the sunrise wondering if anything I was doing in Azerbaijan made any sense. This time, they asked their questions and disappeared. Odd, no?"

"Especially odd since they already knew who we were. Did they ask you about the Count?"

"Absolutely. My interrogator seemed determined to let me know that Andrassy was part of the problem rather than part of the solution."

"So, what do we do next?"

Beth looked over at the room service cart next to the door. "Dinner?"

"Why not? A little adrenaline always makes me hungry."

Beth stood up, stretched like a cat just up from a nap and said, "Me too!"

Barbara's husband sat on the edge of the bed. He looked down at his wife and whispered, "Barbara, you don't want to know. You simply don't want to know. I died in Vienna because they thought I knew too much. They didn't think I was a spy, they just wanted to clean up loose ends and I was one of them."

On the other side of the bed was Peter's father. His face was tragically sad as he looked at his son. "Barbara, you know that pursuing these men is the right thing. They have stolen from a monastery and intend to sell the icon. How do you think they are going to use the money? Crime? Espionage? Terrorism? If you can stop them, you must."

Her husband turned to his father and replied, "That was the last thing you told me before I died. How do you think that turned out? They poisoned me and I had a very long and painful death."

Barbara woke up as she inhaled to scream. She hadn't had a dream that vivid in years and it was the first time that the frustration nightmare involved both her husband and her father-in-law. She was enough of a rationalist to know they weren't talking to her from beyond the grave. Something deep inside her subconscious was trying to tell her something about her current work with Beth. Barbara knew this type of dream was not going to be very helpful. Mostly, it was a warning that something wasn't quite right. She would need to be on her guard. She wondered whether they should just wait until reinforcements arrived. After all, there was nothing like having four retired action heroes around to build your self-confidence.

HERE WE GO AGAIN

Sue watched as the entire team assembled for the first time. It was just past midnight and she was wide awake. The early evening nap might have been the right thing to do so that she was ready to work a night shift, but it also meant that for at least another day, she would be fighting jet lag as her body remained on CONUS East Coast time. She had a mug of strong tea in her hand. If that didn't work, then she could always ask Massoni for some of his coffee. His brew guaranteed sleeplessness for at least twelve hours.

This was the first time she had seen up close the entire Black Sheep team. The previous meeting was at the Panopticon cafeteria and the team kept to themselves. This time there was no way for them to hide. One long table and a single large video screen in the warehouse served as their briefing room. At first glance, the Black Sheep were best described as "of one type." They were a mix of ages from mid 20s to mid 50s. All with short hair and multiple days of beard. Sue's first job in SOF was as a surveillant and it was always important to blend in with the locals, but these men didn't need to blend in. They were locals. Better still, they looked like the underclass of workers that Europeans ignored unless they had plumbing or construction that needed to be completed. They were all dressed in clothes consistent with European workers: either blue coveralls or heavy work shirts and jeans. Probably the only thing that argued against their cover as industrial workers was their footwear. Instead of heavy, steel-toed work boots, they wore a mix of black sneakers or light hiking boots. As Jamie said, the Black Sheep were invisible.

Jamie started the briefing with a simple mission statement. There were three things they needed to accomplish: they needed to identify the entire SWORDFISH team, they needed to identify the target of the SWORDFISH surveillance, and they needed to do their best to identify the team — friend or foe — that was also surveilling the Russians. Once he completed what in the military would have been called the "commander's intent," he turned to the two team leaders of the Black Sheep: Dieter and Jacob.

Dieter stood up and started his part of the briefing. English was clearly not his first language. Sue assumed he was either a Pole or a Slovak, based on his accent. Still, Dieter was comfortable as he prepared the briefing. In his mid 50s, he was a fit, very square man with short hair greying at the temples. He might have easily been a retired NCO or a shop steward in some factory, but either way it was clear he was used to running a team. He used an electronic tablet for the briefing. He tapped the tablet and a pair of individuals appeared on the screen.

"We have determined that this individual is the team leader. We have designated him Bravo 6. He travels with a driver — designated as Bravo 1. Unfortunately, the Russian bed-down location is in a location that we were not able to penetrate. However, we have captured the number of each of the three rental cars." He tapped the tablet screen again and three vehicle license plates appeared on the screen. Sue looked over at Flash who was scribbling in her Moleskine notebook. If anyone on the planet could link the license plates to individuals, Sue was confident that it would be Flash.

Dieter continued. "We tracked them from the BDL to where they set up their surveillance bubble. They were set up in the vicinity of the Belvedere Museum. None of the team attempted to penetrate the museum, so we assumed they were waiting for an individual, most likely an employee, to come out. They are a patient team and they settled into a mix of vehicle and foot movements over the day. They finally moved when the following individual left the Belvedere."

He brought up a picture of a short man in his late 50s or early 60s wearing a black coat and homburg hat. He had a groomed beard. He was walking from the entrance and hailing a cab. "I will continue with the report, but first I think it is best you hear from Jacob." Dieter handed the tablet over to another of the Black Sheep.

Jacob was younger and thinner. In fact, Sue thought he looked like most of the marathon runners she knew. Tall and whip thin. A man who could run all day and all night and show no sign of fatigue. He wore his hair longer than most of the rest of the Black Sheep and his black beard was a stylish two-week growth. Sue thought that Jacob might be the surveillant they used when they needed to follow a target into a bar or a café. She looked over at Flash and realized that her colleague was sizing Jacob up for other reasons entirely. His voice was a mellow version of Dieter's and his accent was hard to pin down. Possibly German? Swiss? Northern Italian? He was a chameleon.

"Our job today was to identify the team that is surveilling the SWORDFISH team. As Dieter said, the SWORDFISH team was most patient and that was our good fortune. The team surveilling the SWORDFISH team was not patient and had a terrible time simply sitting still near the museum. As a result, we were able to identify what we believe to be the entire team." He tapped the tablet and six photos came up on the screen. Each photo captured a man who looked to be of Eastern Mediterranean descent. From the images, Sue couldn't decide if they were Greeks or Turks or Lebanese. "We are calling the six in this team Bravo 12 through Bravo 17. Here are their pictures again with their numbers identified."

Jacob continued. "We also captured photos of their three cars. Please note: one of the cars has diplomatic plates. We checked our database. The grey Mercedes is assigned to the Iranian embassy here in Vienna. As to the other vehicles, here are the license plates." Two photographs appeared of license plates on a red hatchback SEAT and a blue SKODA.

"As I said, they were not patient. Our assessment is that they are not professional surveillants and not used to waiting for long periods of time. Instead, they are simply Iranian assets resident in Vienna. They communicate via cellphone. We used a long lens to capture a text message one of the individuals received when he and his partner left their SKODA to visit a coffee shop." The message appeared on the screen. Sue looked at Flash who, once again, was copying the information from the screen. "While they were in the coffee shop, we were able to deploy a quick plant tracker. We have designated that car Charlie 16 which is associated with Bravo 16 and Bravo 17. I will provide that information to Miss…?"

Flash looked up and smiled. "That would be me, Jacob. And the name is Flash."

Jacob smiled back at Flash and said, "After the briefing then." He continued, "Once the SWORDFISH team was on the move, the Iranian team followed. Honestly, it was like a circus train and Dieter and I agreed that there was no good reason to add to the madness. At that point, we returned to base. One final comment: I have no doubt that the SWORDFISH team know that they are under surveillance." He turned and handed the tablet back to Dieter.

Dieter continued, "Based on Jacob's call, we used the quick plant to track the Iranian team as they followed the SWORDFISH team. As you know already, they all went to a suburb of Vienna — most probably the home of the individual they tracked from the Belvedere Palace. After that, I thought the Russians and the Iranians would return to their respective bed down locations. Only three of the Russians did so. The other three moved toward the city center and visited the Hotel Imperial."

Jamie asked, "Did the Iranians follow the team into the city?"

"They did. However, we don't think they penetrated the hotel when the SWORDFISH team went into the hotel. We watched their three cars and their entire team. Once again, the team that had the tag left their vehicle and found a coffee shop. We decided to recover the tag. We couldn't be sure if they would be going to the Iranian mission. After the SWORDFISH team left, we observed Bravo12 enter the hotel. If he is an Iranian diplomat as we suspect, he may have been able to identify the targets in the hotel."

This time it was Richard who spoke. "Any idea who the SWORDFISH team visited?"

Dieter said, "It was not possible to penetrate the hotel while keeping track of the various Bravos and avoiding any compromise. We can return tomorrow to determine possible contacts."

Jamie said, "Dieter, you keep SWORDFISH as the priority targets. We will visit the hotel tomorrow. If we are lucky, it will be easy to sort out one or more of the guests."

Flash raised her hand and waved. "I suspect I have an answer." Sue smiled. She knew that it was in Flash's nature to be a show-off, but especially when she was targeting a new man. That smile didn't last for long.

"While Dieter was outlining today's surveillance serial, I looked at a couple of the data points. The first one had to do with the SWORDFISH target at the Belvedere. The museum website is most helpful and has a listing of the senior staff with their photos. The target is named Karol Andrassy and he is an expert in Slavic religious art."

Jamie said, "Now that is interesting. I wonder what the SWORDFISH team wants with a museum curator?"

Flash said, "Well, the next bit is equally interesting and is becoming a little on the creepy side."

Sue said, "Creepy?"

"Especially for you, sweetie. The Hotel Imperial guest list is only marginally protected on the web. It was...not a challenge for me to gain access."

Massoni knew that Flash was famous for hiding the lead in her briefings until the last second. He spoke for the first time in the briefing. "Flash, do us all a favor and just spit it out."

Flash seemed hurt that she wouldn't be able to explain how she got the information. She complied. "One of the suites in the hotel is under the name of Ambassador Elizabeth Parsons and her friend, Barbara O'Connell."

Jamie shook his head. "That is definitely not good."

Massoni looked at Sue and said, "Here we go again."

Sue felt the blood rush to her head and her ears started to ring.

FOREIGN COMPLICATIONS

Misha looked at his watch. It was 05hrs. He learned from his father that time wasted was time lost forever. Misha grew up in the military. His father had been a member of the special purpose forces known as the Zeynith, a paramilitary arm of the 1st chief directorate of the KGB. Misha admired his father and wanted to follow in his footsteps. After the collapse of the USSR, the KGB split into multiple organizations. Misha decided instead to follow his own path, first in the Russian Airborne forces, then SPETSNAZ and now in SWORDFISH. Along the way, time discipline became progressively more important. Intelligence operations, like any special operation, had to be performed with precision.

Since the SWORDFISH collective leadership was made up of retired seniors from the GRU, time management in SWORDFISH was strict. Team leaders were judged on their commitment to precision. To date, Misha's team had always delivered results on time and, just as important, in secret. He always started his meetings on time and his teammates understood if you weren't five minutes early to a meeting, you were already late. They were sitting in place, mugs of tea and small notebooks in front of them. As the sweep second hand and minute hand reached twelve on his watch, he started.

"We have three subjects to discuss today. First, a summary of our work so far. Second, the issue related to the foreign complications. Finally, how to move forward on the mission." Even a team as small as his needed to be fully aware of everything that each team member knew. He read that the US military called this situational awareness. The Russian army had a different name of the same idea. They called it information dominance. SWORDFISH teams like his needed to dominate their tiny battlefield. To do so, they needed to share their knowledge. He turned to Ivan and said, "Yesterday?"

"We followed the target from his home to work. It was difficult to physically penetrate the museum administrative areas, but Sasha did go inside. While inside, he was able to use our cyber tools to access the museum's internal networks. Once we did that, we could watch the target through the camera on his computer and the cameras throughout the building. We also used a separate tool, a worm, to access his mobile telephone call records. The target is part of a small cadre involved in the theft and sale of the artwork."

Ivan took a sip from his mug of tea and smiled. "It is so much easier now that The Collective has given us the tech tools."

Misha nodded and said, "Continue."

"We followed the target from the museum to his home. We stayed at that location long enough to identify three of his contacts in Vienna. Two remain unknown. The third was a visitor to Vienna."

Misha said, "We will cover that later. Tell us about the other two contacts."

Ivan turned to Sasha. Sasha was the team's cyber specialist. He was in his forties and served in a SPETSNAZ assault team before transferring to GRU cyber unit 26165. Misha was the SWORDFISH operator who recruited Sasha. In exchange, he asked the SWORD-FISH leadership collective to assign Sasha to his team. He never regretted his request. Sasha had his laptop open and talked to the team over the top of the laptop.

"We now know that the conspiracy is among three different partners. First, we have the manager of the thieves. His name is Abraham Nazzimof. Nazzimof is a Russian exile and now an Israeli citizen. He also holds an American passport. We don't know much about his thieves. His travel records show he traveled to the Egyptian resort community at Sharm el-Sheikh last year. I can only speculate that this was where he met the men who stole the icon from St. Catherine's. That is a best guess. He is currently in Tel Aviv and I doubt that he has the icon."

Misha said, "A logical conclusion. The second contact?"

"He is a well-respected antique dealer in Vienna known as Casper Neufelt. However, he was formerly a German Democratic Republic Stasi officer who worked with the KGB. He was dispatched to Vienna in 1988 to establish a business network in support of the KGB. He disappeared off the records in 1999 and was presumed dead. The FSB would very much like him and any funds returned to the Motherland. We initially identified his office, found that he was out of the country and moved on to our third target."

Misha said, "One mission at a time. Our job is to acquire the icon and deliver it to the Russian embassy here. *If* they decide Neufelt is a target and *if* our company is tasked to accomplish this mission, *then* we will do so." Misha looked at his team. "Of course, if Neufelt or Andrassy get in the way of that mission, we will eliminate that threat. For now, we focus on both targets to see who actually holds the icon." He looked over to another man across the table. "Alex, now for the Persian complication."

Alex nodded. "Vlad and I were covering the south side of the Museum when we noticed an anomaly in our area. There were two separate cars that were moving from one location to another, always within a line of sight of our vehicle. Both cars had two men. At first, we were concerned that we might have come under the scrutiny of the Vienna police or, worse still, Austrian security. However, the four men in the two cars looked like Arabs and they did not act in a professional manner."

"At one point in the day, I decided to get a closer look. We noticed at one point that the driver and passenger of one of the cars abandoned the car to go visit a nearby coffee shop. I walked over to investigate. It was a halal shop run by a Lebanese immigrant. The two men were engaged in a friendly conversation with the owner. I took down the license plate and sent it over to Sasha."

Misha looked over to Sasha. Sasha nodded and said, "It is a rental car rented by the Iranian embassy."

Alex continued, "At your instruction, we pulled away from our location and reset to a location allowing us to watch the Lebanese when they came out of the coffee shop. They were worried when they saw that we were gone. They used their mobile phone to call and report their failure. We were not close enough to hear the discussion, but clearly their supervisor was not amused. They moved to another location where their comrades were watching Sasha and Ivan. We had a better look at their team at this point. Four men, all Lebanese or Persians. We even watched as a third car arrived and a man got out to berate them. He was driving a diplomatic plated car associated with the Iranian embassy." Alex stopped and passed photos of the individuals. "We watched as they watched us. It was amusing."

Misha said, "Not all that amusing. We now have another complication we must address." Misha looked around the table. "What are your thoughts?"

Nicolai spoke for the first time. He was the newest member of the team, a recent arrival at SWORDFISH from one of the Russian Guards Airborne Regiments. To date, Misha had used Nicolai as his driver and personal assistant. Misha knew from his time in SPETSNAZ that new members should not be trusted until they proved themselves. Misha noted that Nicolai had decided that his opinion mattered. Perhaps it did, perhaps not.

Nicolai said, "We could do them harm. Vienna can be a dangerous place."

Misha shook his head. "Nicolai, we have no orders to harm these new spoilers to our operation. Remember, we work for SWORD-FISH and only do the jobs they direct." He looked at the young man. He didn't want to crush him too soon. The rest of the team would likely give him some…counseling later, when they went to the gym. Instead, he said, "I respect your initiative. Short of doing them harm, what could you do?"

At first, Nicolai looked puzzled as if he couldn't imagine what else he might do. He looked at his teammates. They were expecting him to come up with some sort of idea. He said, "Since they are a threat to our mission, we could disable their vehicles. They don't seem very careful about how they manage their coverage of our efforts."

Misha smiled. Perhaps Nicolai wasn't such a wooden-headed paratrooper after all. "Exactly. So, design a plan that draws the two targets into a place where they will abandon their vehicles. However, I do not want anyone to do anything to the Iranian diplomat's car. If his team is disabled, he will no longer be a threat."

He took another sip of his tea and said, "Ivan, report on the American complication."

Ivan looked at Sasha who turned his computer screen around so that all of the team could see pictures of two women. Ivan started after everyone had a good look at the images. "We traced Andrassy to a mobile number registered to an American. There was no effort to disguise the number which was owned by one Elizabeth Parsons. SWORDFISH databases offered significant detail. Parsons is a former senior diplomat who served in Moscow and in several capitals in the near abroad. She has been retired for several years and works for a law firm with offices in Washington, DC, and New York City. Her fellow traveler is Barbara O'Connell. She had a long career in the US special services, primarily in the Middle East."

Misha added, "However, her husband was a Soviet targets officer. He was eliminated when the GRU determined that he had been working as a double agent. Since she retired, O'Connell has been working on contract for Parson's law firm. Most recently, The Collective suspects the two women were involved in disrupting one of our smuggling operations in Germany. There was no certainty on that point and The Collective did not instruct us to eliminate the Americans. Rather, we were to determine by any means necessary their connection with Andrassy. Last night, we identified their hotel and paid them a visit."

Nicolai whispered to Alex, "A real social call." He laughed at his joke until he noticed no one else was laughing.

Misha continued as if Nicolai was not even in the room. "We isolated the two Americans and interrogated them. In both cases, they said the same thing. We are all after the same thing: the icon. They are working for the Orthodox Archdiocese of New York. What they don't know is their contact is not just an expert on Russian icons. He is one of the conspirators."

Vlad asked, "What do we do with the Americans?"

"During my nightly summary, I asked The Collective that same question. They said to ignore the Americans unless they get in the way. The Archdiocese of New York will be informed by Moscow that an official element is on the case. They are to tell the Americans to stop their investigation. That should happen this morning before 1100hrs. If the Americans are wise, they will simply return to the United States and that will be that. If they remain curious, we have authority from The Collective to reduce the risk to our operation."

Nicolai asked, "By any means?"

"The Collective said to use the minimum of force. They do not want the Austrian authorities investigating violence against a former American ambassador. So, we might need to control their actions, but we will not eliminate the Americans. I hope that is clear."

The five men around the table nodded. Misha continued, "So, here is what I recommend. We need to accelerate our plan. The longer we are in Vienna, the more likely we are going to face even more risk. The best plan is to deal with Andrassy on his commute to work. At this point, he is our only target in Vienna. The Collective has instructed us to use whatever means necessary to make Andrassy tell us where the icon is." He looked at Nicolai and said, "It would appear you may have an opportunity for a bit of wet work on this trip."

Nicolai smiled while the rest of the team shook their heads.

Misha ended the meeting. "We meet later in half an hour for the day's plan. We did good work yesterday. Today will be no different."

WHAT ARE YOU DOING HERE?

Richard and Sue left the safe house just before dawn and drove an aggressive surveillance detection route for an hour before parking the car in a public lot in the outskirts of Vienna. For the first few minutes of the drive, neither spoke. Finally, Richard decided to break the silence. He said, "Do you regularly meet with your mom on operations?"

Sue shook her head and said, "It would appear so. Originally, it was because of a vendetta between a Russian family and my own that went back to the 1940s."

"A long time to hold a grudge."

"Tell me about it. I was the one locked in the trunk of a car that was rigged with explosives."

"That sounds bad."

"Well, then they tried to blow me up in the Black Sea in a ship with nuclear waste."

"Worse."

"Then there was the time when my mom was hunting a long-lost cousin who was a Russian wet-work agent. Her operation ran parallel to one that Flash and I..."

"Please stop. I get the picture. This is like a 19th century novel where the characters keep getting into trouble and escape in the nick of time."

Sue smiled. For at least a moment, she had forgotten how angry she was that her mother was involved in another of her operations. She said, "Well, so far."

"Great. Well, I know about the last time. I'm the one who had to toss the bodies over the railing of the hotel and into a snowbank."

"What I don't understand is what is going on with Mom and Beth this time. What are they doing in Vienna and how are they linked to SWORDFISH?"

"Dentmann sent me to work for Beth Parsons for a bit. I suspect it is some sort of international law issue related to theft of something big." Richard looked in the mirrors and then pulled into the parking lot. "We'll know in a bit. We are clean so far. It's time to get on the street and mix it up with public transportation and a bit of a morning walk. Interested in some Viennese pastry?"

Sue smiled. "Always."

"OK, then off we go. We need to be at the hotel around eight, so we can't linger."

For the next hour, they meandered across the old city of Vienna. It was a crisp fall morning and they enjoyed the mix of walking and traveling by electric tram. Richard guided them and made a final stop at Café Leopold. Like Jamie, Richard was fluent in German and ordered them a café mélange, which was the Viennese version of the café latte that was standard fare in US coffeehouses. He also ordered two small pastries that he called mohnzelten. While not in Sue's previous limited German vocabulary, she made sure to write down the name. The coffee and pastry were a perfect pair.

As they walked to the hotel, Sue asked, "Did you and Jamie serve in the 10th together?"

"I'm a young one compared to Jamie. He was in the 10th Group when they were based in Bad Tolz, in Bavaria. I entered after they left Germany and moved to Ft. Carson in Colorado. We still had a European mission and I had some high school German, so they sent me to Monterey Defense Language Institute for a bit." Richard smiled at the memory. "Not that it helped me much in Bosnia or in Afghanistan."

"As Massoni would say: all good training!"

"Leave it to a sergeant major to focus on the positive."

"Until he doesn't."

They arrived at the hotel at precisely 0800hrs. They already knew the room number, so they walked into the lobby and acted like they were a set of guests. Between Jamie's on the ground knowledge and Flash's check of the hotel's computer network, they knew that they were walking in just at shift change at the front desk. As expected, no one took any notice of the well-dressed young couple.

Richard knocked on the suite door and waited. Barbara's voice from the other side of the door said, "Who is it?"

Sue said, "It's me."

The door opened. Mother and daughter faced each other. Barbara was the first to speak. "What are you doing here?"

Richard smiled and said, "Barbara, we might ask you the same question. Can we come in?"

A voice from inside the suite said, "Richard! Oh, am I glad to see you! Come in and have some coffee. Room service just delivered breakfast."

As Sue walked past her mother, she whispered, "This could get messy."

Barbara responded, "Dear, it already is messy."

Beth insisted on playing hostess and they didn't start the discussion until she had poured coffee and offered pastries. Richard took the coffee in the rather dainty cup and saucer, passed on the pastry, and gingerly sat down. Sue could see that he was most concerned about balancing the coffee and not spilling on the furniture or the antique rugs in the suite. Sue learned how to accomplish such a balancing act years ago growing up in a family serving overseas and attending various diplomatic functions. She also knew from years in the field that if you had a chance to eat and drink, you grabbed that opportunity. She took both coffee and pastry and sat down at the couch next to her mother. Sue decided to start the conversation.

"Richard and I are here with a team targeting a Russian hit team that recently arrived in Vienna. Our surveillance team showed the Russians came to the Hotel Imperial last night. I doubt your visit is a coincidence." In an effort not to appear too grumpy over the "coinci-dence," Sue smiled and took a sip from her coffee.

Beth laughed. A long deep laugh that was hardly consistent with Sue's image of *Ambassador* Elizabeth Parsons. After she placed her cup and saucer on the table in front of her chair, Beth said, "Well, it would appear that we have stumbled into another bit of the shadow world."

Richard said, "Beth, it would be useful to know what is going on."

Beth looked at Barbara as if to determine where to begin. Barbara decided to begin at the end of the story. Basically, she wanted to cut to the chase. "We were attacked last night. Interrogated in the room and then released. Most probably by your Russian targets."

Sue paled. She said, "Mother, is this another part of our vendetta with the Beroslavs?"

"Thankfully, no. Just as Beth said, it would appear we have stum-bled into another Russian art theft ring like we did in Germany."

Richard shook his head. "A bit more detail would help."

Beth smiled her most dangerous smile. Barbara always wondered if Beth Parsons knew her demeanor argued that she might both kill and eat her guests. "We were tasked by a client to determine the provenance of a Russian icon up for sale. Based on what we have gathered so far, the icon was stolen. Not stolen from some person, but stolen from St. Catherine's Monastery in the Sinai."

Sue cautiously started what she knew her mother would recog-nize as a debriefing or, perhaps, an interrogation. "Who told you that information?"

Barbara answered, "We met with a Hungarian expert who works at the Belvedere Museum."

Richard nodded, "That's the link."

Beth shook her head. "He is a trusted contact."

Richard said, "Perhaps so, but he is the focus of the Russian team that is here."

"Russian government?" Barbara tried not to show the concern in her voice. She wasn't successful.

Sue shook her head. "Russian mercenaries. SWORDFISH to be exact."

"Shit, shit, shit."

Sue was taken aback because the entire time that she had known Beth Parsons, Sue had never heard her swear.

The conversation was interrupted by the telephone. It was a white ceramic phone with a gold tone cradle. Designed to look like an early 20th century rotary dial telephone, it had a small digital display that showed up when the guest lifted the receiver. Beth said, "Yes?" This was followed by a series of single words interspaced by silence as Beth became more and more agitated. Finally, she said, "I understand. Thanks for calling. We can talk when we return to DC."

Barbara looked up from her coffee. "News?"

"That was one of the Stearns and Mandeville partners. The client has asked us to stop our investigation. The office is satisfied with the results we have provided. The client has paid us a healthy bonus, and want us to return home."

Barbara placed her coffee cup gently home on the saucer. "Well, isn't that interesting."

Beth said, "It looks like we have gotten too close to something that even the Diocese doesn't want to follow."

Richard looked up. He had been carefully balancing the cup and saucer on his right leg and had been eyeing one of the pastries. "The Diocese?"

Barbara nodded. "We are bound by attorney client privilege, but for the sake of this discussion, you need to know that our client was the Russian Orthodox Archdiocese of New York."

This time it was Sue who said, "Isn't that interesting. So, when will you leave?"

Barbara said, "After last night's misadventure, my vote is we leave sooner rather than later. We have something to do in Switzerland before we return home."

Richard smiled. "Visiting your Swiss bankers?"

Beth said, "As it turns out, that is precisely what we are doing."

After Richard and Sue left, Beth looked at Barbara. She said, "We aren't leaving immediately, are we?"

"I said sooner rather than later."

"Exactly. If Andrassy is a creep, I want to know that. And, if he was playing me, I am seriously pissed. I'm sure Hans would love to provide the Austrian authorities with a lead to a valuable Russian icon. It would make everyone happy. I think we need to get a couple of answers before we leave for Switzerland. Longstreet and the team arrive this afternoon. Perhaps a little B&E might be in order."

"In the trade, it isn't called breaking and entering, it is called covert entry."

"Potaytoe, potahtoe."

"Well, we don't leave any traces."

"OK, so that sounds better. I really don't have any contacts in the Austrian police and I'm sure Hans would hate to get a call from a police station."

"So, where do we go? The Museum?"

"What better place to hide a valuable piece of stolen art than in an art museum?"

"Too right. So, we wait until Longstreet arrives?"

"Yes. After last night, I do think we should stay in the hotel tonight."

"Agreed."

Barbara watched as Beth pulled her chair over to the French doors open to the balcony. She turned and said over her shoulder, "Vienna is beautiful in the fall."

WATCH HOW EASY THIS IS

The SWORDFISH team departed their hotel at dawn. Nicolai drove Misha. Ivan and Sasha and Alex and Vlad made up the other two cars. They deployed in a starburst pattern to determine if the Iranian surveillance team was in place and prepared to follow them. It took only a few minutes for Ivan to report. "We are the rabbit."

Misha responded, "Time for the hunters to become the hunted."

In their pre-departure briefing, Misha outlined a relatively simple plan. The team would starburst out of the area, whatever car from the team became the target would take their adversaries for a drive south from the city toward the airport. At the Schwechat junction, they would select highway 10 and set up what would appear to be a fixed surveillance point near Schwadorf. Once in place, they would report back to Misha and the other two cars would close on the Iranian surveillants. Misha hoped that the team was sufficiently amateurish that they wouldn't expect an ambush. In less than an hour, he was proven correct.

Misha thought about the Iranians. His thoughts were not positive and he breathed an audible sigh. Nicolai said, "Chief, is everything all right?"

Misha nodded. "As I checked the time, it brought back memories of Syria. The Iranians are not to be trusted. They proved that in Syria and they are proving that again today." He looked at the young paratrooper. The new team member had probably done only one contract before moving over to SWORDFISH. Perhaps a little fighting in Syria or possibly in Georgia, but nothing like Misha's experience.

161

"The Iranians were supposed to be our allies in Syria. Instead, they left us the shit work. Pacifying the Kurds while they worked against the Syrian renegades. The Kurds are serious warriors, Nicolai, and worse still, they were working with the Americans."

Nicolai nodded. He knew any comment he might offer would be useless.

Misha continued, "We were ordered to partner with Syrian and Iranian special forces in northeastern Syria. The Revolutionary Guards had a long-standing feud with the Kurdish militias. The Kurds accepted no borders but their own. They roamed from Turkey, through Syria into Iran and Iraq. Their politics are complicated. When it was in their interest to ally with the Syrians or the Iranians against the Turks, or in the past, against Baghdad, so be it. When it was in their interest to align with former enemies, they saw no reason not to do so. During the Syrian civil war, fragile alliances and opportunities for treachery were more risk than the Revolutionary Guards leadership in Damascus wished to handle. Better to focus on fighting the Syrian rebel army in central and southern Syria using their own Lebanese proxies from Hizballah.

"That meant we were ordered to pacify the Kurds in the northeast. And the mission resulted in my team riding into the receiving end of the power of the United States Air Force." He fingered the scar again and remembered a dozen colleagues lost and his eye nearly destroyed in one battle. The only positive point was that he was evacuated and did not have to return to Syria. Misha was certain that the catastrophe was due to Revolutionary Guards' perfidy. What better way to eliminate a regional rival than to have the US do the deed?

"We walked right into a killzone. Kurds, US Special Forces and US close air support. Instead of hunting insurgents, we became the hunted." Misha fingered the scar on his face. "It was terrifying. I remember fleeing the fight in two Toyota Hi-Lux trucks, bouncing across the desert, a large field dressing covering half my face. All I could think of, all I prayed for, was that the American aircraft would just let us escape. Worse still, we couldn't recover the bodies of our teammates."

Misha didn't tell Nicolai of the haunting memory of the look in the Syrian medic's eyes as he was pulled from the wreckage of the SWORDFISH armored vehicle. The medic wasn't sure he was going to survive, but Misha had no intention of dying in Syria. "I always knew war was dangerous and brutal. I saw that in Chechnya. But, I have never faced an enemy that had air superiority. No matter how much money you make, the only value to the money is if you survive. If nothing else, the battle in Syria taught me to trust only our team-mates and to hate Americans." He shook his head. He had no room for any other emotions and wasn't sure if Nicolai could understand any of it.

Misha and Nicolai found the first car parked on the side of the road. Both driver and passenger were leaning against the vehicle looking down a hillside where Ivan and Sasha were parked. Misha and Nicolai passed the car and parked a half mile away. They walked back to the two surveillants who were both using binoculars. They never had a chance. Misha dropped the first one with a single punch. It took Nicolai two — one to the sternum and then a second to the chin. After they used nylon cable ties to restrain the unconscious men's hands, they opened the trunk of the car and tossed them in, slamming the trunk shut. Misha took the car keys from the ignition and threw them as far down the hillside as he could. He turned to Nicolai and said, "Easy prey. Let's see if the second set of targets is just as easy."

By the time they reached their car, Vlad was calling. "Our new-found friends have decided to rest for the day."

Misha nodded to Nicolai as they got into the car. He said to Vlad, "Call Ivan. We meet at the target house." Before Vlad could respond, Misha had shut his phone off. He said to Nicolai, "Off to Andrassy's house. No speeding. I know there is adrenaline running through your system, but we don't want any trouble with the traffic police right now."

Nicolai nodded. He wondered if Misha had noticed his hands were trembling slightly on the steering wheel. He thought it was mostly because he was excited about the rest of the day, but Misha may have been correct. He felt as if he had drunk three cans of the energy drinks common in the airborne forces. Perhaps adrenaline was all you need.

Massoni watched the events on the laptop in the safe house. He turned to Jamie and said, "That was pretty slick."

"The way the SWORDFISH dudes dumped their surveillants or the fact that the Black Sheep had cameras on target before that happened?"

"Well, both."

"You're welcome."

"Now we just wait for Richard and Sue to return and we get serious about these creeps."

Flash walked into the room. She was still wearing what was best described as a sleepy face. She was dressed in a black sweat suit and black high-top sneakers. Jamie wasn't entirely sure she had anything on under the sweat suit, but he was absolutely not going to be the one to ask. "Greetings, men! Where is the coffee? Did I miss something?"

Massoni said, "I made the coffee this morning and you absolutely just missed a great show. Coffee is on the counter."

As Flash poured her coffee, she looked over her shoulder and said, "Damn. I was up until nearly three working through the Klingon material searching for some angle we can use against the creeps."

"Find anything?"

"Only some interesting pieces on SWORDFISH recruiting. They really like to grab SPETSNAZ guys and FSB veterans. The analysts back at Langley are convinced they provide their new recruits with additional training in St. Petersburg and then send the new recruits out on seasoned teams. If they don't succeed in their first deployment, they are fired. As I said, interesting but not exactly helpful."

Massoni looked up from his coffee cup and said, "Well, Jamie's crew just filmed the SWORDFISH team take out their surveillance with no difficulty at all."

"Sheesh."

Jamie took a sip from his oversized tea mug and looked at both Massoni and Flash. "What's the news from the Panopticon?"

"Smith called this morning. 0400hrs. It really ruined my workout."

"Sorry we don't have a gym worthy of a sergeant major."

Massoni shook his head. "I didn't expect much. You are civilians after all. I reckon we need to wait until Sue and Richard get back so that I don't have to tell the story twice."

Sue and Richard returned a half hour later. Massoni offered coffee and Jamie offered tea. They didn't take either. After the breakfast in the hotel, safe house beverages weren't all that appealing.

Jamie started the conversation with one word. "And??"

Richard said, "It turns out the SWORDFISH crew visited the ambassador and Sue's mom last night."

Flash looked up from her laptop where she was watching the images of the SWORDFISH team taking out their Iranian surveillants. "Casualties?"

Sue shook her head. "Nope. They just wanted to know why mom and Beth Parsons were fishing in what they see as their pond."

"So, what exactly is their pond?"

"A search for a Russian icon stolen from St. Catherine's Monastery."

Massoni shook his head. "That will definitely piss off some Russian Orthodox priests."

Richard agreed. "And, I suspect whoever runs the show at SWORDFISH. They came in, interrogated the ambassador and Barbara, and then left. Other than using a classic bag over the head, hands and feet restrained, they were gentlemen."

Jamie said, "And who doesn't use a sandbag and cable ties during a polite conversation?"

Massoni said, "Along with a screwdriver in case someone has a screw loose."

Jamie nodded. "Well, there is that. Enough wishful thinking. What were the creeps after?"

Sue re-entered the conversation, "They were after information on a target at the Belvedere Palace Museum, a Karol Andrassy."

Flash said, "A source, a witness, or part of the criminal enterprise?"

"At this point, we don't know. Perhaps you can find out?"

Flash looked back down at her laptop and said, "On it!"

Jamie said, "We watched the SWORDFISH team take down their Iranian shadows with no trouble at all."

Richard nodded. "I expected as much. Whatever they are trying to accomplish, they need to do it without any witnesses. And that means no shadows."

"Except for the Black Sheep."

"Absolutely."

Jamie looked over at Massoni and said, "How about giving us the news from Smith?"

Massoni smiled. "I thought you would never ask."

THE CONSEQUENCES OF TREASON

Massoni looked around the table and said, "Smith called me this morning to let me know they have a pretty good understanding of the leak."

Flash said, "The forensics guys provided the leads?"

Massoni said, "Absolutely. However, it was far more complicated than any of us thought. Here's what he said. The team came in and conducted a full scrub of the last six months of incoming and out-going traffic. That didn't show anything that we didn't already know — that Flash was the fink."

Massoni looked over at Flash as she stuck out her tongue. He ignored her and continued, "Then, under the cover of a scrub for computer viruses, they did a workstation-by-workstation check. Again, no sign of tampering with hardware or software. However, one of the eggheads thought about checking an old-school option — the printer. Now, there is only one printer in the Panopticon designed to print maps and graphics used by analysts or, in the past, TDY teams or local surveillance teams like the MIKEs, the SBS team and Jamie's Black Sheep. Of course, there is a specific log-in procedure and record of printing. Not every workstation is linked to the printers."

Flash nodded, "It wouldn't be easy for unauthorized printing."

Jamie contributed. "Not easy, but not impossible."

Massoni continued, "That's what one of the team thought. Just because there was no software manipulation at the workstation level, didn't mean that someone didn't manipulate the printer software. And it was in the printer software that they found a trojan horse.

Apparently a simple enough beast to allow the printer to believe it was printing for one person when they were printing for someone else."

Flash said, "So who was the chump?"

"Do you mean who was the one that the printer thought was making the request?"

"Yup, the chump."

"Well, it turns out again that it was you, Flash."

Flash turned beet red. Sue had never seen Flash lose her composure or be speechless, but Massoni's comments did the trick.

Jamie said, "That takes some serious stones to piggyback on the most senior analyst in the Panopticon."

Massoni nodded. "I still don't understand how the creep did it, but the forensics guys said it was a very sophisticated hack. All entirely inside the software in the printer and most of it done remotely from the creep's workstation."

Flash finally regained her ability to speak. "Who is it? Who am I going to draw and quarter and then wipe them off the web. Who?"

Jamie said, "See, you were right, we are going to need a screwdriver."

Massoni ignored the comment and said, "Relax, Flash. They already got the guy in custody and flew him out of Germany. Name of Chester Natice. Army E5 who was one of our analysts working the night shift. His focus was on Sunni extremists operating in Germany."

"Where did they take him? I want to give him some…counseling."

Massoni smiled and said, "I think that is my job. But this isn't the real story. After all, just because Natice stole secrets doesn't mean that he sold those secrets."

Richard finally commented. "He took them for…his own amusement?"

"Better still, he took them for what he thought was a super-secret counterintelligence operation managed by a CI team in EUCOM. He was pretty proud of the fact that he pulled files from the system and no one noticed. He saw it as evidence of his skills and hoped to be brought into this specialized EUCOM CI team."

Flash shook her head. "So, not only is he a fink, he is a naïve fink."

Massoni nodded. "This is where the story gets murky. During his initial interrogation which Smith held inside the Panopticon, Natice insisted he was working on a compartmented project for Army CI that was running outside Smith's need to know. As you might imagine, this made our favorite Brigadier furious."

Sue said, "I'm glad I was out of the blast radius when Smith heard that one."

"Smith being Smith, before he went ballistic, he checked with Army CI. He reviewed all the compartmented double-agent programs. He is a thorough guy, our Brigadier. There was no compartmented program."

Jamie smiled. "A false flag operation. You must hand it to our adversaries. That's pretty sneaky."

Richard said, "I have heard of false flags before. One country's agents posing as another. The Russians previously posed as Americans or Israelis while working against a third-world target. But I haven't heard of a false flag operation where the operation was targeting Americans with foreigners claiming to be Americans. How did that work?"

"According to Smith, it was a daisy chain operation. We don't really know the precise end user…yet. Based on the hit of the original German target, we suspect it is the Russian internal security service, the FSB, but that is just speculation. As to the Iranian target, if the Russians had that information, they could use it in trade with the Iranians. We will get that information eventually after the real interrogations begin on Natice's handler."

Sue said, "Jim, you are getting as bad as Flash. You have been hiding the lead on this all along. Who was Natice's handler?"

Massoni said, "It was a pair of Army CI guys working out of USAEUR headquarters in Stuttgart. They had gone rogue…freelance. Selling secrets to…well, just about anyone who would pay for them. A major named Bantler, and his senior NCO named Sherman."

This time, it was Sue who was speechless.

Flash said, "Earl Bantler? Wasn't he part of the search for Daniels a couple of years ago during the MACE OP? I thought he was a waste of space. A do-nothing major with his equally do-nothing senior sergeant."

Richard was sitting next to Sue. He turned and said, "You know him?"

"Yes."

Flash said, "You know we aren't going to accept yes as an answer."

Sue said, "We dated when we both served as warrants at Bragg. I went to selection; he went to OCS. He stayed in conventional military intelligence. He went to the Farm and was working in EUCOM when we were doing the hunt for Daniels. Let's just say the relationship didn't end well."

Jamie shook his head. "Clearly."

Flash took up the conversation. "Jim, I'm hoping Smith has Bantler and Sherman under lock and key."

"I did say it was murky."

Sue's anger exploded. "SHIT! Are you saying they got away?" She stood up as if she wanted to go out and start the search herself.

Jamie said, "Sue, you need to take a breath."

Massoni said in his best sergeant major voice, "Or take a knee, Chief!"

Sue remembered her early days in the Army. Whenever a senior wanted to slow things down or whenever he saw things were getting out of hand, the instruction to "take a knee" meant it was time to take stock of what was going on and spend some time thinking rather than acting. Over the years, Sue had been an imperfect representative of think first then act.

Years ago, and after some required Army counseling, Sue realized she lost her leg because of what Flash at one point had said was the O'Connell marksmanship technique of "ready, fire, aim." Later, while serving on Smith's team, she lost perspective back in Afghanistan when they were searching for Bill Jameson and found that his savior was a Russian nemesis named Beroslav. Sue had worked on controlling her emotions, but again stepped over the line when she confronted her former lover, Jasper Derry, in the Hurtgen Forest.

Derry had gone rogue and provided physical support to a SWORDFISH project while thinking that it would all work out with Sue. Instead, his handlers killed him to keep him quiet. Nearly two years later, she thought her days of flying off the handle were over and she had changed. Now, she realized that inside her head, there was still that person who lost her temper and wanted to act NOW. She decided to slow down and follow Jamie's instructions and take a breath if not a knee. She asked, "Do we know who was directing Bantler?"

Massoni said, "As I said, Smith doesn't know. He suspects either the FSB or the GRU. They used Natice's interrogation and all the computer forensics they could throw at the question with no real luck. Bantler did communicate through a dark web server maintained by SWORDFISH."

"The same guys we are hunting?"

"No, Sue. The SWORDFISH headquarters in St. Petersburg. How that translated into a SWORDFISH hit team wandering around Europe is anyone's guess."

"Earl, are we cooked?"

"Mike, if you mean can we get out of this with our hides intact, the answer is I am sure we can."

Earl Bantler looked through the windshield of the old Opel Astra as he drove along a two-lane road in eastern Germany, headed toward the Austrian border. The car was registered to a source that Bantler ran for nearly five years. It was mechanically sound, but looked just like what it was — a relic of the Cold War. He glanced over at Mike Sherman. They were both dressed in outfits that they purchased in an Augsburg charity secondhand store, consistent with both the car and the aliases on their German passports. Sherman looked as worried as Bantler was confident.

"We have the right documents. We both speak perfect German. Our identities match a cover story that we built over the last two years. We only just picked up the car and identities in Bavaria. Once we are in Austria, we contact the Russians and they will exfil us to Cyprus. We shed these clothes and identities and become wealthy Americans … mysterious men of leisure. All we must do is stay rock steady until we meet with the Russians."

"I just didn't expect it to fall apart quite so quickly."

"That was a surprise, but it was a pretty good run." He looked over at Sherman to check whether his partner was just worried or starting to panic. Bantler decided to take Sherman back to the beginning. "You remember when both of us were passed over for promotion. We knew we only had a couple more years in Germany and then back home. A military pension isn't much money and it certainly wouldn't be enough to live in Germany. What would we do? Run some military club or work at a PX? We both agreed that wasn't for us, remember?"

Bantler watched as Sherman nodded. Sherman had been a steady partner during their work with the Russians. All he needed to do was to keep him steady for another few hours. "I did the approach. We knew one of the GRU sources in Munich. I just approached him and the rest is history. It all went smoothly. We didn't make any face-to-face contact…ever. We delivered the information we wanted to deliver. They paid us. All good. Now, if I had been in charge, I wouldn't have used the same wet work team to hit all the targets, and I certainly wouldn't have hit one of our own. That just brought too much attention from too many different services. After all, we have been trading with the Russians for five years and they have always been far more careful."

"It's the Iranians. It's their fault. Pushing to kill two targets in less than 90 days. Sheesh."

Bantler negotiated a long, slow curve as they headed into the mountains between Germany and Austria. The Opel took the curve at speed, but it required far more concentration than he normally used. He hated to have to abandon his two-year-old E-class Mercedes in Augsburg, but there was nothing to be done about that. As he finished the curve and could relax, he said, "I think our problems started when that idiot Jasper Derry in Stuttgart started doing contract work for that Russian mercenary outfit SWORDFISH. As an MI warrant, he should have known better. It just changed the entire environment in Germany. And then, he was foolish enough to get himself killed in the Hurtgen forest. He should have known that once you decide to leave, they are going to work hard to clean up the mess you leave behind."

"But shouldn't we worry about the same thing?"

"Mike, we have been working for the GRU, not some indiscriminate killing machine called SWORDFISH. The GRU have a vested interest in making the exfil work. Otherwise, their reputation is shitcanned and no one will work for them. Plus, they will want to debrief the living daylights out of us. We are valuable commodities."

Sherman nodded, but Bantler could see he wasn't convinced. He smiled as they started downhill on the road. "Mike, we just entered Austria. Even if the EUCOM notified the Germans, and even if the Germans notified their local colleagues in Munich, it will take weeks for them to get the imagination and bureaucratic courage to notify the Austrians. By that time, we will be in Cyprus, warm and dry."

Sherman looked relieved. Bantler knew that he needed to keep his partner onside for the next few days. After that, if Mike wanted to go his own way, Earl would let him do so. Earl had his own plans and his own money. Mike had been an important part of the plan five years ago, but he was just baggage at this point. Fragile baggage. Bantler concentrated on driving. The speed limits in Austria were far stricter and he couldn't afford a traffic stop at this point. Once they were in Linz, they would ditch the car, get a hotel room and wait to be picked up by the Russians.

Misha and Nicolai were sitting in a carpark two kilometers from Andrassy's residence. Ivan and Sasha were the close team with eyes on the target's house. Alex and Vlad were about 200 meters away, waiting for the signal. They were the snatch team. For this operation, they borrowed one of the vans used by the owner of the gym.

It would be perfect for the snatch. As Misha concentrated on the communications between the two teams, his second mobile started to buzz. Nicolai, alerted to the noise, said, "Headquarters?"

Misha nodded and answered. "Sir."

"New mission. Check your mail."

"Sir, we are in contact."

"Split your team. I am sure you can do more than one thing at a time, Misha."

"Yes, sir." Misha realized he had answered a dead connection.

He picked up the phone used with the team. They had an open chat line. He typed: *Ivan, take over. N&I have a new job. Confirm.*

In seconds, he received one letter response: *C.* He turned to Nicolai and said, "We need to get back to base. New orders. Take your time, we don't want any trouble with the traffic police."

"Sir." Nicolai started the car and drove carefully back to the gymnasium. He smiled as he drove. This sort of change in plans was precisely why he joined SWORDFISH. Once you were in the field, you were expected to act on your own. Nothing like that happened in the VDV when he was serving in Syria. Orders came from the generals to the colonels to the majors to the captains, and if events on the ground changed the situation, you had to wait for the next set of orders to come down from the generals. Meanwhile, the enemy was going down your throat and you were fighting him with your sharpened entrenching tool.

It took a half hour to negotiate Vienna traffic. Eventually, they arrived on site. Misha said to Nicolai, "Wait in the car. If this is some sort of quick response, we will need to leave immediately." Misha noted that Nicolai was acting like a child at Christmas awaiting a new present. He thought to himself: Perhaps he will get that present.

When he opened the laptop and loaded the encryption tool, the message from SWORDFISH Collective arrived. In the past, these sorts of messages were passed by hand from one SWORDFISH operator to another. Clearly this was both high priority and time sensitive.

Mission: meet two clients and end relationship

Where: Vienna main train station, Gleis 12, train from Linz

When: 2300hrs tonight

Following the directive was an attachment. The attachment included four photographs. Two faces and two shots of the individuals walking together. The photographs were enough. Misha understood the directive. Wet work. He looked at his watch. Fifteen hours until contact. It would be complicated balancing Andrassy and the new mission.

"Do we know where they are?"

Jamie watched as Sue did another lap around the table. "Sue, we are waiting on further data. Flash is working her fingers to the bone on her laptop and Massoni is trying to get another call to Smith. By the way, you are making Richard and I dizzy walking laps around the table."

Richard nodded. "This is a case where we need more data before we can do anything."

"And then?" Sue had tried not to sound like a disappointed teenager, but as the words came out, she realized that was what happened.

Jamie took a sip from his mug. "Here's what we are going to do. The Black Sheep can maintain full coverage of the SWORDFISH team. They don't need any supervision. They will observe and report. With a little luck, the SWORDFISH team will do something stupid, we will report them to the Austrian authorities and they will take care of the arrest. Remember, that's our job here. We want to disrupt the SWORDFISH team, get them in custody, and then link them to the murders in Germany. We've both had other ways of doing things in war zones, but this is the way we do things in Europe."

Jamie continued, "Meanwhile, we will work at grabbing Bantler and Sherman and taking them back to the Panopticon for a little conversation with Smith, EUCOM CI agents and the FBI. But first, we must find out where they went."

Sue had completed another lap. She stopped across from Jamie and looked at him. "Well…?"

"Well, what? We have the best team on the planet working on this. You know Flash is going to get the job done and I'm not about to get in their way. Sit down, have some tea, and start to plan how you are going to convince Smith that you should be part of the interrogation. Or you can tell me when your mom is going to get in the way. Richard and I have a bet going. I bet him that in the next six hours we would hear from the Black Sheep that your mom and the ambassador were observed in the mix. He said it would be twelve hours. Neither one of us expect them to just go away."

The mention of her mother stopped Sue in her tracks. "Swell. So, you think they are going to do something stupid."

Richard said, "Not necessarily stupid. Reckless, perhaps. Not stupid."

Jamie nodded. "I have already let Dentmann know we have wild cards on the table. If she is still in Europe, I won't be surprised if she comes to join the party. Dentmann is not someone who will miss this sort of show."

Sue sat down and let out a long, deep breath trying not to make it sound like a sigh. Dentmann was her boss in Cyprus, was deeply involved when Sue and with a joint DoD-CIA team handled the dirty bomb threat, and more recently when they were focusing on a compromise of an anti-satellite weapon. She was a hard-nosed operator who was intolerant of Sue's tendency to color outside the lines. If Dentmann arrived…no, Sue thought *when Dentmann arrived*, Sue would have to be on her best behavior if she wanted to stay in the field.

A FRIENDLY CONVERSATION

Misha and Nicolai were returning to their setup location when Ivan sent a short text in German. It read *Komplett.* He turned to Nicolai. "We need to go back to the gym. They have Andrassy. It's time to get him to talk."

Nicolai smiled. "One way or the other."

"Just remember, a dead man can't help us. Watch how the team works the Hungarian. It will be a good lesson for you. There will be rough work tonight with the other targets, so don't worry. You will have a chance."

They drove the rest of the route in silence.

When they arrived at the gym, everything was already set up. Misha had instructed the owner to close the gym for the day. After all, he received a regular stipend from Russia so he had no problem closing. Also, he really didn't want to know what might happen. So long as the SWORDFISH team cleaned up after they were done, he really didn't care.

Misha and Nicolai walked into the gym. The four other team members were waiting for them. Andrassy was sitting on a wooden chair in the middle of a boxing ring. His arms were restrained behind him with a pair of nylon cable ties. His legs were strapped to the chair legs with the same ties. A thick, black plastic garbage bag covered his head and his shoulders so that all Misha could see of the man was his black wool coat and his stained black wool trousers. Andrassy had already urinated on himself.

Misha looked at the scene. He walked over to Alex and whispered, "What did you do to him?"

"Misha, I swear we haven't touched him. We grabbed him, bagged him, and brought him here. He pissed himself before we got here. I had to stop Vlad from kicking him because Vlad got a handful of wet trouser when he pulled him out of the van. I think the Hungarian is willing to have a conversation."

Misha nodded and walked over to Andrassy. The boxing ring was a perfect venue. There were plenty of blood and sweat stains throughout the ring. So long as he didn't have to kill Andrassy, they would leave no trace. He took care to make as little noise as possible as he approached the seated man from the rear. He carefully raised both hands and boxed the Hungarian's ears. He could have cupped his hands and hit with sufficient force to damage the Hungarian's hearing. That wasn't the purpose of the strike. Rather, it was simply an introduction. Misha leaned over and said, "Are you ready to talk to us?"

A muffled voice came from the bag. It was unintelligible. Was it a plea for his life? Surrender? Something less human? Misha had heard this sort of thing before. Regardless of what the Hungarian had said, he knew for certain the man in the bag would be compliant. That was all he wanted...for now.

Misha said, "We only have a few questions. If you answer them, you may live. If you lie to us, you will most definitely wish to die. Do you understand? Nod your head if you do."

The man in the bag nodded so much, he almost shook the bag off his head. Misha looked at the team. He passed his hand over his face. Each member pulled out a black balaclava and put it on. Misha still hadn't decided whether the Hungarian would live or die, but he would take no chances. Once they were all masked, he pulled the plastic bag off Andrassy's head. Andrassy was a mess. The pomade on his hair had stuck to the bag so that when it was pulled off, the hair on the sides of his balding dome stood straight up. His lips were covered in a disgusting fluid. Was it vomit or simply saliva? Misha didn't care. Long ago he had lost the ability to sympathize with his targets. He wanted results and it was the target's job, his obligation, to provide the answers. He said, "Live or die. Now, question one: Is the icon in Vienna?"

"Yes. I…"

Misha raised the forefinger on his right hand and said, "Speak when I ask you to speak. So, where is the icon?"

"In the archives in the Belvedere Palace."

Misha thought for a moment. On the one hand, hiding stolen property in an art museum archive was a clever ploy. On the other hand, the Hungarian might be playing for time. It was time to put pressure on to find out. He backed away and Vlad put the plastic bag over the Hungarian's head and this time, he tightened the bag around his throat using large industrial tape. It didn't take long for the Hungarian to realize he was about to suffocate. His screams were muffled by the bag.

Misha leaned over and whispered, "Are you ready to talk?"

Andrassy nodded. Misha noted that the Hungarian had urinated on himself again. While disgusting, it was a good sign. Misha pulled out a long thin blade from his belt and used it to cut the tape and the bag away from the Hungarian. He was careful not to cut the Hungarian but equally careful to make sure the cold steel came dreadfully close to the man's neck.

Misha looked at the Hungarian. He smiled and said, "So, now you can tell us the whole story, Karol. From start to finish. Leave nothing out. Tell us about your colleagues Abraham Nazzimof and Casper Neufelt. We want to know everything and, don't worry. We have all the time in the world."

PLANNING FOR THE EVENING

Flash walked back into the room with her closed laptop in one hand and a smile on her face.

"Solution?"

"Yes, indeed. We have the solution to our problem. It wasn't easy, but…"

Jamie interrupted. "Wait one. I just got a message from Dieter." He looked down at his laptop and said, "Well, now we have a solution to an entirely different problem. Come over and watch this." Sue, Richard and Massoni walked over the other side of the table. Flash was last to arrive, in part because Jamie had interrupted what she saw as yet another moment of triumph. The video was split into two parts. The first video was thirty seconds long and showed the SWORDFISH team snatching a man off the street and pulling away in a white van.

Richard shook his head. "Bagged and tagged in less than ten seconds. Pretty slick."

Massoni said, "So long as you aren't the guy tagged."

"Too true."

The second video was less dramatic but from the perspective of their efforts, it was precisely what they wanted. It showed the van pull up to a run-down gym on the outskirts of Vienna and two of the SWORDFISH men pull the bagged man into the gym. A few minutes later, two cars pulled up and the rest of the SWORDFISH team arrived and entered.

Jamie said, "I sent a message for the guys to set up on the building and wait for my signal to pull away. We need to get this to the Austrians…"

Dentmann's voice finished his sentence, "And get these creeps off the streets."

Jamie looked up and smiled, "Boss, I thought you might visit. Sorry, we didn't bake a cake. We do have tea and coffee."

"Cut the crap. It looks like I've got work to do. Who did they kidnap?"

"Looks like a senior at the Belvedere Palace Museum. Probably also a villain who has stolen a Russian icon. But that isn't the point."

"Exactly. OK, you have the coordinates for the building?"

"Coordinates and the address. The Black Sheep are watching the place to see if anyone departs. If they do, then a portion of the team will split and follow."

Dentmann nodded. "OK, I will get station and the Austrians in the game. It is going to take a bit to make sure they don't realize we were working on this for some time."

Richard smirked and said, "Boss, that's what you are good at: Keeping us safe."

Dentmann laughed her distinctive nasal laugh. "It is my curse. Now, before I leave, tell me that you know where our two treasonous creeps are located."

Flash said, "I was just about to say, I know where they are and where they will be at tonight. They have tickets on the train from Linz to Vienna. Arriving at 2300hrs at track 12 in the main train station."

Dentmann said, "No wonder Smith likes you. Any chance you would like to be detailed to the Agency?"

Flash looked up from her laptop like she had received an electric shock. "No offense, Ma'am, but I'm not interested in working for Klingons. I have no problem working *with* Klingons, but not *for* Klingons."

Dentmann nodded. "Fair." She looked at Jamie. "You figure out how you are going to handle the arrival of Bantler and Sherman. I want a low-key operation."

"Boss, you want low key, you get low key with us."

Dentmann laughed again and said, "Sure. Low-key with O'Connell on the team? Well, you can work that out." Dentmann headed for the door.

Massoni called out to her, "That's been my curse, Chief."

Flash said, "Where is she going?"

Jamie said, "Dentmann is going to engage station and the Austrians. She can't start that from here. If she did, the safe house wouldn't be…safe anymore."

"Oh, right. So, do you want to hear how I tracked down our two finks?"

Sue said, "Eventually. Right now, we must figure out how we are going to snatch them."

Richard said, "Well, we could watch how the SWORDFISH guys did their snatch operation and copy that."

"Puhlease," Jamie said. "We are far more subtle than that."

SEARCHING FOR SOMETHING THAT ISN'T THERE

Jake Longstreet and his crew arrived at the hotel mid-morning. Beth booked two double rooms for them and, once settled, they held their initial meeting in the living room of Beth and Barb's room. Beth ordered a large selection of coffee, tea, and pastries and the new arrivals immediately dug in. Beth waited until they had finished their first cups of coffee and then asked, "Have you had a chance to consider our project?"

Mark was the first to comment. Barbara was always amused by the fact that a six-foot tall, two-hundred-pound man could have such a squeaky voice. "We looked at the target. I did a few simple cyber probes. For a place that has so many valuables, their security is crap. The best news is that it is really crap in the storage areas and loading docks. I guess they expect villains to just barge into the front of the museum like something out of the movies. No sense of imagination."

Jake put down his coffee cup and pulled out a schematic of the museum. "We put this together before we left. Entry and exit are not going to be too tough a challenge. What is a challenge will be finding the icon." He pointed to a large space on the level marked U2. "This is the sub-basement. It holds the archived collections. According to Mark, it should be where we find the icon. You will notice it is the length of the entire building. A big space. Bigger than that last version of Aladdin's cave."

Barbara thought back to their last covert entry in Aachen when they were focused on looted art from World War II. She said, "I would hope that the icon would be located with like items."

183

Once again, Mark commented, "That's my thoughts exactly. I pulled up their archived records." He walked over to the schematic and put a very large forefinger in the far-left hand corner of the map. "That's where they are keeping all the 19th century items from the Russian monarchy. If I was trying to hide an icon, it would be in with all this other Russian art. Oh, and by the way, there are over twenty icons in the mix. Do you know what this one looks like?"

Beth said, "We have this picture. It is an icon of an early Metropolitan of Kiev known as Michael I, the Enlightener."

Jake nodded. Mutt, Duke and Joe continued to eat their pastries. Barbara looked over at Mark. He was typing frantically on his laptop. Finally, he said, "No such icon listed in any of the academic records about St. Catherine's Monastery. There is an icon of that name currently listed in a gallery in Moscow."

Barbara looked over at Beth, who seemed completely puzzled. "So, we have been searching for something that isn't there?"

Mark said, "As I said, there are twenty icons listed in the museum basement inventory. None have some provenance from St. Catherine's. If they stole an icon from St. Catherines, it must be something else, or similar to an icon from St. Catherines. Or it simply isn't there at all."

Mutt looked over at Mark. He was smirking when he said, "How did you get so smart?"

Mark replied. "I read a lot." He started quoting a poem, "Yesterday, upon a stair, I met a man who wasn't there! He wasn't there again today. Oh, how I wish he'd go away."

Duke said, "I love that poem."

Joe looked at Barbara and said, "I'm surrounded by erudition!"

Duke said, "I didn't know you knew that word."

Jake had allowed the back and forth for a bit, but now wanted to move forward. He said, "So, are we looking for something that isn't there? Are we just part of a clever effort to con a US client out of his dough?"

Beth finally recovered and said, "If you are trying to sell a forgery, what better way than to make it clear to the client that it might have provenance that makes it hard to show off. Lots of real stolen art goes to collectors who want to possess and enjoy the art in their own home and alone. They tell no one so the art just disappears. If there is an icon in the Belvedere that hasn't been listed or shown for years, saying it came from St. Catherine's just raises the price."

Joe said, "Like chrome bumpers."

Duke nodded. "The perfect con. When we do penetration testing, we often pull that sort of con on the client's staff. Tell them something they want to hear and tell them that it is a secret they can't share. It only takes one selfish creep to buy the story and you are in."

Barbara smiled and said, "Sounds like my old trade. I thought you guys were all about covert-entry operations."

Jake smiled. "Only when we have to."

Beth thought for a minute. "It would seem that the best way to sort this out is not to break into the Belvedere but to have a serious conversation with Andrassy."

Barbara smiled, "Serious, as in violent?"

Joe spoke for the first time, "Only if we have to."

Beth said, "Why don't we call up the Belvedere and see if we can get an appointment with Karol Andrassy?"

Mutt said, "Meanwhile, we will finish the pastries."

Fifteen minutes later, Beth returned to the living room. "Herr Andrassy never made it to work today."

Barbara had been working with Mark on a complex crossword puzzle. She looked up and said, "Perhaps our Russian friends decided to have their own conversation?"

Jake said, "Russians? You didn't tell us about Russians."

Barbara said, "It isn't a long story, but it is a bit complicated."

Mutt looked up from the novel he was reading. He gave Joe an elbow in the ribs, waking his colleague up from his jet-lagged dozing. "I don't suppose it has to do with your daughter."

Beth laughed, "You work with one O'Connell and you get the whole family."

Barbara said, "Perhaps not the whole family. My son is still in DC…I think."

Jake was serious when he said, "How about we hear the entire story."

A few minutes later, Beth and Barbara finished the story from their meeting with Andrassy, through the interrogation by the Russians and ending with the dialogue they had the previous day with Richard and Sue. Longstreet and the team listened and when they were finished, they asked the same questions asked by Richard and Sue: Did they reveal anything other than interest in Andrassy and could Beth or Barbara give any insight into the individuals involved. Just as they had told the Agency team, they could offer little.

Longstreet said, "I think we must decide if we visit the Belvedere tonight or not. Based on Mark's assessment, the entry shouldn't be too difficult. But, I'm not sure at this point what we will be looking for when we get there."

Barbara said, "If it is a con, it would be nice to close the loop for the firm on how much of a con. But, it seems we are doing this more for ourselves than any client."

Beth nodded agreement. "If this is a con, it is a major one. We will get good karma from the Austrians if we can identify a lead and then turn it over to them. Stearns and Mandeville will get serious benefit from the Austrians, which is worth much more than you might imagine."

Mark's squeaky voice whispered, "So long as we don't get caught."

Longstreet said, "There is that. Then we plan on an entry tonight to see what we can find. Based on Mark's research, we only have an hour inside the building before the guards make their standard patrol in the basement. Guard shift change is at 0200hrs local, so we plan for entry at 1 and out at 2." He looked at Beth and asked, "Good to go?"

"Good so long as I get to go."

"This time I think it makes sense because we honestly don't know what we are looking for to make this worthwhile."

Barbara smiled. Only in the last few years had she realized how much of a risk taker Beth was. "Only one adventuress needed in this project. I will stay outside with the security team."

"That will be me," Joe said. "We need to get serious about a map recon to see where we can set up. The Belvedere Palace is on a hill-side, so there should be good fields of vision somewhere close enough for surveillance but far enough away to give us a full view of the various approaches to the building."

Longstreet looked at his watch, an old Rolex GMT that clearly had seem more than a few foreign adventures. "We've got about eight hours to get some sleep and get a plan together. Mutt, Joe and Mark: go put your head down for about three hours. When you come back, Duke and I will do the same." He looked at Barbara and Beth and said, "It is going to be a long night. I recommend you *adventuresses* do the same while Duke and I put together a plan. Do you have any recommendation for a car rental? We are going to need a van. Nothing complicated, just a delivery van that can carry all of us and will fit into any neighborhood."

Beth thought for a minute and then said, "Do you care if we engage a local assistant? He's a retired Austrian security service guy. He won't ask questions but will help get a van in a more discrete way than just calling a rental car company."

"Is he still in the game?"

"He runs a small company that does exactly what you do for a living."

Duke said, "Breaking and entering?"

Barbara said, "We prefer the term covert entry."

Jake offered another term: "I prefer the term penetration testing."

Beth smiled. "I think he would prefer the term corporate security."

Jake nodded. "You are the client. If you think this is the best plan, and it won't get us arrested, then I'm all in."

Barbara looked over at Beth. She was smiling her best Lucretia Borgia smile.

A SWIM IN THE DANUBE?

Misha looked at his team. They had left Andrassy tied up and hooded in the chair next to the boxing ring next door and they were sitting in the office of the gym manager. Misha took the lead. "I want everyone's opinion. One at a time. Is Andrassy telling us the truth?"

Ivan said, "I think he is terrified. I do think he is telling the truth."

Alex said, "I find the idea of this being an enormous scam reasonable. He was going to pass an icon in the archives off as an icon stolen from the monastery. Less risk. But, I don't understand how The Collective missed this point."

Nicolai said, "It really isn't up to The Collective. The client asked for us to sort out a problem. And we have sorted it. Short of doing Andrassy real harm, I can't see how we can expect him to say anything more. I think we have squeezed him like a lemon. He has no more juice." Misha nodded. He was pleased that the youngest man on the team had been listening to the entire interrogation.

Vlad said, "What about the Israeli connection? What role does he play in this story? I don't like it. The Mossad is good at playing complex tricks. Did they do this just to draw us out?"

Sasha was the last to speak. As always, he had been typing away on his laptop the entire time. He looked up from the screen, the blue light illuminating his features. He said, "I have looked up the Israeli. His travel pattern and his background with our special services points to a criminal, not an agent. He is wanted on two different Interpol red notices."

Vlad countered, "Then why haven't the Israelis put him in jail?"

"I suspect it is because the crimes that he is accused of are associated with political corruption in Israel. Amusingly, the two cases are associated with two entirely different Israeli governments from two separate parties in the government. I'm not saying he isn't a source for the Israelis. I'm just saying he isn't an agent and this doesn't look like some Mossad trap."

Misha could see this debate might continue for some time if he didn't offer his own view. "We have another, entirely different contract to accomplish tonight. Here is what I recommend. Vlad, Ivan and Alex will take Andrassy to the Belvedere and have him show you the icon he intended to sell. Apply whatever leverage you wish to make sure he is being truthful. *If* he can show you that it was a piece from the museum collection, then take him back to his residence and make it clear to him that he needs to find someplace else to live. Somewhere where we can never find him again." Misha paused. "Make sure he is convinced."

He paused again and said, "*If* there is any evidence that there really is an icon from St. Catherine's, recover it — carefully to be sure. After that, take Andrassy to the Danube for a little swim." Misha paused for a moment.

He continued, "Agreed?" The men on the team knew that Misha was sincere when he asked for their agreement. This was not an order, but simply a recommendation. They had survived Syria by working on consensus and then conducting the agreed operation. After all, there were only six of them and they should be able to get an agreement with little debate. In this case, they were pleased with the result.

Ivan asked, "What is the other contract?"

Misha said, "Nicolai, Sasha and I are going to meet the American spies at the Vienna train station. The Collective has issued an elimination instruction. I suspect they are considered excess baggage for one of the Russian special services and Moscow wants two things: elimination of the baggage while keeping their hands clean. It should be relatively easy. The Americans have been told they are meeting an exfiltration team." Misha shook his head and said, "In a sense, they are right."

He looked at his watch. "We have several hours before we can accomplish any of this. Sasha and Ivan will take the first watch on our guest while the rest of us will try to get some sleep. In two hours, Alex and Nicolai will take over. Vlad and I will take the last shift."

Misha stood up. The team knew the meeting was over.

NIGHT WORK — PART ONE

Sue watched as the rest of the team suited up for night work. Jamie and Massoni opened two locked Pelican cases with the long promised "toys."

Flash said, "I don't see my long gun case."

Massoni answered, "Smith said no firearms."

"Dentmann said the same," Jamie reiterated. He smiled. His white teeth flashed under his mustache. "Don't worry, Flash. We will carry implements that can do harm."

Once the boxes were opened, the team began a partnered equipment check. Sue was familiar with this routine. It was an essential part of a pre-mission exercise for all SOF operations. Basically, it was a check to be sure that equipment was onboard and in the right place and, probably just as important, in the same place for each operator. Massoni and Flash were partnered in equipment check. Jamie and Richard were doing the same. Once they were done, Jamie would check Sue's equipment.

First, each team member donned a thin vest that included short-range, encrypted radio communications. The radio had voice activated microphones and Bluetooth earpieces. Radio would be their primary communications, with mobile phones to be used only as backup. For the time being, their phones would be on, but placed in thin, Faraday shield bags so they couldn't be tracked. On top of the vest, they donned thin-skin body armor. They didn't expect to get in a gun fight, but Jamie pointed out that they couldn't say for certain. What was certain is the body armor would stop small arms or knife attacks, and would cushion any blows from a fist or a blunt instrument.

After that, they each put on their darkest top designed to disguise the extra bulk from the two previous items. "Dark" was no problem for Flash because as far as Sue knew Flash only owned clothes in black or navy blue. Flash pulled on her black hooded sweatshirt. Jamie and Richard wore navy-blue wool sweaters, Massoni a navy-blue wool shirt. The final piece of kit was a shoulder rig which held a collapsible baton under one armpit and a holstered taser under the other. These items would be covered by whatever jacket they chose to wear. Once they put on that jacket, Jamie handed them two more items — a set of nylon flex cuffs which he insisted should go in the right pocket and a small medical kit the size of a bar of soap for the left pocket.

As he pulled the medical kits out of the Pelican case, he said, "All it has is a pair of heavy-duty bandages and a tourniquet. I'm hoping we won't open these up, but if we do, at least we can stabilize the casualty. Remember, use the kit from the wounded man, not your own!"

Flash said, "Thank you, Dr. Obvious. It isn't as if we haven't been downrange."

Massoni turned serious and used a quiet, sergeant major voice. "It always needs to be said."

When they were ready, they walked over to the long table that had served the last few days as their working "war board" for each of the operations. In this case, it was a large map of the Vienna main train station. Sue asked, "And where did we get this?"

Jamie looked up from the map and said, "Well, we stole it from the Austrians, of course."

Flash said, "Of course."

Richard pointed to the map's special features. "While there are train station maps available, this one shows all the exits — including those that the police and the railroad employees use. You never know where a rat is going to run when you start to chase it."

Massoni nodded. "And these guys are definitely rats."

"Too true, Sergeant Major." Sue had finally calmed down as they moved toward the capture of the two traitors. It took real concentration and some help from Flash, but she was focused on the "how" instead of focusing on her anger about the "why."

Jamie took over the briefing. "Sue, I need you to watch the train as it pulls into the station, but I don't want you to be visible. We all know what their ID card faces looked like, but we don't know if either Bantler or Sherman will be wearing disguises. Only you will know them regardless of how they have tried to change their features. That said, if either of them sees you, they will run, and we don't really want to create a show for the armed Austrian police. The police will not be helpful and might just detain the wrong folks, meaning us. We want Bantler and Sherman to walk off the platform and be moving out of the station when we grab them. Check?"

Sue nodded. Jamie continued, "Richard, I need you as the driver of the van. Ideally, we are going to do the same sort of tag and bag operation that the SWORDFISH guys did. Flash, you will be in the back serving as the necessary muscle when we get them into the van. Check?"

Flash was about to say something, but Massoni gave her a sergeant major stink eye look and she just nodded. He took over for Jamie. "Once Sue has them spotted, we just cozy up to them and convince them to join us. I expect they may try something, but we have the advantage of surprise and weapons if needed. The entire operation shouldn't take more than a few minutes."

Sue nodded and said, "Unless it doesn't."

Massoni nodded. "Exactly. Unless it doesn't. But we all know that if we look organized, we might even be organized."

The lighting in the gymnasium was less than perfect as they sat through their final planning session. Misha looked at his two colleagues. Sasha had served with him in Syria. He might be a tech guru, but he also was part of the worst fighting that Misha saw. He would be good no matter what happened. Nicolai was the wild card. This was his first wet job and Misha knew the first was always the hardest. He opened the locked briefcase and pulled out three suppressed Makarov pistols and three double-edged fighting knives. The blades on the knives were less than four inches long, but that made them perfect for close-in attacks. Used properly, the blade would cause irreparable damage while invisible to all, including the victim. He handed the weapons to Nicolai and Sasha and took a pair for himself.

He looked at both men, though he was speaking to Nicolai. "The pistol is only a last resort. The Austrian police at the railway station have machine pistols. If we must use these pistols, we are certain to get into a deadly firefight that will be hard to win. This will need to be close-in, knife work." He pointed to a sketch map he had drawn of the station. "They will be coming from the train and heading to the exit of the station. You will both be waiting at the end of the platform farthest away from the exit. I will approach the two Americans. Remember, they are expecting contact, so they won't be surprised when I come up to them." Misha paused to look at both men. They nodded. "Once I have come up to shake their hand, I want you both to come up from behind. I want it to look like you have jostled them as you rush out of the station. Remember your training. A simple thrust up under the ribcage, pull down and out and leave. Drop the blade on to the tracks as soon as you are clear. If there is any follow-up needed, I will do the needed extra work. Keep walking at a normal pace and leave the station. Do not look back, do not look for me. We will meet at the RV point two blocks south of the station on Gerhard-Bronner Strasse at the entrance to the Star Inn. This is not how we prefer to do our wet work, but this is the only solution I have. Thoughts?"

Sasha said, "I think it is as good a plan as any. If there is a crowd, it will be easy. It is a late arrival, so there is no doubt the passengers will be rushing to get to the taxis. I am assuming we simply want to cause the injury. We don't have to confirm the death."

"Correct. By the time the authorities realize they are injured, they will already be in critical condition. They won't make it to the hospital."

Nicolai asked, "What about the cameras in the station?"

Misha said, "It is a good question. There is no doubt it will be a challenge. We will have to determine the camera locations when we arrive and do our best to avoid the unblinking eye. We will wear hats and these clear-lens glasses in hopes of minimizing the ability to identify us. Remember, we did not enter Austria through their immigration system and we will not leave Austria by air." He pointed to three pairs of tortoiseshell glasses that would have been stylish in the late 20th century but no longer worn by anyone under the age of fifty. "This is the reason why SWORDFISH serves the Russian state. We will take risks they simply will not take."

European rail stations were always busy. Trains crisscrossed the continent. High speed trains with business travelers raced on special ribbon-rail tracks while local trains trudged along at speeds that a less well-to-do traveler could accomplish by car or bus. One consistency throughout was that the train services were reliable and, most often, arrived and departed on time. Sue O'Connell often used the various European train services while serving as a SOF intelligence collector and more recently as a detailee in her current office affiliated with European operations. Her assignment tonight meant that she needed to be in the Vienna train station before the train from Linz arrived so that she could watch passengers from each coach walk to the station exit. Jamie agreed that their team should deploy at 2240hrs to be certain that they were in place when the train from Linz and their traitors arrived.

While the October days were warm, the temperatures fell quickly in the evening, and the train station was cold and damp when Sue arrived. Sue did her best to keep mobile, stopping at kiosks for cheap and barely drinkable coffee or glancing at the racks of newspapers and magazines. By 2245hrs, the owners of the kiosks were closing shop for the day and Sue was left waiting for the Linz train in a station that was slowly becoming an empty cavern. Just before the last shop closed, Sue bought a small bouquet of flowers. A good prop for someone claiming to be waiting for an arrival. She looked up at electronic display showing arrivals and departures. There were only three trains left to arrive before midnight. The Linz train would be the first.

Sue spent her early days in SOF as a member of Surveillance and Reconnaissance Unit. She remembered the training and her early days before 9/11 when they were hunting Balkan war criminals or Lebanese or Palestinian terrorists. The hardest part of "fixed point" surveillance was deciding how to fit into the crowd. In a crowded business environment, that meant moving along with the traffic. At night, it usually meant finding a hide location, either in a building or an abandoned field. Sue was currently in the worst possible situation: a venue that was closing, filled with a small number of people loitering to either pick up a guest or to take the last train out of town. The security personnel, in this case armed Viennese police, were likely to engage those loitering. Their goal wasn't to find villains. Rather, it was simply to pass the time. As a young woman, Sue expected eventually she would be a likely candidate for a friendly policeman. Since she spoke only a few dozen words in German, she knew that approach would generate even more interest.

To minimize that risk, Sue kept moving along the various platforms while keeping an eye on track 12 for the Linz train. As she walked the platforms, she noticed the arrival of three men who deployed along the track. They came in together, but immediately split up with two heading down to the end of the platform and the third standing close to where the platform met with the main station. They looked to be fit men aware of their surroundings. None of them looked especially pleasant or engaging. Like Sue, they were also working hard to avoid the police.

Sue keyed the microphone and said, "Hey, we may have some new players in the game."

Jamie's voice came through the earbud, "What's up?"

"Three guys. Military or criminals. Honestly, I think they are the SWORDFISH guys we watched on the surveillance videos. They are deploying on our platform and working hard to stay out of the view of both the police and the security cameras. I'm not saying they are after our folks, but if they are SWORDFISH, they aren't a welcome party."

Massoni's voice answered, "On my way."

Jamie said, "Hey, Flash. You got that?"

Flash's voice. "Yup. Trust me, we aren't sleeping."

Sue looked at the faded luminous hands of her grandfather's watch. There was just enough lume on the hands over the black faced dial for her to see the time: 2255hrs. "This is trouble. How do you want to play it?"

Massoni came up next to Sue and said, "We play it the way we always play it. Carefully."

Jamie said, "This might be their exfil team or they intend to erase the finks. It could get ugly. I suspect they don't want a scene on the platform, but neither do we. And, our two targets are more likely to run toward the guys they think are their exfil team than towards you. I'm on my way in as well."

Jamie arrived just as the train from Linz began to pull into the station. Sue said to her two partners, "There are two guys on the end of the platform and then the third guy who is in a navy wool coat standing at our end of the platform."

Jamie peered down the platform and then looked at Massoni. "They are definitely the SWORDFISH team. You want two or you want one?"

Massoni said, "Hey, you are the one with the German language skills. Why don't you start an annoying conversation with the guy at this end. No doubt he is the boss. The other two are simply muscle. Sue and I can distract muscle."

Jamie nodded. He said, "OK. Sue, please do your best not to be seen by Bantler and Sherman. We don't want them to scamper."

Sue smiled, "Got it, Jamie. No scampering. And, if they do, I will make sure they don't scamper far."

Jamie nodded and started walking toward the man in the wool coat. Sue and Massoni worked along the far side of the platform toward the wall of the station and into the shadows.

Jamie came up to the man and asked him in his best German, "Do you know if this train is coming from Munich?"

Misha looked away from the train and toward the man in the

heavy wool sweater and coat. He was not about to get distracted. He responded in German, "No idea."

Jamie persisted, "But if it is coming from Linz, most certainly it must have started in Germany, no?"

Misha tried to push pass the annoying man. As he brushed up against Jamie's left shoulder, Jamie stepped in between the Russian's legs, tripping him. As he fell, Jamie caught him by coat and helped him regain his balance. This time, the Russian was angry and closed in on Jamie and said, "Leave me alone!"

Jamie pushed the barrel of the surpressed Makarov that he just lifted from the Russian's belt holster as he prevented the Russian from falling. He whispered in Russian, "This is not your night. I suggest you and your men leave now before someone gets hurt. Clearly, you were prepared for killing, but the real question you have to ask is whether you are prepared for dying."

Misha looked around the platform. The doors of the train were opening and passengers started to leave the train. Since this was the only train in the station, the police were walking along the platform as well. He looked at the man with his pistol. A professional to be sure. He could see this was a man who had killed and would kill again. Who was he? An Austrian? An American? An Israeli? Was Ivan right earlier this evening? Was this all a setup to eliminate him and his team? As he thought this over, he identified his targets. They were about halfway down the platform. Sasha and Nicolai were already moving toward them.

Misha was used to being in control of the entire environment when he was tasked with wet work. This was different. It was more like a combat environment where there were multiple variables. He also knew that if he failed in this mission, his days in SWORDFISH were over, and most probably, he would have to spend the next few years on the run as The Collective tried to find him and eliminate him as well. That made the choice easier even if it made the job harder. He looked at his adversary and spoke in Russian, "Screw you."

Jamie watched the Russian as he made his mental calculations. Jamie knew the outcome before the Russian did. He expected the

Russian to act aggressively and when the man started to speak, Jamie had already pointed the Makarov at the Russian's left knee. If he was going to throw a punch or a block, it was going to be from a stance that would have his left leg forward. The noise of the train station muffled the already suppressed sound of the Makarov. The Russian's left leg crumpled. Jamie reached over with his left hand and grabbed the Russian by the waist and started to guide him to the closest bench. While he did so, with his right hand, he performed a series of acts. First, he dropped the magazine from the Makarov on the ground and kicked it toward the closest garbage bin. Next, he caught the gun's rear sight along the Russian's pocket and pushed down, working the slide of the pistol and ejecting the round in the chamber. Finally, as he settled the Russian on the bench, he placed the weapon back into the Russian's pocket.

Nicolai and Sasha made their way along the platform, watching their targets and waiting for Misha to make contact. When Misha moved to a bench with another man, they were not sure what this all meant. They had their orders and regardless of what Misha was up to, they were going to complete the mission. It simply meant that they had to walk faster to catch up to the Americans. Both Russians had their knife blades in their right hands, slightly concealed with the blade facing up toward their forearms. It would take a simple twist of the wrist and the blade would slide forward into a killing position.

A man in a large coat bumped into Nicolai. Nicolai looked over in annoyance and then back at his target who was only two meters away. Too far for a knife strike, but easily solved by speeding up his pace. The man who bumped him said something in a foreign language. Not German, not English. Some sort of Asian language. He turned and prepared to give the man the back of his hand. One slap should do and then he could continue the mission. As he pivoted, his entire body seemed to quiver. None of his muscles would respond to his commands. Instead, he found himself on his knees and then on his back. It was a complete puzzle as he stared up at the glass roof of the train station.

Sasha watched both Misha and Nicolai neutralized. He wasn't

entirely sure what was happening, but it certainly wasn't good for the mission. He saw Misha with one foreigner and Nicolai with another. As he turned back to catch up to both targets, he ran headlong into Sue O'Connell carrying flowers. Sasha had no time for a young woman looking for someone on the train. In Sue's other hand was the taser. As she pulled the trigger on the taser and pressed the probes into Sasha's abdomen, she said in English, "Not your night."

Sasha was the only one of the three who had decided to wear lightweight body armor. He wasn't sure why he chose to do so, but that was what saved him from the full force of the Taser's pulse of 50,000 volts. Instead of incapacitation, it was like a serious punch to the head. He was dazed, but not out. As he stepped back, he drew the suppressed Makarov and aimed at the back of his two targets, firing two shots. If Sasha had been his normal self, the two American targets would have been dead. Instead, one of the two rounds hit Sherman in the buttocks. The second round missed completely and struck one of the steel pillars at the end of the platform.

Sasha's second shot might have missed his target, but it ended the gunfight. It struck with a clang that focused the attention of the two Austrian police officers who were walking the platform. They looked over to see a man with a pistol attempting another set of rounds. There were flowers at his feet. Both officers shouted, "POLIZEI" as they aimed their weapons. One of the officers used his Glock 17 pistol. His partner was carrying a Heckler & Koch MP5 machine pistol. Each fired two shots directly into the chest of the armed man. He fell to the ground as they raced to the scene. As if on cue, a dozen Austrian police officers in black tactical uniforms appeared from two different access doors. They surrounded the three Russians. They took all three into custody. All three would need medical care. The medic from the tactical team started working.

Sue and Massoni did their best to disappear into the crowd of late-night train passengers who had not expected to attend a gunfight. In their earbuds, they heard Jamie say, "Stay on Bantler and Sherman!"

Sue easily closed the distance and grabbed Bantler by the elbow.

She said, "They intended to kill you. We just intend to detain you. Which do you think is the better option?"

Sherman was already going into shock from the bullet wounds. He said, "I'm shot."

Sue nodded and said, "We have an ambulance waiting."

In Sue's earbud she heard Flash say, "Now we are an ambulance?"

Jamie said, "You are. Get ready to handle one casualty and one to be detained."

Richard's voice came on saying, "Check."

They walked slowly out of the station as they heard sirens coming from multiple directions. It wouldn't take long for the Viennese police and the Austrian National Police to cordon off the entire area. They needed to get clear quickly. Jamie was still puzzled by the arrival of a tactical unit shortly after their confrontation with the SWORDFISH team. He assumed it was the work of Dentmann. She was always one step ahead of him. He guessed that was why she was the chief and he was just a minion.

Jamie met up with Massoni, Sue and their two captives at the van. Flash had the door open. She took Bantler first, put flex cuffs on his hands and a black sandbag over his head. She used her baton to apply an impolite amount of pressure on a select zone of Bantler's soft tissue and said, "Stay!" Sue and Massoni helped Sherman into the van and closed the door.

Jamie got into the passenger seat of the van and turned to Richard and said, "Let's get out of here. Head south for a bit until we get outside the city and the city cameras. We can loop back to the safe house at that point."

"What about Sherman?"

Sue and Massoni were in the back seat holding Sherman face down while Flash attended to his wounds. She looked over her shoulder at the front seats and said, "He lost a chunk of his ass. He'll live. Take it easy on the drive. We don't want this to become the vomit comet."

Sue nodded, "Amen."

She leaned over and whispered into Bantler's ear, "This is the price of treason, asshole. You are so lucky we were there."

The vehicle was silent for the rest of the trip as it wandered the streets of Vienna.

NIGHT WORK — PART TWO

Beth's contact was true to his word. He provided a simple tradesman's van and asked few questions. Longstreet and Mark checked the van for any electronic tracking or bugs and found none. Mark disabled the van's GPS system and announced he was satisfied. Not necessarily happy, but satisfied.

They loaded into the van 30 minutes after midnight and started a lengthy surveillance detection route. As Jake Longstreet told Beth, "You can't be too careful."

Barbara reiterated the same. "We have to be certain we are clean before we even approach the museum."

Jake was driving with Mark at his side using tracking software to determine if there was any sign of interest in their travels. After a full hour, they started their stair step return to the Belvedere Palace. They parked on a street near the building and split up. Jake, Mark, and Beth headed toward the loading docks of the Museum. Barbara, Mutt, Joe, and Duke worked their way to a location on the Museum grounds that would allow them visibility to the building. Duke said, "The great thing about palaces is they always had gardens. And, gardens are great places to hide."

Mutt nodded. "As long as you keep quiet, you lug."

Joe said, "Hush!"

Barbara smiled at the back and forth. This wasn't the first time she had worked with *Condottieri Malatesta*, but she always felt confident that their teamwork and confidence underscored their level of professionalism. Barbara hadn't brought clothes specifically designed for night work, but her standard wardrobe of earth tones worked well enough on a dark October night. Beth, on the other hand, was challenged until she realized that her navy-blue track suit would work. Longstreet and his team were wearing the perfect night kit for this sort of operation. Cotton navy-colored jackets over sweaters, dark jeans and black trainers. Nothing screamed "I'm a villain," but they easily disappeared into the shadows. Professionals from start to finish.

Mark set up a team SMS net for the night work. The first notice on the net was at 0100hrs. It simply said: *Entry.* Barbara looked over at her three colleagues. They were busy scanning the area using commercial night vision devices that looked more like birdwatching spotting scopes than any military kit. Mutt replied to the SMS: *Starting 60 minute timer...NOW.*

Jake Longstreet wasn't pleased that Beth Parsons was along for the operation. However, she was the client, and he was more than willing to admit that he was not an art expert. Still, not bringing civilians along on operations was one of those cardinal rules that you tried to follow. He noticed that she wasn't too excited and didn't act foolish when Mark used his skills to access the various security protocols and locks at the service entrance. He thought: so far, so good.

Access to the building still meant that they had to find the archives and then search a specific section for Russian icons. This was where he hoped Mark's computer skills and Beth's experience in European museums would come in handy. And, much to Longstreet's surprise, it was. Beth whispered, "Is there a sub-basement to this place?"

Mark looked at his tablet where he had downloaded the Belvedere Palace map. He responded, "Yup. There is a stairwell about twenty meters ahead and to our left. There are two service elevators, but they are both monitored by cameras that I couldn't access. I could spoof the cameras on the various floors, but the service elevators and the main entrance appear to be on a different server. Actually pretty smart when you consider..."

Jake interrupted and said, "Let's save that discussion for later when we sell our security protocols to the Austrians." Jake's phone hummed with an incoming text: *45 minutes.* He looked at the text and took off at a jog toward the stairwell. They walked down the two flights of dimly lighted stairs. Jake used his Surefire flashlight with a red filter lens to keep the stairs lighted enough, so no one was injured. The first door had an alpha-numeric in bright white paint: U1. Mark whispered, "Keep going."

As they headed down to the sub-basement, the air grew far colder and far drier. Beth said, "This must be the right location. Museums keep their paintings and other artifacts at a temperature between five and ten degrees Celsius with an ambient humidity below 20 percent."

Jake nodded and continued down the stairs until he reached the door marked U2. He carefully opened the fire safety door and held it for Mark and Beth. Mark had the archive database pulled up on the tablet. He would lead them through the forest of metal racks toward the stored paintings and then down the rows of wooden and felt racks that held the paintings. Mark was close to the location and about to turn the hunt over to Beth when they heard the voices and saw flashlight beams moving along the floor.

A Russian was speaking heavily accented German. "Show us."

Jake turned to his colleagues and gave them a hand signal to stop. He could see a series of flashlight beams streaking across the ceiling ahead of him. Before he did anything else, he sent a text message to Mutt. It read: *we are not alone.*

Mutt replied, *30 minutes.*

Beth recognized the voice of Karol Andrassy as he responded to the Russian. He said, "Our Russian collection is here. I will pull out the various paintings if you like. We only have two authenticated icons — both from the nineteenth century when Napoleon sacked Ukrainian villages before his army was stopped outside Moscow." There was a pause followed by a cry of pain.

"This was the icon we were going to sell. It is an image of the Metropolitan of Kiev known as the icon of Michael the Enlightener. We have never displayed the icon and it is not the only icon of this image, but it is old enough that the provenance would be impossible to check. We were simply going to say it came from St. Catherine's Monastery to make it more valuable."

Beth heard another cry from her former contact followed by the Russian voice. "Were you really fool enough to improve the value by claiming to have stolen this from a monastery? Did you not think about whether the Orthodox Church might consider a theft from the monastery as a grave sin? Clearly you and your conspirators did not consider the consequences." There was a loud crack as a gloved hand hit a face.

Longstreet was on the floor, slowly creeping along the racks hoping for a brief glimpse of the individuals involved in the conversation. His German language skills were limited, but he knew an interrogation when he heard one, no matter the language. He would have preferred to be above the individuals simply because humans rarely look above their natural line of sight, but he knew crawling up on the racks would make too much noise. Just as he reached the edge of the last rack, he heard the Russian interrogator strike his target hard enough that Andrassy hit the ground, rocking the wooden cases in the racks. As Longstreet's head cleared the rack against the floor, the man on the floor saw him and cried out at the top of his lungs, "Who is that?!"

Longstreet stood up and ran back to Mark and Beth. He didn't need to say anything, the shouting at the end of the racks made it clear what happened. As he ran, he used speed dial to talk to Mutt. "We are compromised. Pull to the RV."

Jake knew that the worst possible thing when you are being chased is to take the time to look over your shoulder. It throws you off stride and it simply doesn't help knowing how close the enemy is — at least if you can assume the enemy isn't armed. The crack of a bullet passing over his head answered that question. This enemy was armed and intended to kill. He shouted to Mark and Beth, "Split up. Go down different corridors. Meet back at the dock." He watched as Beth turned right along a row of metal cabinets and Mark turned left along a series of wooden racks holding Belvedere Palace's paintings that were priceless, but still not important enough to display. Another round slammed into a metal rack next to Jake's head. In the back of his mind, he realized that they weren't stopping to shoot to kill. They were running and shooting at the same time. Not amateurs, but certainly not experts. He knew that if he was on the other side of the equation, he would be dead already.

Jake was trying to calculate time/distance between the stairwell and the door when he heard another shot whiz past his head. The telltale sound of a high-speed round passing nearby was not encouraging. Suddenly, he did hear an encouraging sound — two different voices shouting, "Halt, POLIZEI!" Longstreet turned to watch his pursuer make the wrong decision. The SWORDFISH operator turned to face two Austrians in black raid uniforms, helmets and MP5 machine pistols. The sound of four rounds fired and four rounds hitting a torso with dull thuds was followed by the sound of the individual falling to the ground. Jake realized the police probably knew he was there so he shouted in German, *"Ich ergebe mich,"* and walked out from the metal racks with his hands up. Mark and Beth followed. The police motioned for them to get on their knees, and once they complied, the two officers checked to see if they had neutralized their target. Jake suspected that unless the Russian was wearing body armor, he was very neutralized.

"So, playing cat and mouse with Russian assassins?" Beth recognized the voice of her friend Hans.

She smiled and replied, "I thought you were retired."

"Semi-retired is what I believe I said when you asked."

Jake said, "Can we get off our knees so we can thank you properly?"

Hans turned to the two police officers and nodded. Jake noticed that they had spoken not a single word through the entire confrontation other than to identify themselves as police. It was either a curiosity or a sign of a team that was far more than a simple armed police unit.

Hans walked up to Beth and said, "I hope this wasn't too much trouble. We had to wait until we were certain they had broken as many laws as possible before we detained these men."

In his squeaky voice, Mark said, "You were here all along?"

"Yes. Some were in the racks above you, some in the shadows in the far wall. You know humans rarely look up when they are looking for enemies."

Jake smiled and said, "Yes, I do know that. I considered climbing the racks, but it would have made too much noise."

Hans nodded. "We arrived about thirty minutes before the Russians and Andrassy."

Beth said, "I suspect you had some additional insight."

Hans smiled. "Perhaps."

When Jake sent the compromise message, the surveillance team outside the museum made their way back to the van, planning to leave and head to the dedicated rendezvous point. When they got to the van, a diminutive figure was waiting by the van. "Going somewhere?"

Barbara was the first to identify the figure. "Patty?"

"Yes, dear. I suppose you were just out for an evening stroll with your best friends and wanted to see the gardens after dark."

"Something like that."

"Well, don't worry about your colleagues. They have been rescued by a friend from the Austrian service and his special tactics team. According to their radio chatter, one of the Russians is dead, two are in custody as is Karol Andrassy. They will be facing a long trial and then jail time. Of course, knowing how Russian services like to erase loose ends, it may be in their best interest to work with the Austrians…"

"And you…"

"Yes, Barbara. I had my team give them greater insight into SWORDFISH operations in Europe. By the way, your daughter and her team did a good job tonight as well. Not exactly as clean and quiet as we did at this end, but still a good result. They captured a pair of American traitors and the Austrians captured three more of these mercenaries. Two are in the hospital with gunshot wounds."

Mutt finally decided to ask what he thought was his most important question. "And us? What's next for us?"

Patty laughed loud and long. "Well, my recommendation would be for you all to leave Austria as soon as possible. The Austrian service is certainly willing to forgive and forget for now. Eventually, this is going to be a rather dramatic news story, and at that point, I think they will be under pressure to explain details that they would prefer to leave unanswered. If you are out of the country, that would help them."

"So, we go back to the hotel, check out and get lost."

"That would be my recommendation."

Barbara smiled and said, "Thanks, Patty."

"Barbara, I hope the next time we get together it is over a glass of wine somewhere in the US. Let's not have another party like this one, OK?"

Barbara smiled and said, "I'm with you. Beth and I were planning on leaving for Switzerland, and tomorrow morning sounds like a good time."

"Visiting your Swiss bankers?"

Barbara smiled innocently. "Something like that."

A TRIP TO LUGANO

Barbara had slept little after they returned to the hotel. The adrenaline was still pumping and she wanted a full debriefing from Jake and Beth. They offered it and then asked for an assessment on Dentmann and the plan. She explained Dentmann's role, Barbara's own experience with Dentmann going back years to Dubai, and the fact that if Dentmann made a promise, it was a promise to be kept.

They all agreed that the right answer was to get out of Austria as soon as possible. Jake and the crew went online and booked an early morning high-speed train to Frankfurt and a subsequent direct flight back to Charlotte, North Carolina.

When Barbara was operational in Europe, she did her own reservations based on paperback schedules of train and airlines, checking and rechecking schedules and then calling into an official call center to book the travel. That was over a decade ago. Now, most travelers followed the same plan as Longstreet and his team: open a laptop, identify a schedule, book it. Done. Of course, Beth Parsons was not most travelers.

At six the next morning, Beth called down to the concierge in the Imperial, explained their desire, and hung up. She said, "Anton said he will let us know our options in a few minutes. He also offered an early morning cart of coffee and pastries. I was more than happy to agree."

As promised, in ten minutes, there was a knock on the door and a waiter rolled in a small cart with a silver tureen of coffee, a ceramic pot of tea, and Viennese pastries and a bowl of fresh cut fruit. The waiter handed Beth a small folder with the Hotel Imperial crest. He asked if Beth wanted him to pour their drinks. When she nodded, he did so with a flourish, did a quick bow, and left.

Barbara took a sip of the aromatic Indian tea. She said, "You know, after this I will have a hard time making my own breakfast. It's not even half past six and I am already spoiled."

Beth replied, "Stick with me, dear. We aren't through with the fun yet."

Beth assembled her plate with a croissant and some fruit. She devoured the first croissant with a degree of relish Barbara had not seen in the past. Beth took a small sip from her coffee cup and said, "You know, I really did develop a taste for Viennese pastries. Sadly, I never did develop a deep enough pocketbook."

"So, what did Anton say about a trip to Lugano?"

"He said it depends on how much time we have. There was no easy way to travel from Vienna to Lugano by train. That is a real disappointment. First class travel by train means comfortable seats, excellent food, and a chance to see the countryside in ways that are impossible by car or by plane. Add to that the minimal hassles at train stations compared to airports in a post 9/11 world and it would have been my preferred choice. However, Anton points out that it is over a ten hour trip. I don't think we want to take that much time. After all, your friend Patty made it clear we need to leave soon."

Barbara nodded. "I love trains, but ten hours is probably more than we can afford."

"So, Anton says he can book us on a direct flight from Vienna to Milan this morning and a train to Lugano. It will still be poetic scenery, just not quite an excursion on the Paris-Simplon Orient Express."

"It seems to me that the Orient Express stories always involved violence of one sort or another anyhow."

"We have had enough of that in the last few days. I think Vienna to Milan and then a train to Lugano sounds right. After we do the needful in Lugano, we can take another train to Geneva and fly home from there."

"So, give Anton a call and let him know."

Beth took a moment to devour another bite of her croissant. After another sip of coffee, she said, "Dear, Anton already booked the tickets. He just wanted us to know why he made the choices he did."

"We have been well served."

"As it should be, dear. As it should be."

They left that morning by an Austrian Air flight to Milan. Instead of losing a day on the train or even a day and a night by car, they arrived in Milan in time to take a cab and catch their train to Lugano. Northern Italy was beautiful as it raced by their first-class seating in the train. The fall colors turned the hills a mix of reds, golds and green as they climbed into what geographers might call the "pre-Alps." Snow was already covering the tops of the mountains. The train wound its way through a dozen hillsides and along rivers that fed into the lakes on the Italian-Swiss border: Lake Como to the east and Lake Lugano slightly to the west. It seemed that they had just boarded the train when it pulled into the Lugano train station. Beth said, "If we had more time, I would have rented a car for us in Milan. The drive is glorious, especially this time of year." She smirked and said, "But, sadly work calls and we must get home."

Barbara nodded. "This has been a wonderful little interlude and an ideal way to decompress from last night. It will be interesting to see what happens next when we get to the bank."

"If you like, I will do my international lawyer thing to make sure the Swiss don't try to bully you too much."

Barbara laughed. "You do the international lawyer thing and I will do my best not to use my spy skills. Fair?"

"Like mesmerizing the poor clerks into opening any and all accounts you request?"

"Something like that."

"Deal."

They arrived at Banque Marchande next to the Lugano city hall. The street looked south over Lake Lugano and the surrounding mountains. It was a cool day with the blue sky reflecting in the mirror-calm lake waters. Barbara said, "Next time we are here, we need to take the funicular from the train station to the lakefront."

"Dear, next time we are here, I can imagine far more interesting things to do than ride an ancient trolley. The cathedral is exceptional and there is an art museum that is one of the wonders of the region."

"So, you've been here before?"

"Another of the trips for the firm. There were similar questions of art thefts and replacement forgeries. We were asked to assist the insurance investigation."

"What did you find?"

"Dear, I hate to turn the tables on you, but you really don't have the need to know."

Barbara laughed and said, "I deserved that. Let's go inside and see what we find this time."

They entered the bank and approached the bank manager who was sitting behind a beautifully polished antique desk. In his late 50s, the manager looked like a movie version of a Swiss bureaucrat. He was perfectly groomed, wearing a black wool suit, white shirt and a royal blue and red tie that matched the canton flag that was flying from the city hall. He looked up and greeted the two ladies, first in German and then in Italian.

Beth asked in German if he also spoke English. His response was to be expected: "But of course."

Barbara took over at this point. She said, "I am the owner of a safety deposit box in your bank. It was opened years ago by my family. I would like to review the contents, please."

Both Barbara and Beth were surprised by how quickly they were guided into a small room. The manager asked nothing more than the number of the account, the name on the account, and the key for the account. When Barbara provided all three, he disappeared for a few minutes and returned pushing a trolley with a large metal box that was easily a foot wide, a foot tall and three feet long. He pushed the trolley to the table and asked, "Madame, I am obliged to ask if you want your companion to wait outside while you review the contents."

Barbara said, "No, my companion is my lawyer and we are here to address the contents together." With that, he made a small bow and left.

Barbara looked at the slate-grey box. She turned to Beth and said, "So, this is the moment of truth."

Beth offered, "Remember that phrase is usually used in bullfights when either the bull or the bullfighter loses."

Chastened by that comment, Barbara stood up and opened the box. As she looked inside, she realized why the box was on a trolley.

A TREASURE TROVE

It took Barbara a minute to catch her breath. While working for the Agency, she had handled tens of thousands of dollars. At one point in a counterterrorism mission, she even passed a half million dollars in a green duffle bag to a Lebanese warlord in exchange for his militia to raid a Hizballah camp. The goal was to free a series of hostages in a way that allowed the President to deny that there was any payment to the hostage takers. In the end, the warlord conducted the raid, the hostages were freed, and the White House was pleased with the results. In later discussions, her bosses made the point that a cruise missile fired from a US aircraft would have cost more than the payment with far less likely results. After that, Barbara acknowledged for the rest of her career that a clandestine payment was often a far better way to achieve a result than any military option.

Now, she was out of the Agency and while she did not have to pinch pennies, her access to substantial amounts of cash were in the distant past. Until now. The box had a metal divider. In the front half were large bundles of dollars and Swiss francs. In the back was a leather binder, a Walther PP pistol and a large wristwatch. Long before the pistol became famous in books and film, the Walther was the most common concealed weapon used by Western intelligence officers. It was small, flat sided and the 7.65mm cartridge was available worldwide. Soviet counterparts carried a Makarov which was a less well made, Russian copy of the same weapon. This PP had what looked to be ivory grips rather than the standard hard rubber grips. On the right grip was a dragon similar in design to the one on the gold bangle she found in the concealment at the Chautauqua house. The carving on the other grip was of a Roman short sword with some sort of devil mask in relief over the top. Wrapped through the trigger guard was a worn leather watch strap and a very old watch.

While not a student of horology, Barbara recognized the watch as a 1940s Panerai. The radium dial barely glowed, but the size and the dial were very distinctive to anyone with even a little knowledge of special operations in World War II. It was a watch specially made for Italian frogmen during World War II known as Decima Mas. Like the American A11 watch now on her daughter's wrist, the Radiomir was considered one of the great watches of the 1940s and the earliest of serious dive watches. The caseback was engraved with a single word in gothic lettering: *Gluck.* Barbara put the watch in her pocket, hoped for good luck, and continued her search in the box.

Below the pistol and the watch were two passports — one German and one Portuguese. The German passport was marked with the Nazi eagle.

Beth looked over her shoulder. She asked, "What does it all mean?"

Barbara realized she had been holding her breath and exhaled sharply. "I think I know some of the story based on Peter's journal. As to the money, I have no idea. Perhaps the binder will explain."

Beth looked at her Cartier watch. She said, "I think we have about an hour before we travel to Geneva. Let's do a quick review of what is here, what we can take with us and what needs to stay here."

"Divide and conquer!"

Beth walked over to the box and started counting the bundles of cash. "My thoughts exactly."

Barbara started to flip through the various pages of the binder. The first few pages were related to the contractual relationship between Peter O'Connell and Banque Marchande. They included bank statement entries. Included in the entries were regular, direct deposits to two different international charities. Each of the charities focused on schools and hospitals in Thailand that assisted Thai mountain tribals as well as Laotian and Vietnamese refugees. There was a separate regular payment to a bank account in Los Angeles in the name of Jane Huan. Another mystery to be sure.

Barbara looked at the statements. There was close to ten million

Swiss francs in the account with regular electronic transfers of up to ten thousand per year per charity. Plus another ten thousand per year to Ms. Huan. Barbara did a quick calculation. The account was still very healthy. For now.

In the very back of the box was another journal in Peter's handwriting. Barbara took the journal and put it in her purse. This was neither the time nor the place to read more of Peter's legacy. She quickly noted the bank account number as well as the account number in California, closed the folder, and looked at Beth. "How much?"

"Ballpark? Probably five million Swiss francs in small bundles of five thousand Swiss francs each and two million dollars in bundles of ten thousand dollars each. Oh, did I mention there is gold under the piles of cash?"

"Gold?"

"A mix. Mostly Swiss coins, but also a few British, and some American eagles minted in the 1950s. I have no idea how much they are worth, but they are layered below the cash in cute little felt boxes holding twenty coins each."

"Sheesh. OK, now I need some advice. Is it appropriate for me to take some of this money and ask for the manager to deposit it into the account?"

Beth laughed. "Are you kidding? This is your money. If you want to put it into the account, the manager will be thrilled. It is that account that he is using to pay your fees to the bank. What else do they do with it?"

"It turns out they have been paying thousands of dollars a year to charities going back to the late 1960s as well as an annuity to a lady in California."

"Any other creditors?"

"Not according to the bank statements."

"So, Peter O'Connell was a silent donor to charities?"

"Children's charities to be precise."

"So, you want to take some of the money and put it back into the account to be sure it doesn't run out of cash."

"Precisely."

"Well, if it was me, I would use the dollars first. You never know when you might want to have some Swiss francs." Beth smiled.

Barbara said, "OK, so we empty the dollars out of the box, and have it deposited in the account. We close up the box and leave for Geneva."

"Not going to grab some Swiss francs?"

"For what?"

"I don't know. Consider it mad money? Perhaps watch shopping in Switzerland?"

Barbara giggled. "You do realize how absurd this all is?"

"I do, but it's not the most absurd thing you O'Connells have shown me."

"Hmm, like the Russian vendetta or the cousin who was an assassin for hire?"

"Exactly." Beth took one of the bundles of Swiss francs and put it in Barbara's purse. "Are you going to leave the pistol here?"

"I am."

"And the passports?"

"For that next trip when we come here on vacation."

"Fair enough. As your lawyer, here is my recommendation. Pull out the bundles of US cash. Leave them on the table. Close the box and I will go out to the lobby and call the manager. We will do this in order. First, he returns the box to his vault, gives you the key, and then we talk deposits. Clear?"

Barbara nodded.

Beth stood up, straightened her black wool sweater and black wool trousers and headed out the door.

Barbara looked up at the ceiling and spoke to the ghost of Peter O'Connell, "I hope you have a reasonable explanation for all of this."

WHAT'S NEXT?

Massoni sat next to Flash in the Panopticon cafeteria. He said, "Smith found the results satisfactory. The two traitors are already singing away during their initial interrogation. GRU handlers, tradecraft and targeting will be disrupted in Europe for a bit."

Flash shook her head. "True, we got Bantler and Sherman and they will eventually end up in a supermax prison forever and there are fewer SWORDFISH creeps in the world."

"Do you think the Russians are going to be happy about the results? I suspect the SWORDFISH creeps need to worry more about their Russian pals than Austrian authorities."

Flash shook her head. "I hadn't thought about that. You think SWORDFISH will clean up after themselves?"

"If not, then the GRU will. After all, the job was to kill Bantler and Sherman so they wouldn't talk. That didn't go as planned."

"Still, it's not closure for us."

"Flash, when have we ever received closure? We just do our best each time. Back when I was a young Green Beret…"

Flash smiled. "Sergeant Major, you were young once?"

Massoni ignored Flash and continued. "As I was saying, back when I was a young Green Beret, I had a sergeant major tell me something that I have taken to heart."

Smith's voice suddenly added to the mix. "Sergeant Major, you have a heart?"

They turned to see Smith at the coffee urn filling his mug. While Smith might have been slowed by his wounds, he remained as stealthy as ever. Neither of them had heard his arrival. He said, "Continue, Sergeant Major. I want to hear the lesson."

"My sergeant major had joined SF in the late 1970s. He had been involved in multiple deployments in Central America. He transferred to 1st Group and was the Battalion Sergeant Major with multiple deployments in the Philippines working against the communist insurgency there."

As always, Flash was impatient. She wanted the bottom line. "AND?"

"And, he said to me: Massoni, there were villains in the world when you were born, there are villains here now, there will be villains in the world when you die. All you can do is focus every day on doing your best. Accept little successes as the nature of our trade and understand that it is all you can do."

Smith put his hand on Massoni's shoulder. "Very much stoic philosophy."

Massoni smiled, "I thought it was Confucian philosophy."

Flash said, "I still want to crush the SWORDFISH network."

Smith nodded, "Funny you should say that. The Command thinks the same way. Now, stop pondering the nature of the universe and get back to work. We need to find the main headquarters of SWORD-FISH and disrupt their operations, permanently."

Massoni looked at Flash and said, "You heard the Boss. Get to work!"

Sue was completing the substantial paperwork required at the end of any trip. She wasn't sure which bureaucracy was worse: the Agency or DoD. Richard could hear her grumbling in the cubicle next to his. He said, "It is the price of admission for being a globe-trotting spy. You come back and there is paperwork. Now, stop your whining and just get it done. Who knows when the next call will come."

Sue smiled at the voice from the other side of the wall. Richard was right. The paperwork wasn't that onerous, and she did like the work. When she was working, she was working in Europe. When she was back, she could live in the Potomac River House. She would even get a chance to spend time with her family for the holidays. For the first time in years, they would all be in the same time zone, and they had all agreed to meet at the Potomac River House for Christmas and then go to her brother's house in Georgetown for New Year's Eve. In the meantime, paperwork.

Jamie's voice echoed in the office. "Sue, you need to join me for an SVTC with the Boss."

Secure Video Teleconference. Sue thought: Another job already? At least it meant she didn't have to dress properly and go to CIA headquarters. She stood up, stretched a bit to loosen up her left leg and reset her balance off her prosthetic and headed to the box where SVTCs were held.

When she got there, there were two mugs of tea, two notepads and Jamie. Clearly, he was expecting a fairly long, detailed session. When the screen filled with Dentmann's face, she was certain that Jamie was right.

Like Smith, Dentmann was never interested in starting a discussion with pleasantries. She just started the conversation with the main topic. No warm-up. And, like Smith, when she was done, the screen would go blank without even an acknowledgment that the conversation was over. Dentmann began, "I just wanted to let you know what has happened since you returned. Bantler and Sherman are singing like robins at dawn. We are getting names, dates, and places of their meetings with the GRU handlers and the type of intelligence they passed. It won't minimize their sentencing, but it may allow them more privileges in supermax. It was a good result for us. At least for now, the leak has been plugged."

Sue looked at Jamie. He shrugged and took a sip of tea. Sue couldn't help herself. She said, "For now?"

Dentmann's face on the screen looked puzzled. Sue couldn't tell if that was just the distortion from the camera or if Dentmann was truly surprised at her question. "Sue, this is the never-ending battle. We recruit one of theirs, they recruit one of ours. We catch one. We work hard to prevent them from catching one of ours. It just never stops. You can count on the fact the Russians, the Chinese, the Iranians, and our other adversaries are always out there trying to find a weakness in our personnel, in our computer systems, in our tradecraft. Now that we also have intelligence mercenaries out there willing to work for anyone so long as they pay, it is even worse. It just never stops. We accept little successes, but we never can declare victory."

Sue nodded. The trade goes on. She should realize that by now. After all, she was a third-generation spy.

Dentmann's screen image looked at Jamie. "There is a short trip on the schedule. I want you to travel with me to the UK. The focus will be on the threat from mercenary organizations like SWORDFISH. You will be my subject-matter expert. It is a joint CIA-DoD trip to meet with every UK counterpart who will attend from their most senior Joint Intelligence Committee down to representatives from the various services. I am going to push to get Smith to serve as my counterpart, but you never know with the Pentagon and a high-profile trip to London. Either way, we leave next week."

"Check, Chief."

"Pack a suit, Schenk. I mean it. Not your normal Euro-trash outfit. A suit. A couple of dress shirts and a tie."

Jamie was less enthusiastic in his response this time. "Check, Chief."

Dentmann looked at Sue. "I have another job for you, O'Connell."

"I don't get to join you and the Brits?"

"I don't get a vote in this one, Sue. I got the orders straight from my director and the SOF CG."

Sue's stomach churned. Every time in her career that she had been in proximity with seniors, it had been an unpleasant experience. She opted to say nothing and wait.

"Normally, detailees are allowed to stay with the Agency for three years before returning to their respective service. You just finished your first year in OSU, so I thought we would be able to keep you with the Division for two more. I was wrong."

Sue looked down at the pad on her desk. Here it comes.

"You have new orders. You are staying with the Agency, but in a different job. After the holidays, you are going to be an instructor at the Farm. The CG has followed your work for years and he wants an experienced operator at the Farm to serve as a mentor for his students and to showcase the partnership between the Agency and SOF. Once you have finished the paperwork from the trip, you need to go down to the Farm and check in. The next class starts after the new year, so all they want you to do for now is start the admin paperwork, getting the appropriate access and logons to their system and meet your colleagues. After that, you can spend the holidays with your family. And, please try to keep your mother out of trouble."

"But…"

"Sue, this was not my decision. It was a decision that the CG made. He personally asked the Director. I do think it is a good decision for our two services, and I also think it will be good for you to serve as an instructor and a mentor. You are a senior now. You have been on every sort of operation from war zone to classic espionage to counterintelligence. We need you to teach the next generation." Dentmann took a sip from a coffee cup. It said *I'm the Boss.* Dentmann continued, "How many years do you have in service now?"

"Eighteen."

"So, you complete two years at the Farm and then, assuming you still want to work in the field, we bring you on board like Jamie and Richard. I think everyone wins."

"Except me."

Jamie looked over at Sue and whispered, "Don't whine. It is an order, remember?"

Sue looked up at the screen. She said, "Check, Boss. I will let you know when I head down to the Farm. How do I get in?"

Dentmann smiled. "The same way you got in the last time you were there. Name, driver's license, and your smiling face. They will be ready for you." The screen went blank.

Jamie said, "Well, congratulations. No one has ever said I would be a good choice to mentor the next generation."

Sue smirked. "With good reason."

"Hey, I've got feelings."

"Where?"

"In a rucksack someplace. Now, let's get back to Richard and tell him the news."

THE COLLECTIVE

An emergency meeting of The Collective was not common. The members were forced to stop their regular work for SWORDFISH and travel to Stockholm for the meeting. For most, it was a short flight from St. Petersburg or from Prague. For one of the seniors, it was a long haul from Bamako to Paris and from Paris to Stockholm. At least on the time zone but a long series of flights. He arrived directly from the airport in a rumpled suit and an equally rumpled disposition.

November is the beginning of the bleak time in Sweden. Whether the short days are filled with rain, sleet or snow is dependent on the North Sea. What is dependable is the loss of daylight. By mid-December, Stockholm has either grey skies or black night skies. The SWORDFISH offices were already operating under artificial light during office hours and the windows in the conference room looked out over a grey day with sleet hitting the plate glass and running down the side of the building. After the heat of equatorial Africa, the retired SPETSNAZ officer was chilled to the bone by the time he arrived in the conference room.

The senior of The Collective took his place and looked at his watch. The sweep second had reached twelve and the minute hand clicked into place. It was time for the meeting. He started to speak. "The Vienna affair was unfortunate. We lost an operator and we did not accomplish any of the missions. Our GRU client is furious that we did not eliminate their former assets. While the Orthodox Church was pleased to hear that the icon was not stolen from St. Catherine's, they also were not pleased at the arrest of our operators in the Belvedere Palace. After all, they hired us for a discrete operation. Finally, the Iranians have complained that the operators in Vienna manhandled their men. Does anyone have details?"

The former member of the Eighth Directorate of the GRU known more commonly as SPETSNAZ and the senior who just came from Africa said, "The team made mistakes."

"Explain."

"They violated tradecraft and used the same communications equipment in Germany and Austria. They were tracked by one or several services while involved in the GRU-cleaning operation. We think it was a joint US and Austrian operation."

"And the Iranians?"

"The Iranians decided to track our men as well. Then, the IRGC officer in Vienna decided he wanted to determine what our team was doing after the Frankfurt operation. I have no information on why the Iranians would choose to do so, but we know for certain from our penetration from the Iranian embassy in Vienna that they did decide to interfere. They got in the way of the team. I think the team showed remarkable control. They did not do any severe damage to the Iranian surveillance team while they were surveilling the target in the icon operation. The IRGC officer involved was ordered to return to Tehran. His colleagues believe his actions were tracked by the Americans or the Austrians, or both. I believe the Iranians compromised the icon operation."

The senior in The Collective nodded.

Across the table was the former member of the Second Chief Directorate. "I met with the GRU in Prague. They gave us the mission to eliminate their former sources in Vienna. I have no information to suggest they may have compromised the request, but our reporting from the Vienna police suggests that the Austrian and American special services were waiting for the arrival of the two targets. I do not think Misha and his team were at fault there. I think the GRU tradecraft was flawed. Their contact with their American sources was through open telephone contact. The GRU senior in Prague said his counterpart in Berlin will be sanctioned."

The FSB veteran looked at the head of the table and continued.

"Here is what we know for certain. The two targets were taken by the US special services and flown to the US. There is already a sealed indictment against the two targets. They have pled guilty and will likely talk. I fear the GRU handlers involved may be compromised as well as any GRU tradecraft used in Germany."

He stopped to look at the senior manager to see his response. As always, the manager's face gave away nothing. He might as well have been listening to a discussion of Russian poetry or classical music. The FSB veteran continued, "Our penetrations of the Austrian police reported the Austrians have designed a cover story for the events at the Vienna train station. They kept the events at the Belvedere Palace a secret. They presented a case to the court that our team had been involved in the kidnapping and interrogation of a member of the Belvedere Palace Museum with the goal of the theft of several paint-ings in the museum's collection. The criminal Andrassy agreed to cooperate with this story in exchange for the Austrians not looking too carefully at his own plan to steal a painting and sell it on the black market."

The manager next to the former FSB officer spoke for the first time. His background was known to all at the table. He was a former member of the KGB Zenith team and, after the collapse of the USSR, a member of the FSB Alpha Group known for their successes in assassinations and other active measures. "I traveled to Vienna when I heard of the problem. I eliminated the witness. It will look like he committed suicide rather than face a trial and jail time. Since the criminal Andrassy is unable to testify in support of the case against the SWORDFISH members, our team members have received lesser charges and yesterday they were released on bail. Our bankers in Vienna provided the bail and the necessary means for the team to disappear. My question now is what do we do with them?"

The SPETSNAZ side of the table looked uncomfortable. The most likely answer from The Collective would be termination. Both SPETSNAZ veterans knew Misha and his team. After a few moments of silence, the senior SPETSNAZ officer said, "There are two choices. The easy choice is termination. However, I would suggest that we offer Misha and his remaining team another chance by sending them to Mali. I just came from there and there is work to be done and money to be made. If they refuse the offer, then it will be on their heads."

The Alpha Team veteran across the table nodded. "I think that is entirely fair. Africa is a reasonable exile. They will have a chance to earn our trust again."

The senior looked down the length of the table. He considered the possibilities. On the one hand, he needed these four men to work with him. They were his eyes and ears and managed the various SWORD-FISH teams. On the other hand, he considered failure of this grand scale unacceptable. He looked up and said, "Syria."

The men along both sides of the table realized that this was a compromise between termination and reconciliation. Syria was a war zone. SWORDFISH men had died there and likely would die in the future. But, it meant he wouldn't task one of them to terminate a SWORDFISH team. The second SPETSNAZ veteran decided to give his partner support. He said, "I will work with our team in Austria to begin the exfiltration today. They will be transferred directly to Latakia via our ship operations in the Adriatic and then on to Northern Syria. "

The senior manager turned to the rest of The Collective. "Do we know the names of any of our adversaries, either Americans or Austrians?"

The FSB senior said, "We have tracked some travel of Americans. The names are familiar. At the train station were two who have given us difficulties in the past: Schenk and O'Connell."

The Alpha Team leader added, "And in the case of the museum, another O'Connell. This time the wife of Peter O'Connell. A target I eliminated years ago."

The senior manager nodded. "Is there any profit in erasing these individuals? I have no interest in revenge, only profit."

The SPETSNAZ senior said, "I will engage my GRU colleagues. I think they will be interested in Schenk and O'Connell. I have no idea if they have any interest in the elder O'Connell."

The senior manager said, "Excellent. Remember, we are only interested if they are willing to pay well for this sort of high-risk work." He paused for a second and looked around the room. "Speaking of the GRU, we must compensate the GRU for our failure in Vienna. I have already told them that we will each give up one hundred thousand Euros as a rebate for the failure. I hope you are all in agreement."

The men at the table understood. One hundred thousand Euros was far easier to accept than facing their own termination.

J.R. SEEGER is a western New York native who served as a US Army paratrooper and as a CIA case officer for a total of 27 years of federal service. In October 2001, Mr. Seeger led a CIA paramilitary team into Afghanistan. He splits his time between western New York and Central New Mexico.

www.ingramcontent.com/pod-product-compliance
Lightning Source LLC
Chambersburg PA
CBHW022138240626
47153CB00007B/2414